Under a Maltese Sky

Nicola Kearns

Under a Maltese Sky

This edition published June 2017

Copyright © Nicola Kearns 2015

The moral right of the author has been asserted.

All rights reserved. No part of this publication may be reproduced, stored in a retrieval system, or transmitted, in any form and by any means, electronic, mechanical, photocopying, recording or otherwise, without the prior permission of the author.

For my sons, Darragh & Adam

'And when they had escaped, they then learned that the island was called Malta. And the barbarous people showed us no little kindness, for they kindled a fire and received us every one, because of the present rain and because of the cold.'

Acts 28:1-2

PROLOGUE
~ Malta 2001 ~

Ana was very happy. Today she had met Pope John Paul II and as she told her grand-daughter, if she died now, she would do so contentedly. As the rest of the group were busy chatting and drinking wine, Ana gazed out the window. From her seat she could see down into Grand Harbour. Although it was dark, Fort St. Elmo was lit up as was the whole harbour below. She wondered what had happened to all the people she had loved on this island. Where was the man who had never been far from her thoughts for over fifty years? Where were the girls she had been to school with, the nurses she trained beside and lived with through those terrible war years? She remembered vividly the horror of the war. It was almost impossible to visualize battleships moored where there was now a pretty marina, or to imagine the frightening sound of an air raid siren, breaking the silence of the night to warn them of yet another air raid.

Sadly Ana knew the fate of some of the friends she had loved in her time here during the war. Looking over at her grand-daughter she smiled to herself as she realised that when she was Jessy's age, she had been here in this country of sunshine and sadness, of laughter and loss and love. Thanks to her grand-daughter she was now back in Malta. Although she had been shocked and excited when she realised she was to return to the island, Ana was happy now that she had come. The place she had tried to forget for years was still familiar and just as beautiful.

PART I
~ *Ernie* ~
1

Apart from seeing friends and comrades killed almost daily, everything else about the war excited Ernie McGuill. He loved being in the Army. Joining up at eighteen was the most exhilarating thing he had ever done in his boring life. The feel of the heavy uniform against his skin and the weight of sturdy boots on his feet filled him with a sense of purpose and place in the world that he had never known. For the first time in his life he felt that he was somebody and not just a lackey for his father and brother Joe on the farm. He greatly enjoyed the camaraderie of the other men. When they had got over their jibes at his Irish brogue and innocence regarding the ways of the world outside his country village, they accepted him for the hard working eager lad that he was.

Ernie made it a goal to rid himself of his country accent and within a few years of being surrounded by his English comrades now that he was based in England, he was able to pass for one of them. He stood just shy of six foot four and had an unruly mop of dark hair which he had to cut almost weekly in keeping with army regulations. Years of hard work on the farm had given him a well-muscled body and he could take on any man that dared to tease him. Those who tried did so only once.

Rising quickly through the ranks due to his driving ambition, Ernie gained the respect and admiration of his peers for his abhorrence of alcohol. In doing so he proved that not all Irish men were hard drinkers. His complete lack of fear both amused and awed his superiors and there was no job or mission that Ernie McGuill would not take on and excel in. He was always first to volunteer no matter what or where the task took him. His willingness to give assistance to colleagues when needed, justly earned his promotion when it came time for his first deployment.

From the day he turned his back on his father's farm he never returned. He was a soldier in the British Army now and he didn't feel the slightest bit guilty for 'taking the Kings Shilling' and being labelled a traitor to his country. Ernie didn't care. His country had never done anything for him. He had watched as his young friends enlisted into the Irish Republican Army and had seen families, farms and homes torn apart for a so-called Free United Ireland. Men who had fought side by side against the British found themselves fighting against each other in a horrific Civil War.

Ernie had been brought up listening to his father rant and rave about the 1916 martyrs and had also heard the heartrending cries of mothers at too many funerals as they buried their sons. He decided he wanted no part in any of it. He remembered well the sound of gunfire on the hill in 1921 when seven young men, some of them neighbours, had been shot down by the British when they came upon an ambush of the Irish Republican Army. At ten years old he had been helping his father repair fencing when he heard the rat-tat-tat of the British guns as they fired on the young IRA men. He had dropped his handful of nails in terror as his father pushed him face down on the dewy grass.

'See that.'

His father pointed and Ernie gasped aloud. A British soldier hit one of the young IRA men who already looked dead over the head with the butt of his gun.

'That's the animal we are fighting against. The dirty swine! You wouldn't do that to a bloody dog.' Later when he sat around the kitchen table with Joe and his father along with several of the village men, he was shocked to hear his father say he hadn't seen a thing.

'No, meself and the young lad had gone home for the breakfast then. We could hear the gunfire alright but we never seen anything. That right Ernie?'

Ernie gulped his tea and almost scalded his throat.

'Ay, that's right Da.'

He knew by his father's face that he couldn't dare contradict him.

'Not a word outa you about this morning, I'm warning ye,' Pat Joe McGuill shook his fist as he headed out the door to feed the cattle. 'We don't want the Brits round here asking any questions. Heed me now.'

Over the next few days Ernie couldn't believe that there was no further talk about the ambush he had watched play out in front of him. The locals went about their business as though the killings had never happened. He never heard his mother mention a single word about it. News came that at least six of the men were dead and one was un-accounted for. Apart from these bits of stories, Ernie never heard another word about the horrific event.

Seven years later he still felt sadness at the deaths of his countrymen. Some of them had joined the meitheal of men who had worked in the fields with his father many times. But more than sadness, he felt just despair at their foolhardiness. No, it wasn't a good thing that the British killed them, but it was a 'them or us' situation and that was something he could understand.

Ernie had not joined the British army because he had nowhere else to go. Being forced to leave school at thirteen and work day and night on his father's small bit of land, with never a penny in his pocket was not what he wanted to do with his life. He had loved to listen to his mother's stories about her brother Ernest McKeown, who had gained a medal for valour in the First World War and after whom he had been named. A life that would give him respect, while providing challenge and danger was what attracted him. This was what the British Army offered.

When his mother died there was nothing to keep him on the farm. His closeness to her was the only thing that that had kept him there. Knowing that he had been a comfort to her was his only reason to stay. As a second son he would never have any say or any right to the land. He would always be under the orders of his father as long as he lived beneath his roof. When his father passed on he would then have to answer to his brother Joe. He knew he would be made to feel guilty for looking for work elsewhere. Rather than endure that kind of a life he'd have joined the bloody Krauts. He would have done anything to get away.

2

By the time Ernie joined the British Army in 1928, Ireland had been known as the Irish Free State, with its own government for just six years. Joining the British Army meant he had to travel the long distance to Ballykinler in County Down and sign up at the Barracks there. This regiment was originally part of the Inniskillings Regiment at St. Lucia Barracks in Omagh, County Tyrone. Following Ireland's Independence, the 2nd Battalion 89th (The Princess Victoria's) Regiment of Foot was formerly adopted in Northern Ireland which remained under British jurisdiction. This battalion was eager to get young Irish men to join up. After months of tough training, the stern faced Officer in front of him raised an eyebrow when Ernie looked straight ahead and swore allegiance to the King.

He didn't feel loyal to any country or King or government. He felt only a loyalty to himself. He wasn't going to waste his life. His lack of fear was fuelled by knowing that he had nothing to lose. There was no sweetheart clinging to him, or kids to provide for and he no longer had anybody he cared about back in Ireland. It would be better to die fighting for a life he believed in, than die working a land that would never be his.

Strangely enough his father didn't question his long absences. In fact, it almost seemed as though he approved. Ernie was ready for a row every time he left the house, but instead his father made comments such as 'Good on ye, our lad' which puzzled Ernie no end. Joe was the one who showed his temper when Ernie put out his hand yet again to grab the coat and cap hanging on the back of the door.

'Where the bloody hell are ye off to now? There's a sight of work to be done yet and you're off fancy footing around. I'm sick of doing all the donkey work around here.'

'Hee haw,' Ernie shouted back. He heard the scuffle behind

the door he had just banged shut. This meant that Joe had jumped up to thrash him. He could hear the shouting between father and son as he threw his leg over the bike for the long journey to the Barracks. Joe roared that it wasn't fair while his father admonished him, telling him to his fury to leave the lad be. Ernie chuckled to himself, 'Oh how the tide has turned.' He never minded the long cycle ahead of him. Instead he whistled on the way, knowing he was heading to better things. Before he knew it he was in with the lads and the farm was far from his thoughts. He actually felt excitement, albeit with a mixture of trepidation thrown in about telling his Father the news that he had joined up. He was now officially a member of The British Defence Forces serving his Majesty King George V.

Ever since the sad death of his mother last summer, life on the farm had become intolerable. The knowledge that she was on his side always saved the day. After his work in the fields, he knew that she would be waiting for him with a mug of tea and some homemade soda bread. She knew the way he liked it with the strawberry jam dripping out of the huge chunks she served him.

'Arra love,' she'd say, gently rubbing his back with her weathered hands, just as she had done when he was a child. 'Sure don't be minding him at all, his bark is worse than his bite and he loves you in his own way.'

Her soft spoken words would take the sting out of any abuse his father had shouted at him that day. By the time the men had sat down in front of the hearth with their tobacco tins and roll ups, peace would reign, more or less. Now there was nobody waiting at home to soothe him and there was no more soda bread. Instead, the men fended for themselves at whatever time they came in and the evidence of their housekeeping was all around. The once spotlessly clean kitchen tended lovingly for years by his mother was now hardly fit to live in.

'Would you get on and get yourself bloody married man,' was all his father could be heard roaring at him when he took in the state of the scullery. Crumbs and food covered the floor and the fire was not yet lit. 'The only good thing in keeping you here at all is if you'd get some young one in to clean this place up.'

Ernie clenched his fists and cursed inwardly as he raised his eyes to heaven before storming out and loudly banging the cottage door, almost taking it off its hinges. If he had heard that fatherly advice once, it must have been a thousand times since the death of his mother. He imagined the impossibility of bringing some young girl in here. She would be treated like a slave, cooking and cleaning and washing up after three men. Even if he had any interest in marrying, he sure as hell wouldn't bring a bride back here.

It was important that his father didn't find out about his trips to the Barracks before he had a chance to tell him. Ernie was sure his father thought he was courting because he always smartened up before he left. The care he took in shaving left no sign of whiskers and the black curly mop of hair that his mother had loved was now cut close to his head. His nails were also cut short and he picked away at the dirt under his fingernails with a nail until he drew blood. This was what was required as a soldier of the British army. Because Pat Joe didn't comment on his changed appearance Ernie hoped his father believed he had a girl. There would be hell and more to pay if Patrick Joe McGuill had to hear it in the village that his youngest son had been training with the Brits. The IRA watched those who went in and out of the Barracks and he was surprised that not a word had been said to him yet, or worse. The fact that he hadn't been brought before a kangaroo court and shot there and then for being a traitor was a miracle. The quicker he broke it to his father and got the boat out of this godforsaken place the better.

'You'll amount to nothing ye young traitor ye,' Pat Joe fired the hoe he had been working with into the muddy soil and marched down the meadow into the house. He knew if he stayed any longer arguing, he would have killed Ernie with his own bare hands. The shame of a son turning his coat and going off to fight with the Brits would be the death of him. He had been feeling proud of his son these last few months. He had been sure these disappearances at strange hours of the day, oftentimes overnight, were because Ernie had joined the Irish Republican Army, like many of the other idealistic young men in his county. To discover that he had in fact done the very opposite and joined the British Army was too much to bear. As far as he was concerned Ernie was dead and now he had only one son.

Ernie McGuill boarded the ferry from Larne a few short hours later and when Ireland became just a dot on the horizon, he felt no sadness.

3

Cranwell, Great Britain, 1939

'You are getting to do it because you are a flaming nutcase,' Billy Cortis retorted as he fired the cigarette pack in Ernie's direction. 'I mean, there's not one of us here would do it, unless under orders. Isn't that right boys?'

The other men in the room murmured in agreement. Ernie lit a cigarette and lay back on his bunk. This was exactly what he had been waiting for. He had put his name down for the Empire Air Training Scheme with the other lads when the recruitment advertising for pilots came out, but never imagined he'd have a hope. Usually it was the Oxford or Cambridge boys who got to do the pilot training. He was thrilled beyond imagining when he was accepted to do the intensive training course in the RAF College Flying Training School in Cranwell. However Ernie was well aware that it was only because of the urgency of the war that he was lucky enough to be transferred from his present regiment, to that of an Officer of the Royal Air Force. He knew there were a lot of soldiers eager for this chance and there was some ill feeling among the men. He vowed to prove his worth and had already surpassed the others by getting his Wings in record time. Flight training courses were shortened due to the war and as a result some of his fellow trainee pilots had been killed during their flying lessons. The Training School was awkwardly located for flyers in attempting to find their landing position. Because of this many of the pilots mistook the red light on top of the college as a marker for the runway and were killed in the event. Some of them had also got into a lot of trouble for flying their planes right through the aircraft hangars. However grounding pilots as a punishment was no longer feasible. They needed men in the air and as fast as possible.

Now his dream was coming true. Fancy him, Ernie McGuill from a small farm in Ireland going to be a pilot for the Royal Air Force! For a fleeting moment he wished he could let his father and brother know how well he was doing, but quickly put thoughts of them out of his mind. He'd had no contact with them since the day he left the farm eleven years ago. The RAF was his family now and he wanted no other life.

'Personally I'd prefer to be carrying guns in my plane than a darn camera,' Billy was Ernie's right hand man in all things but this. He thought Ernie was 'off his head' as he kept telling him, 'I mean, what's the use of a Spitfire that doesn't fire?'

'It's a challenge,' was Ernie's simple response, 'the information I can gather about what those Germans are up to is gonna win us this war.'

'But you have no guns, no radio back-up. All you will have is a map and a damn compass. Jeez the boy scouts are better equipped. And you will freeze your ass off mate, let me tell you. Also do you know how low you have to fly to get any type of decent snap? It's a suicide mission. They must be trying to get rid of you,' he sniggered, 'I bet you wish you'd never got into photography now eh?'

On the contrary Ernie was delighted that his little pastime had earned him the position he now held. Reconnaissance pilots were few and far between. Flying at high altitudes with a plane that was stripped to the bare minimum was not a mission favoured by most pilots. It was highly dangerous and most recon pilots risked death every time they got into a cockpit. Unlike other pilots, they had to fly deep into the enemy's airspace, photograph targets and return to base without the aid of radio contact. The weather was also his enemy, as he might have to fly above a cloud bank for hours before seeing any significant landmark. This had the added danger of using valuable fuel while waiting for unpredictable weather to clear. Monitoring of the gauge was very important and many never returned due to lack of fuel. Not for nothing was this kind of operation called 'Dicing' as in dicing with death.

'Hey Irish. Why don't you get us a few good pics of those German frauleins when you're up there? Take us back something to put on our walls mate,' bawled Billy Cortis from the shower room, 'I could do with a change of scenery in here.'

Ernie assured him that he would and stubbing his cigarette out in the ashtray on his chest, he pushed it under the bed and turned to the wall. Sleep came easy to him as always.

~

RAF Benson South Oxfordshire, Great Britain, October 1939

'This particular mission is a hairy one, McGuill. You fly out from here to Germany and you are requested to photograph the lot. What I mean by that is I want targets. I want any goings-on whether on land or sea and I mean anything. If it moves I want a photo of it. Do you understand?' Wing-Commander Laurence Mellor sat back in his seat and faced the tall handsome man standing in front of him. Two of his other best pilots had already refused the mission and he had placed a black mark against their name for this.

'Copy sir,' was Ernie's uncomplicated reply and with that he saluted and took his leave.

Laurence Mellor never failed to be surprised by the young Irishman. He hadn't blinked an eyelid while hearing of the dangerous mission assigned him. If anything he seemed to embrace the danger. Mellor had a high regard for Flight Lieutenant McGuill and since his arrival at Cranwell and subsequent move to Benson recently he had been keeping a close eye on his career. This young officer's complete lack of fear showed him to be exactly the type of man Mellor needed for the job in hand. Most reconnaissance pilots were regrettably shot down during their first couple of assignments. To have photographic evidence of enemy targets and activity on land and sea was of extreme importance. The worrying fact was that the pilots had to get extremely close to the terrain and in doing so were easily spotted by German fighter planes. They flew without radio back-up so no assistance could be requested which basically meant they were on their own. When Mellor discovered that Ernest liked to take pictures as a hobby and that the photographs covering the walls of the Officer's mess had been taken by him, he knew instantly what job he would assign him to. He also knew instantly that Ernest would take it on.

~

'Would you come out for just one night?' Billy cajoled his friend. 'There are three women to every man, booze, dancing. You name it you can have it. One night and I won't ask you again? After what you've been through you deserve it.'

Ernie could think of nothing he'd want less. The only thing he did want was to get back on that plane instead of being forced to take leave. Mellor thought he was doing him a favour giving him some long overdue time off, but in reality Ernie was only happy when he was in the sky.

'Go have some fun Ernest boy, find a girl, let loose.' The Wing-Commander intended to do just that himself as soon as he got the opportunity. War was a mucky business and a man had to find something to occupy his mind. Later that evening he was happy to see the young officer jump into the truck with the others as they drove into town.

When Ernest's plane failed to return next day they all feared he was dead.

'It isn't possible that he still has fuel,' alleged the officer sitting next to Mellor. 'He should have been back forty-five minutes ago. There are no sightings of his plane at any of the airfields.'

4

Wing-Commander Mellor was relieved when Ernest reported to his office.

'You had us all quite worried old boy, for a while.'

He was not only relieved because he would hate to lose a good recon pilot like Ernest, but because this particular reconnaissance plane was a kind of guinea pig for the others that had been ordered for the war. From now on they had decided to strip any Spitfires used in recon missions down to the bare bones to enable high altitudes. That included no radio and no ammo. If Ernest McGuill couldn't get this one home, none of them would.

Ernie had had the time of his life, even though he was scared to death when he saw the German Messerschmitts zoom like a swarm of bees behind him. For ages there was nothing. He had clear skies, perfect for the task in hand and he hovered as close as possible, taking photo after photo of military airfields. All in all it was a very successful mission he thought, turning his plane back towards Benson. That was when he noticed he had company. Due to the plane having been stripped of everything possible to ensure it was light, although an additional fuel tank had been added to extend its range, Ernie was able to gather speed and soar high above the fighter planes attacking him. He was conscious that he had been hit on at least one occasion. It was a long way home. By the time he landed Ernie felt frozen, thanks to there being no heating system in his plane. Because of his height of well over six feet his body was almost stiff with cramps from being confined for so many hours in an uncomfortably small cockpit. When he was helped out of his seat and straps by his fellow pilots he saw that his plane was peppered with holes where he had been hit, not just once but several times. He smiled to himself as he felt sure that his mother was watching over him from heaven as she promised she always would, guiding him home.

Billy-boy as he was nicknamed by the men, got his wish and Ernie joined him and the others on a trip to the Sunrise Ballroom. 'Good name for it,' Billy laughed, 'because it's always sunrise by the time we leave.'

The place was absolutely jammed to capacity. A cloud of smoke wafted in the air above the heads of the dancers and despite the doors and windows opened to the cold night air the hall was sweltering.

'Don't knock the heat Ernie mate,' Billy warned him, 'you will be happy to know it causes the girls to start taking off cardigans and sometimes even unbuttoning the tops of their dresses to cool themselves down. Keep the home fires burning I say,' he laughed and clapped Ernie hard on the back before disappearing into the heaving throng.

Ernie accepted a glass of lemonade from Ted Langley, one of the other pilots. With his other hand he fished in his trouser pocket for his matches while balancing a cigarette in between his lips.

'Light, soldier?' Ernie was asked by a young woman in front of him, who was holding a silver lighter up to his mouth. He nodded and she deftly lit his cigarette. Then cheekily she took it from his lips and placed it in between her own, her white teeth gleaming against ruby red lipstick which had been liberally applied. She giggled coquettishly up at him while he regarded her with disdain. She then took the glass from his hand and proceeded to take a long swig from it, leaving to his horror a dark lipstick stain on the rim.

'It's just lemonade!' she exclaimed in disbelief.

'Ten out of ten for your observation,' Ernie replied sarcastically.

'Don't you drink?' she enquired, offering him back the glass.

He shook his head and as he turned to go back to the bar, he was accosted by his mate;

'You have a right goer there,' Billy whispered into his ear. 'She looks like she could show a man a good time if you know what I mean?'

Ernie did know what he meant and he couldn't have cared less. He had no more interest in women than a fish had with a dog. This was a fact that he had carefully kept hidden since he had joined the army eleven years ago. In spite of living in close quarters with men every day, they had no idea that women were not what made his blood hot. Since his adolescence he had been aware that he was 'different' from other boys. Growing up he had listened to his young friends as they discussed the mystery of sex and he was conscious that he just did not share the same interest as they did in girls. Peering in neighbours windows as the young daughters of the house bathed in front of an open fire, didn't excite him as it did the other fellows. However this was something he quickly learned to conceal. He often questioned himself as to whether this had been a motive for joining the Army, to be in an environment that was predominantly male. However, living and sleeping in close proximity with other men did not cause him any lustful thoughts. It was akin to a fisherman being in a lake where the fish jumped up to be caught. No, he wanted the thrill of a chase, the appeal of the forbidden fruit. To have possession of that which was denied him. Like his missions, he coveted the most dangerous, the most illicit of all. It was a desire that if acted on and discovered, would result in instant dismissal and imprisonment. This was something he wanted to avoid at all costs.

5

'So Billy-boy, did you strike it lucky last night then?' Ernie reckoned he already knew the answer to that question, seeing as his friend had only returned to Barracks in the early hours and was still lying in his bed in full uniform.

Billy reluctantly turned around in his bunk, 'I did mate and I'm frigged.'

'Why's that?'

'I'm in love.'

Ernie laughed, 'Again?'

Billy was a hopeless romantic. He was never short of a girl owing to his sultry dark looks. Although he was quite short in stature, he had strong muscled shoulders and arms which made him appear taller than he was. He was Maltese and had joined up as soon as he turned 17. All the women were crazy about him. Although Ernie himself was a good looking man, Billy had a charm that Ernie didn't possess. He could make the girls swoon with his romantic words. As a great singer he also had an added '*Je ne sais quoi.*' He could serenade them, which he did with aplomb at any opportunity. Although able to play several musical instruments, he refused to take part in the bands at the dances. He believed it would limit his chances to chat up women if he wasn't in the midst of the dancing. Billy was also a great dancer. He could do the jitterbug, lindy hop, swing, jive. Ernie on the other hand had two left feet.

'This time it's different mate,' Billy assured him. 'This girl is not like the others.' 'Oh, and why is that then?' Ernie asked,

'Because she doesn't like me.' was Billy's honest reply.

'She doesn't like you?'

'Nope. She said I was a…. what were the words? An ignorant, conceited peacock' - the sexiest thing I ever heard come out of a woman's mouth.'

'So, go on. Tell me how this made you fall in love? I'm all ears. And also, why did she call you that? What were you doing?'

'One question at a time please mate! Jeez, respect for the hangover. I was dancing, and she was on the floor with another guy. I cut in and said that her partner's skills on the dance-floor left a lot to be desired and she'd do better with me. So I grabbed her round the waist, threw her in the air and proceeded to do the rest of the dance with her, but she hit me an awful clatter round the chops and that's when she said those words to me.'

Ernie roared laughing, 'And now you are in love with her?'

'Yes. I told her that I'm going to marry her. But first I have to find out her name and where she can be found.'

Ernie raised his eyes to heaven. And this was one of the men supposed to be looking out for him in the skies. God help him.

~

'You are being deployed to Malta,' Mellor informed Ernie. 'You leave via aircraft carrier tomorrow following a sub. This journey won't be without danger.'

Ernie felt his heart sink. There was nothing happening in Malta. Only the older military men or young recruits went there. He racked his brains to think of any reason why he was suddenly being taken off the reconnaissance assignments. There were no transgressions on his part and his flight record was exemplary. Perhaps he was being sent to train younger pilots.

'I know you are wondering why this sudden decision. I don't have to explain, but I will. I believe you deserve an explanation. It is looking more likely that Mussolini is going to drag Italy into this war, whether she wants to or not. If he does, Malta is in a strategic position for us. We need to know what Il Duce is planning and what his defences are like, whether by air or sea. It's important that we know what we are up against McGuill, and we need to know fast. There are no recon pilots in Malta and you are the best we have. Up until now you weren't under orders. I am afraid to tell you, this time you are, but I have a feeling you won't let me down. Am I wrong?

'No sir,' was Ernie's immediate answer.

'I will be your Wing Commander there too. Malta is my primary base. I was drafted in here as you know to give you youngsters some of my wisdom and expertise,' he winked conspiratorially at Ernie. 'It's a good place to be. I will see you on board, McGuill.'

Ernie saluted and left. He was going to Malta.

■■■

6

'I couldn't let you go alone now could I? You don't even speak the language,' Billy had been deployed also, owing to his Maltese origins.

'Don't they all speak English there? Isn't it a British colony?' Ernie was still reeling from his orders to go to Malta but wouldn't complain to anybody, not even Billy. Knowing his mate was also going there made things a lot easier to swallow.

'Yes of course, most of them do. But it is still a different country with a different language. You will love it there Ern. The sun always shines, you can swim in the ocean and fish. The local women aren't bad either. Though I have to warn you, they are a lot different from the girls here. Not as forward if you know what I mean. But there are English girls there too, so never fear.'

Ernie wasn't a bit fearful. In fact he didn't think there was one thing in life he did fear, except perhaps ever losing his wings. God forbid.

'What does Katie think of you going then?'

Billy and Katie had been married at Christmas, just a few short weeks ago with Ernie acting as best man, before the deployment orders came through. Billy had been distraught at the thought of having to leave his new bride at home. He didn't think Katie would want to leave her mother and friends to follow him across to the Mediterranean. However she surprised him by saying to his delight that he was her husband and where he went, she would go. The plan was that Katie would follow Billy sometime in February, when the naval ship carrying military personnel would make the journey to Malta.

'Not too happy mate, I can tell you. You know her. She doesn't hold back what she thinks. We were just settling into the married quarters, she'd frilly curtains and the works up and now its pack up your kit bag. Except Katie doesn't have a kit bag does she? She's been ripping up stuff and sewing summer clothes like there's no tomorrow. She says the only good thing about leaving here is that she will get to meet my family and that there will be sun. My mother wanted her to live with them, but Katie wouldn't have it. She wants to stay by my side at the family Barracks. Loves me, indeed she does,' said Billy happily.

~

They had to leave sooner than expected. Apparently there were security concerns. Plans of dates for aircraft ships to depart for the Mediterranean in a few weeks had somehow become known to the enemy and orders were to be prepared to leave within hours. Luckily each man was ready to do so at short notice and soon they were on board the huge naval ship. Billy was bereft. He had no time to say goodbye to Katie and although he had arranged that she be told of his sudden departure, she would not be given this information until he had arrived in Malta, again for security reasons. He knew that she would probably come up with this solution herself as he had forewarned her of the possibility, but he still felt bad for her. Ernie on the other hand was quite pleased to be setting off. He hated hanging around waiting on a mission to begin. He was an impatient man and he preferred to be in the action than not. His comrades were the opposite. They enjoyed the time off before their deployment and he was sick listening to them whine like schoolboys when they had to leave suddenly.

Conditions on board were adequate. He was used to sharing a room with the other men and being in cramped conditions in a cockpit. However, he was not prepared for the sea-sickness which embarrassingly gripped him within hours.

'Give me a blasted plane any day,' he grumbled as he hung

over the side of the ship, holding on to the rail for dear life. He could have quite happily jumped off into the sea below to be rid of the awful gut clenching nausea he was experiencing. 'Thank God I didn't join the navy,' he moaned as another vomiting bout overtook him. After the first few days he felt much better, but he had to suffer the jibes of the other more sea-worthy men who riled him relentlessly about his lack of sea-legs.

'You should have had a few drinks like us,' Billy laughed. 'We've all had a few every day and not one of us has been ill like you.'

Taking alcohol just to ward off sea-sickness didn't tempt Ernie. He knew first-hand what the drink did to his father and he had vowed from a young age never to touch the stuff. He was disgusted by the way his father would rant and rave when he'd had a 'few bevies' as the lads called it, terrorising his mother and sons with his cruel words. Hearing the physical abuse that his mother endured after one of his father's binges filled him with rage. No woman should have to put up with that. Only once did he intervene by banging ferociously on the wall, to be told by his mother in the morning that what happened between a man and his wife was nobody's business and how did he think he was born otherwise? He swore he'd never do that to a woman and was glad that he never felt the urge to do anything to induce such vile behavior. Ernie thought his father's lust was repugnant and not manly in the least. He didn't ever want to be like that.

He spent most of his time on deck. Looking out at the sea and the land he occasionally spotted prevented him feeling nauseous. Then one afternoon Mellor joined him.

'I am afraid that I will be returning to Britain on the delivery of this ship.'

Ernie looked aghast. 'May I ask why sir?'

His Wing-Commander looked down for a brief moment, then raising his head and looking straight out to sea he continued,

'My wife has died.'

Ernie was shocked. He didn't even know that Mellor was married.

'I must return to see to things at home. I have a daughter.'

Ernie sympathized with him but protocol meant that there was a line you did not cross. To shake his Wing-Commander's hand in condolence without its being first offered would be considered a liberty.

'Because of this incident I will informally tell you that you are to be promoted to Squadron Leader.'

Ernie was dumb-founded.

'I am aware of the irregularity of this but we are in irregular circumstances. I am unsure as to my return yet, but it is likely it will be alongside the military personnel who are being shipped to Malta in a few weeks. My men know you and respect you. They need a face they trust and recognize to be answerable to over there. I have a feeling it is not going to be the easy ride they think it is.'

Ernie was very much aware that being taken into the Wing-Commander's confidence like this was an honour and one he would be sure to repay by his undivided loyalty to the RAF and to Mellor personally. Having the Commander's respect meant everything in the world to him and he surprised himself by feeling tears come to his eyes. He hoped that his superior would think that it was because of his own sad news and not because Ernie was so touched by the complimentary words with regard to himself.

~

Billy was put out by Ernie's promotion.

'He definitely has you in his favour,' he said sulkily when Ernie imparted the news to him. 'What did you do, offer to polish his boots with your tongue or something?'

Ernie was angry at his friend's obvious jealousy, but he had already suffered the taunts of men from his previous regiment when he was transferred to join the RAF and he could put up with more. Having to take it from Billy was harder.

'So I guess this means you will be giving me the orders now, right?'

Billy was stung by this knowledge. 'Flamin' typical,' he shouted and slammed his fist into the cabin door. 'I have a wife to support and you get the darned promotion. Even you Irish are higher in the eyes of the powers that be than the Maltese. Whose island is it anyway? Who better to protect it than us?'

Ernie didn't disagree with him. However he had a task to accomplish and this was what occupied his thoughts at the moment. They had just berthed in Malta and he was to report to the Air-Vice-Marshall Maynard at Luqa Airbase immediately. Maynard had been in Malta just a week before Ernie and the other pilots arrived. He was not very enthusiastic about his posting. When he took over his role there was practically nothing for him to command apart from old bi-planes used for target-throwing duties. There were three airfields, none of which were fully operational. Luqa airfield itself was still being built. Takali airfield in the west was nothing more than a dried out lake. This together with a radar system on the Dingli cliffs, south of the island made his mission a depressing one. So far Malta was not somewhere he was happy to be. Although pleased to see the arrival of pilots to the island, he couldn't see how he was to continue to train them without any aircraft.

On receiving word that Mellor was returning to Britain immediately he was in foul humour by the time newly promoted Squadron Leader McGuill stood in front of him. Ernie's file had not yet been delivered to him and he was unaware of the high regard in which this pilot was known for his dangerous and successful reconnaissance missions.

'So,' he declared, looking the tall man in front of him up and down, 'I suppose you came here for the sun. Well it's not arrived yet. All we have so far is rain so I suggest you find another way to fill your time while you are here.'

Ernie stared straight ahead, wishing he could clench his fists so as not to knock the cap of the sarcastic man facing him. However, he was at attention and therefore had to keep his palms professionally down at his sides. He reminded himself of his rank and the ambition that someday he would be sitting in the chair of the man in front so he remained silent.

'I don't know if you are aware, but we have no aircraft for you to fly. Why they sent me pilots and no planes is beyond me, but perhaps we can find something for you to do. I haven't seen your file so I have no idea who or what you are, so maybe you would enlighten me.'

Ernie did as he was asked. Conscious of not wanting to boast of his achievements, something which was frowned upon in the RAF, he listed his flying missions to date and when he had finished he was relieved when told to take a chair.

'A recon pilot eh?' this excited Captain Maynard more. 'I could do with one of those. You know there is talk of Italy joining the war?' Ernie indicated that yes he was aware.

'It would be interesting to see exactly what those Eyeties are up too.'

Ernie did not want to enlighten Maynard by informing him that he had already been notified by Mellor of his mission. He was also aware of the plan that Spitfires were to be sent to Malta but again he kept this information to himself. Apparently he had been privy to more facts than the Air-Vice-Marshall he was assigned to. He didn't think this was something he should share.

'You are lucky enough to be stationed at Luqa Barracks with me,' Maynard jibed. 'It is quite basic there and also quite relaxed, for the time being. Physical training is required. Route marches, that sort of thing, as is the preliminary training in navigation, aircraft recognition, Morse code, service law etc. With your rank you will be assigned to train the younger pilots in these areas until I have another task for you. Good luck McGuill.'

Ernie decided that the interview had gone well enough. Even if he did feel Maynard was slating him in the beginning, he realized quickly that if anything the older man just seemed frustrated. Like Ernie, he was here to do a job without the tools to do so. He understood that. Waiting around for something to happen drove him crazy and he supposed that if he had been in the other man's shoes he would behave in the same manner.

7

Ernie found that he loved Malta. He marvelled at the walled fortress around St. Elmo and the waterfront. He was in awe of the high solid walls and the majestic citadels, beautiful churches and palaces. Usually he didn't take much notice of his surroundings, but one couldn't help doing so in Malta.

When the ship had ferried them into Valletta harbour just a few days ago, he was standing on deck with his mouth gaping open at the beauty before him. The sun was just beginning to set as they arrived and the city was clothed in an orange glow. It was something he had imagined from hearing stories as a child about far-away lands, Arabian nights and ancient cities. It looked like a picture out of one of those books. He immediately ran below deck to grab his camera and by the time they pulled into port he had a dozen photographs already taken. Over the next few days Ernie didn't go anywhere without his camera strung around his neck as he toured the island with some of the other men. His *Leica IIIa* was his pride and joy and he had a selection of other cameras also back at the Barracks. He hoped he could add to his collection while in Malta.

Kalkara and the three cities of Copsicua, Vittoriosa and Senglea took his breath away. It seemed that everywhere he turned there were wondrous sights to behold. He clicked away continuously, with the other men having great fun striking different poses for him. He had got Billy back on side when he showed him the photographs he had taken of his wedding to Katie at Christmas. He had brought the film over with him as he did not have time to get them developed before they left. It appeared getting photographs developed was cheaper in Malta, as everything else seemed to be, much to the men's delight.

As Maynard had told him, things were quite relaxed at Luqa

Barracks, although it was not without some loathing that he and the men had to physically build runways themselves. Carting heavy stone about all day was not what they had envisaged on their deployment to Malta. As Ernie wanted to be regarded as one of the men he also did the back-breaking work with them. As a result they all wore blisters on their hands and complained of aching joints. The one good thing about it though was that it passed the day and they all knew that if they wanted to fly, then they had to have runways.

It was thirsty work. As soon as the men downed tools when the dusk began to draw in, everybody showered and changed and headed into the nearest bar for some beers. Ernie occasionally joined them, but like anybody who doesn't drink, after a few hours when everybody else is swaying and talking rubbish three octaves higher than their usual speech, it stops being fun. Instead he unsuccessfully tried to coax his men to go home.

Later of course he had to listen to them arrive back to Barracks, singing and shouting at one another. In the morning they were reluctant to get up. They always managed it though, even if it meant that they moaned and groaned, complaining of hangovers the whole next day. His men were good chaps however. They looked out for each other all the time and if there was some jealousy initially at Ernie's promotion, it was quickly dissipated by his also taking on any physical work they were asked to do. As one of the men said:

'Ernie wouldn't give you a chore he wouldn't do himself.'

It was true. Having the respect of his men was of utmost importance to him.

~ *Ana* ~
1

England, February 1940

Ana felt guilty that she was more upset about leaving England and her friends than she was about her mother's death. She also felt terribly guilty because of all the fights with her mother over petty things, sometimes even telling her mother that she hoped she would die. Now Ana wondered if somehow it was she that had willed it to happen. Every time she thought that, a chill would go right through her body and an awful feeling would develop in the pit of her stomach. This feeling was much worse than 'butterflies' before going into an exam. She still felt consumed with guilt despite her school chaplain's attempt to relieve it. Although she had cried at Mama's funeral and was genuinely shocked and saddened at her mother's sudden death, she still could not meet her father's eye. Ana was sure that with one look at her he would know that Mama's death was all her fault.

Just four days ago she had woken up to the usual sounds of other girls in the dormitory chatting and laughing. She found her slippers with her feet and wrapped her warm woollen dressing-gown around her. On this chilly February morning, she wondered whether to finish her essay or to sneak outside for a cigarette with Juliette before breakfast.

Now as Ana stood in the rain-soaked cemetery, looking over at her Father's bulky form opposite, she tried to make sense of how her life had changed so drastically in such a short time. She hadn't even realized it was raining until she got into the back of the sombre black funeral car and the driver rather unkindly made her sit on a rug so that she wouldn't get his seats wet.

Sr. Emmanuel's entrance into her form room on Monday morning filled Ana with a horrible sense of foreboding. She watched as Rev. Mother whispered something into the form-tutor's ear and she knew immediately that this time it wasn't because she had been caught smoking again. Sadly, she wasn't the first girl to be called out of class in the last few months. When their classmate didn't return everybody knew that it was because somebody had been killed. It was usually a beloved father or brother fighting in France. Each girl felt both a mixture of sadness for the person who was bereaved and a huge sense of relief that this time it wasn't one of her own family members. Usually the girl would disappear for a few days and come back quiet and subdued. Some didn't come back at all. By February, just a mere five months after the outbreak of the war, many people had been killed but so far nobody that Ana knew. To her it was something that happened to other people. Her heart beat wildly in her chest as she followed Sr. Emmanuel to her office. As the Head closed the door behind her and beckoned Ana to sit she cried out,

'It is father isn't it? He has been killed, but how? Malta isn't in the war.' Then she collapsed into the chair while the kindly nun put her arms around her,

'No my dear, your father is quite safe in Malta. I am afraid it is bad news about your mother.'

~

When she arrived into the large drawing room at home where her mother always sat reading and doing her correspondence, the vacant chair didn't conjure up any sudden feelings of loss. Mama was often away on Ana's weekends at home, engaged in war work or visiting friends and shopping in London. It was one of the reasons for their many arguments. Ana didn't understand why she had to leave her beloved St. Leonard's–on-Sea (or St. Len's as it was known to the boarders) where weekends could be spent walking in town with her friends, having refreshments in one of the many tea-rooms and hopefully meeting some of the young men from the nearby college. Instead, Mama insisted that Ana make the journey by train to Yorkshire each Friday evening, often not arriving home until very late at night if trains were cancelled or delayed. Ana also couldn't understand the point of the long trip just to be bored in a dull house all weekend on her own. Most of the time if Mama was busy, her only outing was to Mass on Sunday morning with Kitty, her adored housekeeper. Occasionally Mama would have neighbours or friends visiting. Ana had to join them in the drawing-room and listen to tedious village talk until she was dismissed to her bedroom for the night. Then she would curl up on her window seat, cigarette in one hand, a book in the other, and blow the smoke out into the cold night air. Little did she know last Saturday night that it would be the last time she would do so.

Now she was at home to pack and this evening she and her father were taking the Southern Railway train to Southhampton port. From there they had to make the long and dangerous journey to Malta on a Royal Navy ship. In the past she and her mother had taken the ferry to Calais on their annual holiday, followed by the train journey down through France where they would take a ship from Marseilles to Malta. However now because of the war, they would have to sail the whole way. Ana was looking forward to going on board a naval ship. Although her father had taken her on one some years before just to have a look, this was the first time she would actually sail on one.

She was leaving home. Saying goodbye to Kitty was the worst part of it all. She had been in Ana's life since she was born. Although officially the family housekeeper, she had been more of a nursemaid in Ana's early years. Her comforting presence in the house was still the only thing that made it home to Ana. It was Kitty who always knew that she liked her milk put in before the tea was poured and couldn't bear the skin that formed on the top of her hot chocolate. It was also Kitty who matter of factly and consolingly explained that she was not bleeding to death, but having a 'totally normal monthly event like all the other women in the world in order to carry babies.' Her mother had awkwardly told her that it was part of the curse of being a woman and something never to be mentioned or talked about, ever. But Kitty could not be coerced into going, despite her heartache at losing her 'wee dote' Ana.

'I'd rather the divil I know than the divil I don't,' was Kitty's simple answer to Father's request that she accompany them back to Malta. 'And anyways, this place needs somebody looking after it for you 'til you get back.'

Kitty had not lost her lilting Irish accent despite her many years in England. As she hugged Ana to her ample chest she whispered she had packed away some of those cigarettes that Ana pretended she didn't smoke, as well her own well-used rosary beads and some holy water to keep her safe. Ana blushed, thanked her, promised to write regularly and said she would see her soon. Hopefully this would be at Christmas time. To this Kitty replied as she wiped Ana's eyes just as she had done when she was a little girl. 'That's only if God spares us all child. Sure only He knows what's in store. What do I always tell you? People make plans and God laughs.'

2

Ana hated all of it. The sea-sickness, the smells, especially the ones that she knew were her own. She had only seen her father twice since this hateful journey. He had come into her cabin the evening of her first day on board to enquire as to her well-being. She had hastily pulled the scratchy blanket up over herself to disguise the fact that her nightdress was covered in her last meal. Retching into a bowl with nowhere to get rid of the evidence afterwards was not the kind of pastime she had envisaged when her father told her of the trip to Malta. In her innocence she had been looking forward to fun times on deck like the last time she had visited the island with Mama. During those voyages they had dressed for evening meals with the Captain and sea-sickness was treated with kindness and soup in bed. Travelling on a military ship was quite different. Her first shock was the realisation that she had to share a cabin with several other young women. They had volunteered as nurses on the outbreak of war, naively thinking that doing their service abroad would be more exciting. The majority of them, like Ana, spent the whole time so far throwing up and wishing they had stayed in dear old England. On boarding at first she was treated with sympathy owing to the black armband over her coat sleeve showing that she had been recently bereaved. Being the daughter of a Wing-Commander had also afforded her a certain type of treatment. However, after only one day she was pushed aside just as quickly as the others when it came to a stampede for a 'sick bowl.'

Except for the assistance of a young woman named Katie Cortis whom she had met on her first day of boarding, she didn't know how she would have coped on the long torturous journey. Katie was just twenty-one years old but seemed much more mature than Ana. She was from London and had recently married a Maltese pilot named William, or Billy as Katie called him.

'Oh he is the most handsome man I have ever seen,' Katie crooned as she showed Ana a wedding photograph. 'He practically stole me of the fellow I was seeing at the time, right there on the dance-floor. He told me he was going to marry me the first time we spoke and he was right.'

Katie was making the journey to join her husband who had been posted to Malta in January, having gained his pilot's licence in Cranwell. Katie couldn't wait to see him again. Ana thought it was all so romantic and looked forward to meeting the man her new friend talked about day and night. The two young women became inseparable on the voyage. Katie swapped bunks with another girl so she could be closer to Ana when she became ill. She held her hair back from her face when she got sick and sponged her down day and night, never leaving her side unless it was to fetch something that Ana needed.

'I don't know how I would have managed without you,' Ana said. 'I have only seen my father twice since we started the journey and he knows how ill I am. He hates sickness though.'

'Oh men are useless when women are taken poorly,' Katie retorted. 'But when they are sick, it's a different kettle of fish altogether.'

Katie's optimism and good spirits cheered Ana considerably and she didn't mind when Katie confided her concerns about going to live in a foreign country.

'I've never been anywhere really see, especially not by myself. There are eight of us in my family and everywhere I go I'm always with some of them. I'm terrified to tell you the truth about going over there. I mean, I don't even speak the language.'

'You don't need to worry about that,' Ana reassured her. 'They all speak English because of Malta being a British colony.'

'See, I didn't even know that,' Katie replied making both of them giggle.

By the time they arrived in Malta both women were fast friends having spent every waking minute together. Despite the differences in their ages and backgrounds, they became almost as close as sisters and vowed to see as much of each other as possible in Malta.

Up to the time that sickness took hold Ana had been feeling sad about leaving England and her friends, especially Kitty who was more like a mother than a housekeeper. This sadness was coupled with the excitement of going to live in Malta. She loved it over there. The sun, the sea and the parties given by the wives of her father's colleagues made her hate to leave when it came time to return to boarding school. Although once she had settled back in and enjoyed the catching up with the other girls, the summer in Malta was soon forgotten. She did have several friends in Malta. These were daughters of her father's colleagues whose mothers had chosen to remain on the island while their husbands were stationed there. Her friends went to English schools and some of them boarded like her. They wrote to each other during the school year and she looked forward to meeting up with them again when she arrived. However, this time it was different. Now she was going back to Malta to live there, perhaps even forever.

When the ship pulled into Valletta the first thing Ana noticed that was different were the enormous battleships moored around Grand Harbour. Instead of the luxurious cruise liners and lovely little colourful fishing boats which usually hugged the area around the water's edge, these ships loomed large and intimidating. Jutting up out of the sea, their ugly greyness immediately caused a sombre quietness on deck, which up until now was beginning to hum with the excitement of passengers happy at last to get on land.

'Look at the barbed wire,' Katie whispered, her manicured hand shaking as she pointed towards the harbour.

Ana looked to where her friend indicated but was blinded for a few seconds by the glare of the sun. Each time she arrived in Malta she was shocked by its dazzling brightness which caused black spots to float in front of her eyes, making her squint. Even in February she could already feel the heat from its rays.

Stop doing that darling,' her mother used to exclaim, as she rubbed the spot in between Ana's eyes were already there was a slight crease developing. 'You will get wrinkles and no man wants a woman with wrinkles.'

Her mother wasn't here to prevent her squinting now. Placing her hand up over her forehead she peered at what looked like rows of huge balls of silver twine. They made a rainbow effect on the blue water and their reflection shimmering in the sun looked so pretty, causing a kaleidoscope of colours in the sea in front of them. Then Ana's eyes adjusted to the sunshine and she could see that they were actually thick angry balls of steel. The sharp nasty looking points of wire promised bodily harm if anybody approached. But the thing that shocked Ana most of all were the signs which were dotted every couple of yards. On wooden posts in large red capital letters, written in both English and Maltese with a huge X in the centre, were the words:

'PPROJBIT GHAWM U SAJD '
'FORBIDDEN SWIMMING & FISHING'

Ana was puzzled. Malta was far from the war in England, Germany and France. There was nothing in the newspapers about the Germans having any interest in Malta, so why was this beautiful city of Valletta being so obviously protected? Protected from whom? Ana felt quite confident that she was knowledgeable about the war. Having a father who was a RAF

Wing-Commander meant that she was privy to some information not even mentioned in the newspapers or newsreels she saw in the picture house. Although Father never 'spoke shop' in front of her, she often heard snippets of his war talk and her silence as she hid behind a book meant she could eavesdrop without anybody realising she was there. Usually war talk bored her and much of what she heard went over her head. Despite her feelings about leaving England, she was quite relieved to get away from the threat of air raids and the restraints of war. Knowing that she would soon be far away from it was comforting.

3

From what Ana could gather Malta was apparently at war as it was under the monarchy of King George VI. But like Ireland, which she knew had some parts belonging to Britain, there was no talk of Hitler invading it. Hadn't she heard her mother talk to her friends about how relieved she was that Father was stationed in Malta and not in France or Poland or somewhere like that, where the 'real fighting' was taking place.

'I hope it's not going to be like this everywhere Ana. I couldn't bear it,' Katie exclaimed as she climbed into the dgħajs which was going to ferry them to the harbour.

Ana had already snagged her stockings trying rather ungracefully to climb aboard. She put out a hand to steady her friend.

'I do hope Billy is waiting for me. I'm dying to see my new home and get a decent meal. Aren't you hungry? I'm starving.'

'Oh gosh yes,' Ana nodded her head, 'It seems ages since breakfast time, but a hot bath is what I am looking forward to most of all.'

Katie had never been to Malta before and was dismayed that her first impressions were not good ones. Billy hadn't warned her about it looking so grim. Yes, the scenery was breath-taking, anybody could see that. But Valletta harbour had scared her to death with all the battleships and warning signs and barbed wire. It wasn't what she was expecting at all. Ana had told her how beautiful it was and spoke fondly of the hustle and bustle of the marinas. Katie was also looking forward to the fun social life Ana told her about, the parties and picnics. It sounded like just the type of lifestyle she always desired and it made married life seem much more thrilling. But so far Malta looked disappointingly like a war zone. She thought she had left that far behind her.

'Oh, do come with us Ana,' Katie cried coaxingly to her friend who was still patiently waiting at the sea front for her father to disembark. 'He's probably gone off somewhere with all the other military. Don't you know where you are going?'

'What is the name of the school?' Billy was anxious to get his young wife to himself. 'We can drop you there if you like?'

Ana opened her smart black leather shoulder bag and brought out the letter from the school. Centred at the top of the cream embossed paper in beautiful print were the words: Verdala Esteemed Boarding School for Young Ladies, Valletta.

She handed the letter to Billy who nodded to indicate that he knew where it was.

'Champion school, we will have you there in no time. Climb aboard.'

'What about my luggage?'

'Oh that will be sent on presently. Don't worry about that.' Billy started up the army truck he had borrowed for the occasion.

As the truck whizzed along the roads, Ana could see many changes since last summer when she had visited her father. Evidence of service personnel was all around. There were many more soldiers walking about in uniform than she had ever noticed before. All along the waterfront were naval ships and cargo boats. The usual fishing boats jostled for space in between them. She fleetingly thought about the painted eye on all the little Maltese boats that was supposed to ward off evil spirits. She was sure the local fishermen weren't happy with the invasion of their ports.

Billy drove up a long driveway lined with trees. The boarding school itself looked just like one of the small palaces that were in evidence all around in Valletta. It was ornately decorated with the baroque design distinctive of most Maltese traditional buildings. Walking around the grounds, which were not so typically green, were many young girls and women, some linking arms and others reading while they walked. Other girls could be seen in the distance on a tennis court.

'It does like nice. Doesn't it?' Katie asked. 'It's much better than the horrible looking school buildings at home.'

Ana was about to agree but she realised that Katie was actually saying this to Billy. Her friend had clung possessively to her husband's arm, chattering continuously to him while they drove the short journey to the school. She mostly complained about missing him and Billy had made consoling noises while trying to concentrate on weaving the truck in and out of the busy roads. By this stage Ana was exhausted and didn't care if she was being left in the charge of a prison warden right now. She was just eager to get washed and into bed and any bed would be preferable to a swaying bunk. Nonetheless when Katie and Billy drove back up the driveway having waved goodbye, Ana felt quite bereft. Up until now she had never been alone. On the ship Katie was her constant companion and she felt a touch of jealousy seeing her go off with Billy.

The Headmistress, Miss Honeyman welcomed her at Reception. As Ana followed her up the stairs she realised she was on her own now with strangers.

'Strangers are friends you have yet to meet,' is what she knew Kitty would have said. She had a saying for everything and Ana often found herself repeating these same sayings at various times in her life.

'I am afraid that my luggage is in transit,' she informed Miss Honeyman.

'Don't worry,' the glamorous looking older woman informed her. 'We are prepared for these little emergencies.'

Pointing at a door that said 'Provisions', she told Ana to help herself to whatever she needed. 'We simply ask that clothes are returned washed and ironed and toiletries replaced when you are in a position to do so. Until then, you may take what you want, as you need it.'

Ana thanked her and then gasped with surprise when Miss Honeyman opened one of the doors on the spacious landing and said, 'This shall be your room. I trust it is to your liking?'

Ana was thrilled with the large feminine room which had a small balcony overlooking the back of the building with the sea in the distance, but she simply nodded and replied,

'Yes, it is very nice, thank you.'

However when another door off the bedroom was opened, she almost squealed with delight. Inside was a small pink flowery bathroom, complete with a tub. She was overjoyed at this luxury. This place was more like a hotel than a school and Ana was sorry she would only be here until her final exams in May. What her father had planned for her after that was still unknown. Mama had organised a year in France at the finishing school where she herself had gone. However the war had changed all that and nobody knew if it would all be over by May.

~

It was almost a week later before Father called to see her. Miss Honeyman, or Honey as the girls called her owing to her buxom shape, showed him into the Reception Room where tea and cakes were laid out.

'My dear Anabel, how are you finding Verdala?'

Wing-Commander Mellor laid his cap on the side table. As a tall man he cut quite a dashing figure in his uniform. Although now beginning to grey a little around the temples, this served to give him an air of distinction along with the piercing blue eyes which Ana had inherited. She was often aware of women casting a second glance at him wherever he went. Her father was away so often that when she met up with him she felt every time that she had to get to know him all over again. This was tiresome and she always felt scrutinised as though up for inspection like one of his officers. He had quite a deep loud voice also and although this was an asset as Wing-Commander, it was very intimidating to a young girl growing up. As a result, Ana always kept well out of his way when she could on his visits home.

Since Mama's death the family consisted just of herself and her father and for this reason Ana resolved to get to know him. She was no longer a child and hoped that they could begin to have some type of relationship with each other. He never spoke of her mother's death. When Laurence Mellor arrived at their stately home for his wife's funeral he was exhausted from the long journey. He had flown most of the way in quite dangerous conditions and appeared older than usual. He had formally shaken Ana's hand when he found her seated with Mama's friends in the drawing room and said that it was a 'bad business.'

It was Kitty who had told her about the impending trip to Malta. Although she was happy that her father was not going to abandon her, she was anxious about leaving and longed to ask her father so many questions. She wanted to ask about things that were important to her, but perhaps not so much to him, like where she was going to live or if she would continue school.

'You're going to be going to a fancy boarding school over there so ye are,' Kitty told her as she folded some of Ana's undergarments and placed them in a suitcase. 'I'm packing the lot. It's still February,' Kitty continued doggedly when Ana protested that she never needed woollen vests in Malta.

'Better to be prepared. Anyway, I believe that this boarding school is the best that there is. Daughters of the officers go to it and it's supposed to be even better than that fancy finishing place your mother was for sending you to. I think there's even royalty goes to it.'

'When will I see you again Kitty?' Ana threw her arms around the stout woman's body and began to sob.

'Ach my wee love,' Kitty whispered as she rocked Ana to and fro against her soft bosom. 'When it's God's will,' was her simple reply and she began to hum softly to the sweet girl that to her was always a child. Looking out the huge bay window at the rain pouring down outside Kitty wondered when exactly that might be.

4

The girls in the school were obsessed with romance. They were worse than those Ana had left behind in St. Len's. Here boys were the topic of almost every conversation. Perhaps since her previous school had been run by nuns, any talk of boys had been confined to weekend trips to the tea-rooms in town.

The girls were waiting for the rickety bus that was to take them to Mtarfa in Rabat which was on the west of the Island. Miss Honeyman had organised that anybody wishing to train as a nurse could attend an interview today with the matron of the Military Hospital. They had been assured that young ladies from a privileged establishment like Verdala would be welcomed with open arms. Nursing was not a profession that was high on Ana's list of chosen careers. She still had hopes of returning to England and perhaps eventually joining her friends in France at the finishing school. In fact she detested the sight of blood and seeing it sometimes made her feel faint, especially if it was her own. However father had decided that Mtarfa was a good place to go after her final exams in May. Right now any idea of returning to England was quite definitely out of the question. Although nursing was not considered the noblest of professions for a young lady, there were opportunities to travel. Miss Honeyman knew that Ana was keen to experience this and because of the war, nurses were needed everywhere. Besides, she had nowhere else to go. Jeany, her school-friend was also going to Mtarfa, as were several others. Admittedly they were more excited about the opportunity of meeting trainee doctors than in assisting the sick.

There was a dance on that evening at the Regent Hotel in Sliema for the Easter celebrations and they all were hoping to get back from Mtarfa in plenty of time to prepare for this thrilling event. The young RAF officers would be there and talk of what to wear and how to do their hair had been the topic of the girls chat all week.

'Golly,' exclaimed Ana, as the bus wound its way up the hill towards the hospital. 'It's huge isn't it?' Jeany nodded her head in agreement. 'It's the biggest hospital in Malta I think,' she added. 'There are bound to be plenty of doctors here.'

Matron Saliba was the scariest looking woman Ana had ever seen. She was about 14 stone and her blue uniform, complete with white apron on which was a large red cross looked as though it was going to burst at the seams. Her hair was scraped back under a white veil and despite her robust frame she had a thin pinched face with beady eyes that looked like she could read your mind. This caused Ana to colour a little, immediately bringing her to the Matron's attention.

'Do you require medical assistance?' she asked in a booming voice.

Ana stammered a reply that she was quite well, just tired from the journey. Matron answered,

'If you look like that after a bus ride, I wouldn't like to see you after a shift in my hospital.'

Ana considered herself severely rebuked and with a blushing face she followed the other girls into a spacious room which was obviously Matron's office.

'Gosh Ana, she sure had it in for you didn't she?' exclaimed Jeany later as they walked back towards the bus stop.

'I don't think she liked me,' Ana agreed forlornly. 'She looked at me the whole time she told us about the rules, as if she was expecting me to break every one of them.'

'Oh, don't mind her,' Jeany replied soothingly. 'My sister said her bark is worse than her bite and that she's alright really. Vicky was here for a year before she got married and she loved it. Though I have to admit, it does seem quite strict. It's more like a school than the one we are at already. Do you think it's just like that during training? I mean, how are we ever going to meet a husband if we can't get out of there to meet anybody?'

'Let's not talk about that now Jeany. We have a dance to get ready for!'

Ana didn't want to think any more about the fierce looking woman or her catalogue of rules. She couldn't wait to go dancing tonight. In two short months they would start their exams and if she didn't do well, father had warned that she would have to repeat the whole year. She didn't want to see all her new friends move on without her.

'Maybe tonight you will get to kiss somebody,' Jeany said as she attempted to do a victory roll in Ana's hair from a magazine she had laid out on the bed. 'Well not a boy I mean, a young man. I can't believe you never have.'

'I can't believe you have kissed three,' was Ana's sharp reply. 'Where did you meet them all?'

'Oh, that's the good thing about having several sisters,' was Jeany's response. 'They always need a chaperone when out with a man and of course I always volunteer. However, the plan is that their beau takes a chaperone too and we both pair off. That way everybody is happy and everybody gets kissed.'

Once again Ana was reminded of being an only child. She greatly envied her friend with her large family of brothers and sisters. Jeany was always off with one of them and she got invited to lots of fun excursions. Ana, on the other hand had to stay behind patiently waiting to hear all the gossip when Jeany returned. She had accompanied Jeany several times to her family home at the busy seaside village of St. Julian's and loved the noise and banter of a noisy household. However Jeany assured her that it wasn't always fun.

'It is impossible to have any time to oneself,' she grumbled. 'That is why I begged for permission to come here. At home there are always parties and appointments to be kept or people visiting. It's tiresome. At least here I can study in peace.'

Luckily for Ana, her father was very generous with his allowance. Along with Jeany, she was one of the few girls who had private rooms at Verdala. Jeany's family was very wealthy and she was in fact one of the royals that Kitty had mentioned. Although she wasn't 'royal' in the same sense as the young Princesses Elizabeth and Margaret, Jeany belonged to one of the families known as Nobles. Ana wasn't exactly sure what that meant.

Jeany's home was an actual palace. Built in the 1570s it had been in the family name of Castelletti for centuries. Although the huge front gates opened right onto the street, there was then quite a walk through a courtyard to the actual palace itself. Behind the palace were magnificent gardens and a swimming pool. The family had servants including the butler who always opened the gates. Ana had been extremely awed when she first was invited to Jeany's home. However, Madame Castelletti and her family were very friendly and they all made sure that Ana felt quite at home on her visits. Unlike some of Jeany's other friends, she and her sisters were encouraged to live independent lives, to become educated and have a career. Jeany's father told them both that the world as they now knew it was changing, and he believed that young women needed to be self-reliant.

The girls had new dresses for the dance. There was no rationing on clothes or food in Malta and they were lucky enough to be able to shop in the best clothing stores in Valletta. A shopping expedition was the most enjoyable way to spend a day and they tried on dress after dress, testing the patience of shop assistants to the limit.

Eventually their choices had been made. Katie, with whom Ana had spent much time since they arrived, had been delighted to accompany them on their outing. A respectable married woman was considered a suitable chaperone for the two young ladies and Katie was eager to get out of the Barracks for the day.

'Oh, it is so good to be away out of that place,' she sighed as she linked arms in-between the two girls. 'I hardly ever see Billy and I've been feeling wretched this last month or so. I don't think the food over here suits me at all. I can't wait to go dancing tonight. Did I tell you Billy is a fantastic dancer?'

Ana assured Katie that she heard on several occasions how Billy had won her over on the dance floor.

'Though not that I let him know that then of course,' her friend revealed. 'I wanted him to think he was the last man on earth I would go out with, but I had already decided that I was going to be Mrs William Cortis the second I set eyes on him.'

'Why did you want him to think you didn't like him?' Jeany innocently asked.

'Because men always want what they think they can't have. Always remember that,' was Katie's candid answer.

5

'Billy, you remember Ana?'

He nodded his head and handed them both a glass of white wine.

'Course I do. Do you like your new school?' he asked her.

'Yes, I am very happy there thank you. This is my good friend Miss Jeannette Castelletti. She is a boarder there too.'

Billy's face changed colour immediately. He mumbled something about getting another a glass and disappeared into the crowd.

'What was that about?' Katie asked suspiciously. 'Do you both know each other?'

'Yes, he is from the same village as me,' answered Jeany.

'Do you two have a romantic history or something?' Katie continued, her suspicions growing.

'Good Lord no,' Jeany laughed, 'His parents work for us.' Then she was the one whose face changed colour. 'I mean, our families are acquainted.'

But it was apparent to both girls listening to her what had transpired. Billy obviously felt out of his depth. Jeany was a 'Noble' whereas he was the son of her servants. No wonder he had looked embarrassed just now.

'I'd better go after him,' Katie said, feeling cross at her husband's embarrassment. Not cross with him, but at anybody who made him feel inferior. To her he was amazing just as he was. He was the kindest, most loving man she had ever met and way better than anybody else. Wasn't her mum a waitress in a coffee shop, so what was the big deal?

When Katie left, Jeany turned to her friend, obviously upset at what had just taken place.

'I feel so bad,' she confided in Ana. 'He looked so shocked to see me. His family have been with us for years and years. We love the Cortis family. They are very honourable and I have known Billy all my life. We played together as children, until my father thought it was inappropriate when we reached our teens.'

'Oh, I am sure he will get over it,' replied Ana, trying to console her friend. 'For now, let's have some fun. I for one am longing to get on the dance-floor.'

The two girls proved quite popular with the young officers who kept them busy dancing all night, until Katie came running over and practically dragged them both off the floor.

'I have to go home. I've been the whole night in the ladies room out back throwing up. I can't get Billy awake. He's passed out on the seats over there.' Katie indicated to the leather covered booths in the back of the hall where people sat with their drinks.

The three girls headed over to where Billy lay slumped, his head resting face down on the table in front, obviously full of drink.

'I can't drive,' Katie implored. 'Can either of you?'

Both young women shook their heads.

'How hard can it be though, right?' Katie asked, 'I mean, you just steer don't you? Billy's truck is out front.'

But the girls realised then that they didn't have keys. Katie searched in Billy's trouser pockets but to no avail.

'Oh for goodness sake, they must be in his jacket,' she puffed and went over to the bar where Billy had been sitting earlier with his friends. As she moved along the stools aimlessly picking up one jacket after another she spotted the friend he had introduced to her earlier. Approaching him she asked if he knew where Billy's jacket was.

'It's here. I've been sitting on it all night. Keeping it warm for him, you know,' he answered, laughing at his own joke. 'Hey, are you okay? You look a bit green around the gills?'

'No. I feel sick and Billy is out cold. The girls and I are going to try to drive his truck but none of us know how.'

'I'll take care of it. Get the girls and I'll meet you outside. But first I'm going to get some of the lads to give me a hand getting Billy up. The poor sod never could hold his drink and he has been flying all night too. I'd say he is more exhausted than drunk.'

Minutes later they all met outside. The men already had Billy in the truck. Katie climbed in beside him and the two other girls got in front.

'Where to ladies?' asked the driver.

'I'll show you the way.' Jeany laughed. 'Ana has no sense of direction.'

Ana could feel Jeany pinching her in the side. She glared at her friend, asking with her eyes what she meant. Jeany rolled her eyes back in the direction of the handsome driver who sat beside her, expertly manoeuvring the truck in and out of the traffic which was quite busy even at this late hour. Ana took a good look at the tall man behind the steering wheel and admitted that he was very dishy. She nodded and smiled at Jeany, sure that her friend would not need much encouragement to make her intentions clear to him.

She sure didn't, for within seconds she struck up a conversation;

'Where are you based?' Jeany asked him.

'At Luqa,' he answered.

'Have you been here long?'

'I came over with Billy. So about two and a half months. How long are you here?'

'Oh just about the same length of time as you. We arrived in February.'

'You must have come over on the same ship as my Wing-Commander then.'

At this Ana's ears pricked up and she asked, 'Who is your

Wing-Commander?'

'Laurence Mellor.'

'He is my father.'

'Then I must offer my sincere condolences on the loss of your mother Miss Mellor.'

'Pretty girl,' he thought. She had her father's eyes, but her hair was blond whereas her father's was dark.

'Thank you,' Ana answered, and remained quiet for the duration of the journey.

'Well,' Jeany asked as soon as the truck had driven off, leaving the girls at the front door. 'Wasn't he dishy?'

'Yes, he was,' Ana agreed. But she was concerned that he knew her father. First of all her father wouldn't like to know she had been at a dance and drinking alcohol. Also, he wouldn't like to know she had been out so late and had to be driven home by one of his officers. She hoped this man wouldn't say anything to him.

However, thoughts of Ana were far from this officer's head when he finally got to bed. He was exhausted. It had taken him and two other men to get Billy into his married quarters without waking up the whole Barracks. To his horror, Katie had thrown up in the truck, not once but twice. That would have to be hosed out tomorrow and he knew just the man for the job.

6

'It is totally your decision,' explained Miss Honeyman. 'Matron wanted me to ask you all. Nobody is expected to go if they don't wish to. You all have exams and some of you could do with more time than others to study.'

The matron at Mtarfa had requested that any of the girls who were free would begin their training a little earlier than originally planned. There was a need to train up nurses as quickly as possible. She had suggested that they go to the hospital from Thursday evening to Sunday, which still allowed them four days in school to prepare for the upcoming exams.

Ana volunteered and was surprised when Jeany declined.

'My parents wouldn't be happy,' she explained, 'they are adamant that I do well in these exams. I don't want to let them down.'

None of the other girls wanted to give up their weekends either and Ana found herself the only one going off the following Thursday on the bus journey to Rabat. She needed to get a connecting bus from Sliema and found herself walking up and down the road looking for the correct one. She was getting worried now, concerned about arriving late on her first evening. Matron already seemed to have a poor opinion of her.

Once again as she began the walk up the street opposite the harbour, carefully reading each bus-stop sign as she did so, a young man approached her.

'Are you lost?' he asked.

Ana took a breath. He was so handsome, in a rugged sort of way.

'No, I mean yes. I am rather, I am afraid.' she stammered. 'I am trying to find the bus to Rabat.'

'Oh that is too bad,' he replied. 'The last bus to Rabat left about ten minutes ago, from there,' and he pointed at the corner where Ana, to her embarrassment saw a clearly written sign saying, RABAT BUS-STOP.

'Oh, I was sure the last time I got one it was outside the Regent,' she said, worried now that she was not going to be able to make it to the hospital tonight.

'Yes, you are correct in that. However, it only goes from there at the weekend. Any other day it stops here. I can give you a lift if you like.'

Ana did like, but she was concerned about being unchaperoned with a man, especially a man she didn't know.

'I don't mean a lift the whole way to Rabat. I mean, I can follow the bus,' the man explained to her, seeing her worried expression.

Ana agreed and he told her to wait, saying he would be back in a moment.

Minutes later Ana was a little alarmed to see that they would not be travelling by motorcar, but by horse and cart. She had never ridden this way. Not wanting the man to witness her discomfiture, she grabbed the hand he offered and with a toss of her head, climbed into the seat beside him. The journey took just about fifteen minutes. As promised, the man who introduced himself as Franco Vella, did manage to catch up with the old yellow bus and yelled at the driver to pull over.

'I hope everything goes well for you at the hospital,' he said as he helped her down.

Ana explained her haste to get to Mtarfa. She corrected him when he thought she had a sick relative.

'Oh no, I am beginning my nursing training this evening,' she told him, 'and I think the matron already doesn't like me.'

'I can't see why that would be,' was his somewhat forward reply. 'But I am hoping that if I ever have a terrible fishing accident I will be taken to your hospital to be looked after.'

Saying this however, he crossed himself to prevent bad luck. Ana waved goodbye to him as she climbed into the bus and continued on her way. As she approached Mtarfa, she could see that Matron was waiting at the entrance of the hospital.

'Oh no,' she thought, 'I am in trouble.'

However, to her surprise, Matron was simply waiting to welcome Ana and kindly offered her some tea and cake before she began the first evening of training.

'It is very good of you to volunteer,' Matron declared, 'we are terribly under-staffed at the moment and there has been a bout of gastritis among the local children. I need you to help out with general care in the men's ward. For now you can just keep a close eye on the patients. Let me or the other nurses know if you see anything that might need attention. Soon you will have simple duties like taking temperatures, bandaging and that sort of thing.'

When they finished their tea, Matron called a nurse who showed Ana to her dormitory. It was a long spacious room with eight neatly made beds, each complete with a locker and narrow wardrobe at either side. There were curtains in between each cubicle, like in a ward, and some beds had brightly coloured blankets thrown over them. On the lockers were a selection of toiletries and some photographs in frames, but overall there was a sense of order and neatness in the room. It was however quite different from her plush bedroom at Verdala. Her bed was pointed out and Ana was happy to see it was next to a window. She followed the quietly spoken nurse back across a court-yard to the main hospital. Here she was given a uniform which fitted her perfectly. The veil however was trickier to place on her head and she wandered out in the corridor with it in her hand, until a nurse came running over and chastised her gently.

'Don't ever let Matron see you come out here like that,' she remonstrated kindly, 'she would have an attack of rage and that's a scary sight, let me tell you. We must look immaculately dressed at all times, no matter what is happening. If our uniforms get dirty, we have to go immediately we get a chance and change. Here, let me help you. You'll get used to putting the veil on in no time.'

After her first evening and night, Ana was exhausted. There were two other girls asleep in the dormitory when she finally got to bed sometime after 2am. Matron had told her to go at midnight. Then four soldiers who had been injured when their truck overturned on the Dingli cliffs were brought in and it was all hands on deck. None of the men was in a serious condition, but Ana was needed to record temperatures and other vital statistics, to give them some hot sweet tea and distribute blankets. When the four were declared well enough to be discharged it was almost 2am and Matron once again told Ana to go to bed which she did gladly.

The seven o'clock call came very quickly and by eight Ana was once again on duty. This morning she was in training which meant she had to watch and assist the other experienced nurses when required. After lunch she was transferred to the admissions section where she was to receive basic training in dressings. Following the evening meal Ana's time was spent between the wards where she was most needed. It appeared that most of her training was going to be very much on a 'watch and learn' basis. Matron kept a very close eye on her, as did the other sisters on the wards. They were all very nice to her however and seemed to be grateful for the extra pair of hands.

By the time Ana returned to Verdala on Sunday night she was tired, but felt a great sense of purpose which she had never experienced before. She found that she was actually sad to leave the hospital. Her favourite part of the work was sitting chatting with the patients, especially those who seemed nervous or worried. She had a very calming influence on them and when some of the older women sat up in their beds with their rosary beads to pray, Ana often joined them. Her own beads which Kitty had kindly packed for her were always in her apron pocket and the older women seemed comforted to know that a 'mara ta fidi' as they called her, or 'woman of faith' was nursing them.

It did not go unnoticed by Matron that Ana took time out to sit with the patients. As far as she was concerned this separated the women for whom nursing was a job from those to whom nursing was a vocation. She could tell that Ana had a vocation. She had a natural affinity with people, especially vulnerable people and was quick to ascertain when somebody was frightened, even if they thought they hid it well. She saw Ana hold the hands of the older patients and carefully fix a blanket here and a pillow there to make them more comfortable. This was all natural to her and something that could not be taught in nursing training. Despite her sadness at leaving the hospital that evening, Ana was happy to be back in Verdala hearing all about how her friends had got on at the weekend dance which she missed.

'That friend of Billy's who drove us home at Easter was at the dance.' Jeany told her as soon as she arrived back. 'Katie wasn't there though. Billy said she has been quite ill.'

Hearing this Ana was worried and decided to go and visit her friend as soon as she got the opportunity.

'That chap is a cold fish though,' Jeany complained. 'You have to drag any conversation out of him. Lilian and I spent over an hour at their table and he never offered to take either of us out for a dance. Billy didn't dance either. He was too worried about Katie and was even less fun than his friend. He must have a girlfriend. Whoever she is, I envy her. He is so good looking and is definitely on his way up in the RAF. That was one subject he will talk about forever. I questioned Billy though and he said he has never known him to have a girl ever. He said that he just lives for flying.'

'Just like Father,' Ana said. 'My mother told me that she hardly ever saw him in their early married life. He was always off on a flying mission somewhere. It was only when he got promoted later on that we used to come to visit him here in Malta. I often thought she must have missed him so much. Maybe it's better not to get involved with a pilot Jeany. You don't seem to be the type who likes to wait around for a man.'

Jeany nodded her head emphatically. 'You are right there Miss Nightingale. What's the point of being married to spend all your time alone? Your friend Katie doesn't seem to see much of Billy.'

Ana agreed. She was worried about her friend. Katie had told her that she wasn't feeling well at the Easter dance and now she still appears to be ill. After the next day's lessons at Verdala, Ana took the bus to St. George's Barracks. She carried some flowers for Katie which she picked up at a little stall just outside the gates of her school and hoped they would last the journey. It wasn't very far, but the heat on the bus was making her wilt, never mind having the same effect on the bunch of flowers. She also took some magazines which she thought Katie would enjoy, knowing that her friend found it quite tedious at the Barracks and hard to keep herself occupied.

An older woman who got off at the same stop introduced herself as Mrs Catherine Johnson.

'Are you visiting someone at the Barracks?'

Ana nodded.

'Come with me then. It can be difficult to find anyone there if you don't know where you are going. What is your friend's name?' she enquired.

'Mrs Cortis. Katie Cortis,' Ana told her.

'Oh. Katie. She is a darling. She helps me with my kiddies. She is a lovely girl. To be honest with you Miss... What is your name dear?' she asked.

'Ana, Ana Mellor.'

'Are you anything to that handsome Wing-Commander, Laurence Mellor?'

'Yes. He is my father.'

'Oh he is a big hit with the ladies. So sorry about your dear mother though. That was bad news. But regarding your friend, she has been sick almost since she got here.'

Ana accepted her kind offers of condolence and followed her into the Barracks where she was shown into a huge courtyard with many different buildings. Catherine was correct. She would certainly never have found Katie on her own. The older lady showed her exactly where to go and left her to it. Ana knocked on the door but when there was no reply she pushed it and the door opened easily.

She knew this must be Katie's home, as the room she entered had frilly curtains on the windows and she was aware of the faint fragrance of Blue Grass perfume by Elizabeth Arden which her friend always wore.

She called out and Katie answered immediately.

'Ana, is that you? Oh you darling. Come in here.'

Ana followed the voice and entered into a smaller, yet prettier room and saw her friend beginning to sit herself up in the double bed which was covered in various pieces of material she was busy cutting up.

'Oh it is so good to see you,' Katie cried, throwing her arms open to Ana. The two women hugged and Ana sat down on the bed beside her. Ana was shocked at her friend's appearance.

'I heard you are still not feeling well. What do you think is wrong with you? I am a nurse now you know,' she giggled, holding on to her friend's hand, whilst also taking in the pale complexion and thinner looking face.

'I have no idea,' Katie replied while letting go of Ana's hand she ran her fingers through the hair which she knew was badly in need of a wash. 'I've been trying to keep my mind off it by making a new dress, as you can see with all this sewing paraphernalia on the bed.'

'You know there is a bad bout of gastritis among the children here. I met a woman named Catherine Johnson on the bus and she said you had spent time with her family. Maybe you picked up the same condition?'

'Yes, I heard that. Catherine's kids do have it. Her youngest son James was really bad and I was with him a lot before he went to Mtarfa hospital.'

'That's what you have then,' Ana confirmed. Though at the same time, she couldn't help but notice that Katie's lips were horribly cracked and dry. 'Have you been drinking enough water? In the few days I spent at the hospital I saw several cases of dehydration.'

'I can't keep it down,' Katie told her. 'Though one good thing, it has made me even thinner, which I am quite happy about.'

Ana laughed at her friend, vanity always came first with Katie. Nevertheless, she decided to ask Matron about her on Thursday when she returned to the hospital.

~ *Ernie* ~
8

Malta May 1940

'At last some exciting news to tell you Ernest my boy. Take a seat,' said Maynard, indicating that Ernie sit on the chair opposite his desk.

Ernie was all ears. Anything exciting was welcome. Life at Luqa Barracks was a bit boring to say the least. The runways were operational now and he was having trouble keeping the men occupied.

'We've just received seven Gladiator planes from the airfield at Hal Far, which is close to Kalafrana. You know of it I presume?'

Ernie nodded.

'Funny business at the start though.' Maynard continued, 'They were sent here at the end of April. I kept this information to myself as no sooner had they arrived, even before I had a chance to notify you, the Navy decided they needed them instead and they were shipped back over to that lot. Now they have sent seven back. They need stripping as they are full of Navy modifications and some other bits and pieces need to be added, but I am sure you and your team are up to the job?'

Ernie was thrilled. They finally had something worthwhile to do.

'Yes, without a doubt,' then he added, 'though I am a man down. Ted Langley contacted malaria in Egypt some time ago and he appears to have suffered a relapse. He is in Mtarfa hospital, in a bad enough way, so I'm told sir.'

'Hmm, I will have to ask for a volunteer from my own men then. Leave it with me. In the meantime I need you and your boys tomorrow at Grand Harbour 06.00 to meet the transport ship. I will see you over there.'

The other men were in high spirits when Ernie broke the news of their early morning task.

'Thank God,' Billy said, throwing his hat in the air. 'I was going stir crazy. Though whether I can operate a plane with these hands is questionable.'

He held his hand up to show the blisters he incurred while breaking stone for the runway at Luqa. However, nobody had sympathy for him as they all suffered with the same affliction.

'I will get some creams for you big girls when I go to check up on Ted later at the hospital,' Ernie told them, grinning as he did so. 'Let the nice nurses up there know that my chaps like to keep their hands soft!'

He ducked when boots and tin cups flew through the air in his direction and ran out the door to cadge a truck for the journey.

~

Ana recognized him as soon as he came into the ward. He was the man from the dance who had driven herself and Katie home. Feeling instantly self-conscious in her new uniform, she smoothed down the front of her apron and fixing her veil back in place, she strode with a confidence she didn't feel down the long row of beds towards him.

'Hello,' she said quietly, 'Are you visiting somebody?'

Ernie looked at the fresh faced nurse in front of him and tried to remember where he had seen her before. Then noticing her eyes he realised who she was. She was Wing-Commander Mellor's daughter.

'Oh, this is where you are now is it Miss Mellor?' he asked her. 'School out already then?'

'No. They needed volunteers for a few months so here I am. I love it though, much better than school.'

'Very good, very good,' he nodded his head, 'I'm here to see young Ted Langley. How is he?'

'Oh yes, Ted,' she blushed.

Ted had been quite a bit amorous with her earlier when his drugs took hold and had declared his undying love for the pretty nurse. Now he was sleeping it off and she reckoned he would be feeling a bit embarrassed on awakening. That was if he even remembered.

'He is asleep at the moment.'

'Is the matron about so I could find out how he is holding up?' Ernie questioned, looking around as he did so.

'If you wait just a minute I will try and find her,' and Ana walked briskly down the corridor ahead of him in search of Matron Saliba. The matron wasn't as bad as she had feared she was going to be. In fact she was nothing if not very pleasant to Ana, the only girl who had volunteered to begin her training now instead of at the beginning of June. Matron knew this meant that the young woman had to take a bus ride late on Thursday evening alone to Rabat and then walk to the hospital from there and begin working immediately on arriving. The hospital was short-staffed and Ana worked long hours without complaint, receiving in exchange just bed and board in the dormitories. Matron respected her for this and she admitted, but only to herself, that her first impression of Ana had been wrong.

After a brief conversation with the matron, Ernie returned to the ward to find Ted still sleeping and Ana unsuccessfully trying to clean the wound of a young soldier in the bed next to him.

'Are you alright?' he asked her, noticing that she looked rather pale. The soldier was in good humour having an attractive nurse sitting on his bed, so he didn't notice that she was making a mess of the job in hand.

'Yes of course,' Ana replied rather brusquely and began

walking towards the sink where she washed her hands. When he followed her, she whispered to him, 'Don't laugh, I know I am a nurse, or supposed to be. But I hate the sight of blood. It makes me feel ill. I really don't want to faint in here.'

Ernie didn't laugh. Instead he made a suggestion to her.

'When I worked on the farm at home, we had to do all sorts of things with the animals and it sickened me, but my mother used to tell me a trick that worked.'

Ana looked up expectantly at him and he continued.

'Pretend it is jam. Pretend it is sticky jam that you need to clean up as quickly as possible. Think of strawberry jam. It sounds ridiculous but it does help.'

Ana giggled, 'I will try, but if I faint on top of the soldier Matron will kill me.'

'If you do,' Ernie chortled, 'I am quite sure you will raise his temperature and his blood pressure also.'

~

Wing-Commander Mellor was also at the harbour front in the morning, as eager as the other men to see the Gladiators arrive. On spotting Ernie he approached him to say that he wished to speak with him later. Ernie was intrigued to know what this could be about, but right now his interests lay in the transport ship that was unloading the much needed aircraft.

~

'I am quite certain that you have not forgotten why I posted you to Malta in January,' Laurence Mellor said as lit his pipe and settled down in the armchair facing Ernie.

'You noticed that we unloaded a Spitfire today? The time has come for you to perform the mission we spoke about some months ago. It is imperative that we get reconnaissance facts about what Italy is planning and we need that information on the double, do you follow me?'

'Yes indeed sir,' Ernie concurred, 'When do you want me to leave?'

'You fly out first thing in the morning. I can read your mind Ernest and I can imagine your concerns after that close shave you had in Germany, so let me enlighten you. Supermarine engineers have come up with an ingenious invention for the Spitfire. Ninety gallon jettisonable fuel tanks will be carried under the fuselage of the plane. It will also be fitted with dust filters for carburetor air intakes. Isn't that genius? Not like the tin cans you used to fly eh? I am sure that little bit of information has made you a bit more eager to take to the skies. You will still be without radio back-up however, but I am sure you are aware of that. I think we should celebrate.'

Retrieving two whiskey glasses and a bottle from his desk he offered one to Ernie and as he uncorked the lid ready to pour, to his surprise Ernie told him that he not drink alcohol.

'Well even better then, for the job you have.' Pushing the cork back into the bottle he proclaimed, 'This will keep. I will drink to your good health upon your return.'

Arriving at the airfield the next morning Ernie was greeted by Maynard.

'I have a man for you. Burges is his name, my personal assistant actually. Good chap. He has volunteered to join the Fighter Flight with you. Another thing, don't take unnecessary risks up there. You are more important to us alive than dead. If something comes on your tail or you think you are low on juice, get out of there.'

Ernie saluted smartly. He appreciated his superior's concern, but he had no intentions of coming back empty-handed.

~

The heat in the cockpit was ferocious as he set up the camera equipment. Some of the other chaps came over to watch him prepare for take-off and he was moved by their support. Flying conditions were excellent and it wasn't long before Sicily was below him and the foot of Italy in the distance. Flying closer than he should have dared, for his efforts he fulfilled in record time what he had been asked to do. He had photographs of several airfields, at least three in the North at Palermo, Trapani and Comiso in the South, with another two further East. By the time Ernie hit the runway in Luqa on his return, he had evidence that he knew would be very important at this time and he felt satisfied his first mission from Malta was successful.

~ *Ana* ~
7

May brought even stronger sunshine to Malta. When it came time for their finals, the girls were told to their dismay that for some reason the exams had been re-scheduled to an earlier date. Ana however was no longer overly concerned with her results. By now she was almost a fully-fledged auxillary nurse at Mtarfa Military Hospital. This was where her true loyalties lay. Ana had completely thrown herself into her training and while she sat the exams, her thoughts were of her patients. She was not particularly worried about the poor preparation she had done.

'If I fail, my father is going to make me repeat,' wailed Jeany. I don't want to be in the same classroom as my younger sister Olivia. That would drive me crazy.'

Thankfully neither girls failed. Miss Honeyman had organized a dance at The Regent in Sliema in honour of her graduated students. When the worry of exams was over and all the young ladies had luckily passed, their main concern now was who was to chaperon them. 'I would dearly like that friend of Billy's to escort me!' said Jeany wistfully. 'I wonder what his name is? Who would you like to have take you Ana?'

The only man that Ana would have liked was the handsome fisherman she had met in Sliema on the first day of her training. Unfortunately she hadn't set eyes on him since. She knew it was quite unladylike, but she had started to leave early on Thursday evenings to catch the connecting bus to Rabat in the hope of meeting Franco Vella again.

Ana thought that it might be a good idea if her father agreed to ask Ted Langley to accompany her to the dance. Despite flirting with her while on medication, Ted had seemed quite indifferent to her afterwards. She thought perhaps it was due to embarrassment. He was the young RAF pilot who had been in Mtarfa with malaria but was now discharged from the hospital.

'Otherwise I shall just go with my father,' she replied to the astonishment of her friend. 'At least that way he will see that I am not throwing myself at men and maybe he will allow me to get my own little place which I'd love to have. He can afford it and it's not as if I will be living at Mtarfa forever.'

'Oh, imagine the parties we could have,' Jeany answered gleefully.

Unfortunately for Jeany parties were not what Ana was planning when she dreamed of her own place. She just wanted somewhere of her own, where she could be independent.

However it didn't enter her head that if her father organised somewhere for her to live, it realistically it would not be her own. Practical matters, such as how to buy food and pay for other necessary bills, did not occur to her. Ana's life was a comfortable one and always had been. She never needed to think about where everything she ate and used and wore came from nor did she have any idea how much rent or food cost. Her only experience of money was on simple daily expenses, the allowance from her father covering fripperies like cosmetics and dances. Wherever she shopped a bill was sent to her father. After that Ana had no more concerns.

A few days later she was disappointed to hear that her father was otherwise engaged the night of the Graduation Dance. Instead he had arranged for one of his officers to accompany his daughter. To Ana's surprise the man who arrived at the hotel with flowers and chocolates and attired in full RAF dress uniform was the same man she had just recently met again at the hospital and introduced himself as Ernest McGuill. He looked extremely handsome as though he had really made an effort to spruce up. Ana had gone to a lot of trouble also, though not necessarily on his account. She had just been caught up in the frenzy with the other girls while shopping. Although the dress code was white for the ladies, they all somehow managed to be groomed in original dresses. Because Ana was so fair and her pale skin wasn't much enhanced by the white dress, she wore a red flower in her blonde hair and a sash of bright red ribbon around her waist. This made her stand out among the others.

'You look very beautiful Miss Mellor,' he said sincerely as she came down the stairs to greet him and accept his gifts. Ana blushed and thanked him.

The dance hall was full to capacity. Some people were standing around having a drink, others were already out on the dance floor. Ana spotted Jeany who looked quite satisfied with her chaperon named Alexander, a friend of one of her brothers. She waved to Ana as he swung her around the dance floor. Most of the officers seemed to be there, apart from Ted Langley who had been re-admitted to hospital following a relapse.

Ana took her first cigarette in Malta that evening and felt quite dizzy, so she ventured outside for some fresh air. She hadn't smoked since the voyage over. Being stuck in the cabin with constant smokers had only added to her sea-sickness. The sea opposite the hotel looked wondrously cool. Ana carefully walked across the busy road, taking in some much needed fresh air. She wanted to brush off the school-girl image and embrace one of a career woman instead. Part of this transition meant that she had to learn to smoke properly, inhaling fully and blowing it out expertly. Everybody here seemed to smoke. The film stars in the pictures always looked so sophisticated with a cigarette in their hand.

Her feet ached after all the dancing. As she got closer to the sea she walked up to a little jetty not restricted by the horrible barbed wire. Sitting down, she unstrapped her high heeled shoes and eagerly placed her feet in the cool water below.

Ana leaned back against an up-turned boat and blowing the

smoke from her cigarette high up into the air, she listened to the sounds of the busy harbour town all around her. From here she could still hear the shrieks and cries of joviality across the road and she felt totally at peace as she lay there looking up under a Maltese sky.

Unknown to her though, a fisherman just coming into harbour on his simple little fishing boat was watching the beautiful woman clothed in red and white. He felt he had seen a vision, a mermaid of his very own in front of his eyes! He recognised her immediately by the toss of her head which he had noticed one time before, when she had jumped awkwardly into his horse and cart.

~ *Ernie* ~
9

'Stukas!'

Wing-Commander Mellor leaned over the table which was littered with the black & white reconnaissance photographs taken by Ernest McGuill.

'So Mussolini wants to pay us a little surprise visit does he?'

~

On Tuesday morning 11th June 1940, the feast day of St. Barnabas, Ernie and the other fighter pilots were rudely awakened by the sound of the air-raid siren shattering the silence of this sunny morning. Since Mussolini had announced that Italy had joined the war the previous day, most soldiers and pilots alike slept in their uniforms after having been given orders to be ready for attack. Some men were already running along the airfield while the skies opened above their heads as the first bombs rained down and they hopped into planes, taking off in pursuit of the enemy. Within minutes of being airborne their airfield of Hal-Far was already bombed and in the distance they could see the black spirals of smoke as it rose above Grand Harbour.

Malta was at war.

~

Ernie was full of adrenaline as he chased the bombers across the sky back towards Sicily, furiously firing his machine guns and eventually causing the bombers to swiftly disappear. From the mirror, he could see three Gladiator planes in a rapid chase behind him, intent like him on bringing down the bombers who had invaded their skies with terror. Relentlessly the *Regio Aeronautica* (Italian Air Force) kept Ernie and his comrades busy that first day of their attack on Malta. In all they attacked the island eight times. The three airfields, Luqa, Ta-kali and Hal-Far had been hit as had the dockyards at Grand Harbour and the Three Cities. Dust permeated the air and sirens wailed on and off all day until finally giving rest after the last assault around seven thirty that evening.

Expertly landing his plane among the rubble of what was once a runway, Ernie McGuill was aghast at the damage inflicted in just one day. Exhausted and starving, he wearily climbed out of the cockpit and walked towards the men who were smoking well needed cigarettes, huddled at the edge of the airstrip. In the midst of the group was his Wing-Commander. As he approached him Ernie knew that Mellor wasn't here just to welcome the boys back from their duty.

'McGuill, I have a job for you,' he said.

The two men walked towards the Barracks and despite his hopes of some food, Ernie was directed into a room were Maynard and another man were seated, all looking grim as he walked in.

'Today was a bad business,' Mellor said, 'and it's going to get a lot worse. We are sending you over there again. This time you will have a radio fitted but once you have reported what you see, you are not to use the radio again. Is that clear?'

Ernie gestured with a nod of his head that it was clear. He was being put on a suicide mission.

~

Ernie's successful reconnaissance photography proved what Mellor already knew, that Malta was in no way equipped to deal with the aircraft attack Italy was already launching and intended to continue to initiate, on the exposed and vulnerable island.

The day after the first air raid attack the pilots took it in shifts to sit inside the cockpit, wanting to waste no time getting into the air at the first sightings of enemy aircraft. The men baked in their seats while grounded, but the extra few minutes it afforded them meant the difference literally between life and death for the island's inhabitants.

Apart from one brief scare, when an Italian reconnaissance plane was spotted flying overhead, possibly to assess the damage of yesterday's onslaught, no more raids took place that day, or indeed the next few days owing to low cloud. This gave the RAF some much needed time to make plans. New aircraft was needed immediately. The Navy sent over two more planes but unfortunately one crashed on landing and the other at take-off. Cleverly they managed to make one plane out of the two but one was not enough. Six aircraft en route to Egypt were drafted in to Malta instead, much to the dismay of the pilots who to their annoyance had not been briefed that they were to join the Malta Fighter Flight in an island under siege.

On 22nd June thousands of people in Valletta and Sliema watched in astounded silence as an air battle was fought in the sky above their heads. An Italian bomber was hit by one of the Maltese Gladiators. The islanders looked on as it took a perilous dive towards the sea below and then they merrily cheered at the first victory to Malta's Fighter Flight. Their victory was short-lived though as the island continued to be shelled almost continuously, even now at night-time, suffering an astounding fifty-three more air raids during the ensuing weeks.

Ernie and his men were either in the sky or in their beds, where they tried to get some much needed sleep before returning to the air in a few short hours. They now slept in air raid trenches, which were basically underground tunnels that served as their living quarters. When their comrades landed they were waiting to take over their places in the cockpit, ready for take-off at the next air raid warning.

Billy was now living with the rest of the crew, while Katie had been moved to the married quarters at St. George's Barracks which was close to St. Julian's. She seemed quite happy there among the other wives and children and she met up with Ana occasionally. Billy worried about her though and every time the air raid siren wailed he wondered if she was safe. Ernie had nobody else to worry about and this suited him well. His sole concern was his main occupation of achieving photographic information so the personnel at Lascaris War Rooms could keep on top of what the enemies were up to. When he wasn't on a reconnaissance flight then he was in the air in combat. Luckily he didn't seem to require much sleep and any he did take was when he was practically ordered to do so.

'Dead men are no good to me,' Mellor informed him. 'You might think you are invincible, but take it from me, those Italians are getting their sleep and they are relying on you not getting any. Why do you think they have started to play hard ball by keeping us up all darned night as well as day now? When I tell you to go get some lie down time, I want you to take it. Understand?'

Ernie reluctantly agreed and not long afterwards, within seconds of laying his head on the bunk he was asleep. Some of the other chaps had terrible trouble sleeping. They were so focused on the job they had to do that when they were grounded they couldn't unwind. A few of them resorted to sleeping pills which they obtained in the local pharmacies until Ernie got news of this and gave them a telling off.

'Those pills are only good if you can sleep until you decide to wake up. That's not the case here unfortunately for you lot.

What's the use of pilots up there who are half asleep on pills? If you have trouble sleeping I suggest you count flaming sheep instead!'

He couldn't come down too hard on the men though. They were giving everything they had to the Fighter Flight and they were badly needed. The problem was that there just weren't enough of them.

~

At the end of July sadly Ernie lost one of his pilots. He had just landed the same plane himself. As he conversed with the other men who also just grounded, they raised their heads to watch as their friend and comrade got involved in a dog-fight above them just minutes after becoming airborne. They applauded as the attacking plane was successfully hit and veered towards the sea. Seconds later their glee was short-lived. Their Gladiator burst into flames and shocked, they silently watched as it disappeared. Everyone was in a sombre mood for the next few days as this was the first loss from their team. The mood was lifted slightly by the welcome announcement that twelve more Hurricane planes and pilots were due to be delivered on the 2nd August. This took a lot of the pressure of the Malta Fighter Flight which although now grown in numbers, were still not nearly sufficient to defend the island of Malta from the Italians.

~ *Ana* ~
8

On Tuesday morning, the 11th June 1940, Ana was at Mtarfa hospital with Jeany and the other nurses. They had heard the startling news the night before that Italy had joined the war and soon the word had spread among the patients also. There was not much sleep for anybody at Mtarfa that night. Nevertheless thoughts of the war were not in Ana's mind. It was almost seven o'clock on a beautiful sunny day. The young nurses were enjoying a cigarette and cup of tea in the garden before their shift began. There were fantastic views from the hospital and they could easily see the towns of Mdina and Mosta in the distance, basking sleepily under the rays of the morning sun. Ana didn't get to see much of the outdoors anymore as she was working non-stop since she began full-time training the previous Monday. Any breaks she had, she took outside to soak up some sunshine and this morning she was waiting for her hair to dry in time for the 8am start. Normally the shift would end at four. The other shifts were from four to twelve and from midnight to eight in the morning. However, she often over-ran her hours and by now she was well used to one shift overlapping another and simply grabbed some sleep when she could. Ana had a little bit of experience of this, but Jeany who just began last week and her other two friends from Verdala were finding it hard to cope with the working schedule.

'This is a lot tougher than I expected,' Jeany moaned, 'and the doctors are all so old.'

They weren't so old really. The youngest was perhaps in his early thirties. They were also working long hours and there weren't enough of them to go around either. When the air raid siren sounded the girls all looked at each other in alarm but nobody said a word. They waited with baited breath to see what would happen next or to be told what to do by somebody in the know. Jeany handed her another cigarette and Ana noticed that both their hands were shaking as they lit up.

Within what seemed like a few moments, they could hear the drone of airplanes overhead and suddenly like huge angry birds of steel, the Italian air-force planes came into view. The young women dumbly sat watching incredulously the show above their heads, until another older nurse came running out in a panic and told them to get to the air raid shelter. However, as the girls jumped up to do as she demanded, Ana decided to go in search of Matron first. She was here long enough to know that she daren't move without Matron telling her to do so.

She found Matron exactly where she should be at eight on a Monday morning. She was at the nurse's station, waiting to give them their instruction for the day. This saw the start of each shift, and if Matron was not on that particular shift, the sister next to her in rank would do so instead. This involved a detailed account of the patients on a particular ward that morning and how they had been through the night. They were informed of procedures to be carried out that day. Matron also inspected each nurse to ensure that everyone was fit and looked presentable for duty.

This morning was no different. Matron directed Ana to get the other nurses in immediately saying, that this side of the island was not under attack. There was nothing of any consequence for the Italians here and patients were waiting to be looked after. Ana went out to inform the others but seeing no sign of them she ran back in again, until she got as far the hospital corridor where she knew running was forbidden. Matron had told her that come hell or high water, a nurse must never be seen running or nervous or concerned about anything other than her patient.

During the day Ana heard the air raid go off perhaps seven or eight more times. She could hear the noise of the aircraft above as she tried to coax the excited patients to remain in their beds and keep calm. Doing this kept her so busy that she hadn't time to connect with the fear that was bubbling away inside her somewhere. However in the male surgical ward it was almost impossible to maintain any semblance of order. Men who were fit enough wanted to be discharged immediately. Many threatened to discharge themselves only to be told that this was forbidden as they were in his Majesty's Service and under orders. Sick men were no good to friend or foe they were told by Matron.

Ana didn't know how Matron could keep so calm throughout the day. She herself was a bundle of nerves and had a knot in her stomach that she knew was no more than pure fear. She was not able to eat at break time and instead smoked about five cigarettes in quick succession. The other girls, Jeany included, had resurfaced and were told by Matron that when she gave instructions to go to the air raid shelter, only then should they go and their patients with them. Until then they stick to their stations.

The first casualty brought in by the Italian shelling was at around two o'clock, but Ana didn't get to see who it was or what the injuries were. The patient was taken immediately to surgery and she didn't get to hear anything else. By the time Ana got to bed that night she was exhausted from lack of sleep the night before, a long day on her feet and from pure fright. She slept soundly that night and for the next few days the air raids thankfully seemed to have ended.

~

Ana did speak to Matron about her friend Katie's condition as promised. When it was suggested that she bring Katie in to be looked over, she made the journey once again to St. George's

Barracks to see her friend. Katie was up and having some bread and milk when Ana arrived and she told her that she would go to see a doctor at the hospital in the morning. Ana promised that she would meet her there. The next morning as both women waited to see a doctor an air raid siren went off.

'Isn't it terrifying,' Katie cried, 'I think it could be sheer fear that has made me ill you know. I thought I had left all this malarkey at home in England and now it has followed us here and all. Don't we need to go to the shelter?'

'You can do if you like,' Ana answered, 'but they haven't dropped any bombs this way yet. It seems to be Valletta and the Three Cities and Sliema that have got the most of it. Wasn't St. Julian's hit too?'

Katie confirmed that it had been, but only once so far. At the Barracks the women and children had been safe enough, though she did usually go to the shelters if she wasn't feeling too ill, mainly to help Catherine with the kiddies. Her neighbour went into a screaming fit of terror every time an air raid siren went off and this only resulted in frightening her children even more.

Just then a nurse came out to inform them that the doctor was ready for Katie and as Ana was a nurse she was allowed to accompany her friend in. She held Katie's hand as the doctor probed and prodded much to both girl's horror. She was still holding her friend's hand when he announced that Katie was perhaps three months pregnant. Katie promptly burst into tears as Ana hugged her;

'Oh, thank God,' she cried to Ana, 'thank God. I thought I was done for you know. My poor old aunt Dora started throwing up like I was. When the doctor took a look at her he said she had a huge growth inside of her stomach and she was dead within weeks. I was sure that I had the same thing. That it was hereditary like. A baby! Oh, Billy will be well pleased.'

After she congratulated her friend, Ana showed her to the

women's ward and helped her to get comfortable. Doctor Falzone wished to admit her for a few days to ensure she didn't become dehydrated. She promised Katie that both Billy and Catherine would be informed of her admittance to hospital and that she would come back later to check up on her. Katie was relieved that Ana had thought of telling her to bring an overnight case, otherwise she would have to wear one of those horrible hospital gowns and she shuddered to think that maybe somebody had died in one!

Later that evening Jeany asked Ana if she would like to join her family at the Festa of Santa Maria the following Thursday, the 15th of August, in Mosta. Ana readily agreed to go and was happy to be invited. Any invitation on behalf of the Castelletti family was an honour. She had been to these festivals before with her mother. They usually went to Gudja however as her mother had friends there. It was the Feast of the Assumption of Our Lady into Heaven and a public holiday in Malta. The towns and villages were gaily decorated for the occasion, especially the Catholic churches and there were always elaborate processions with thousands of people coming out for the celebrations. As Malta was a Catholic country, many of its feast days were celebrated by a festival, but today's one was a special favourite of the Maltese and not even a war could prevent them from marking this day. Many businesses closed for a week during this period or at the very least, workers took some days off and went to the beach or visited relatives. There was a real party atmosphere and fireworks in the towns where processions were held.

Ana was worried that she might have to work that day and to her dismay she discovered that unfortunately she did. She was on the early shift but Jeany luckily had the whole day off. Ana surmised that Matron was under no illusion, that to prevent the daughter of the Castellettis from being able to join her family on this important day would not be a good move for the hospital. Especially since her father, Alessandro Castelletti donated hugely to the hospital annually.

~ *Ernie* ~
10

Ernie was exhausted, physically and mentally. Seeing his friend's plane disintegrate before his very eyes, had shocked him to the core. He had already lost some other friends on the very first day of the war who were serving at Fort St. Elmo's. Although not of his team, all the military were familiar with each other and rank had no meaning when they met socially. It was the first time however that he lost one of his own. This was somebody whom he had personally trained, ate and chatted with. The men's morale was low after seeing one of their own shot down and Ernie argued with himself about how to handle it. He wasn't sure whether to go with the military approach of 'that's war and what we are here to do' or gather with the men after the horrible sight in the bar afterwards and talk it to death. He was glad of Mellor coming to his aid on this one.

'He is your first loss McGuill,' his Wing-Commander said, putting a fatherly hand on Ernie's shoulder, 'and unfortunately in this business, it won't be your last. Now you have to stand up to the mark and take it on the chin.'

Ernie looked at him with distaste. Had the man no heart?

'I know you think that I am taking this lightly Ernest, but believe me when I tell you that every man we lose causes me much distress. I am more than aware of what it is like to lose somebody in a rotten war and all I can advise you is this. You remind those chaps what your friend achieved. He took out an enemy plane. In doing so, he saved the lives of perhaps hundreds of people as that plane was over here to drop bombs on Malta. Thanks to your brave friend, the enemy didn't get the chance. Now you go out there and you remind them of that.'

So Ernie did just that. However, he realised that gaining the men's respect in his role as their Squadron Leader meant that he also had to gain it with his empathy in their grief. When Billy handed him a very full glass of whiskey and asked him to drink to their lost friend's life he had no choice but to do so. The sharp liquid burned his throat on the way down and as he raised his glass to his men he already felt the headiness it caused. Nevertheless, the men cheered and slapped his back and he knew he had done some good.

~

When Billy approached him to ask for some time off to visit his wife who was in hospital Ernie readily agreed.

'Of course, but we need you back in the morning,' he requested. 'We don't want to be another man down in case those lovely neighbours of ours plan on popping in for breakfast.'

Billy assured him he would be back in time and hastily jumped into the truck which he had borrowed for the trip to Mtarfa. On arrival he was greeted at the door by Ana, who he remembered meeting way back in Easter. He didn't realize that she was now working in the hospital where Katie was a patient.

'Come with me Billy,' she volunteered, 'she is waiting for you.'

When Billy entered the long hospital ward at first he didn't recognize his wife. She looked so wan and pale against the white bedclothes though he noticed she still had her familiar red lipstick on. This made him feel a bit lighter in his heart as he hadn't been sure what to expect.

'How is my girl?' he asked, as he put his arms around his frail looking wife, taking in her scent as he did so.

'Oh, I am terrific,' she replied, fixing his collar like she always did, as he always had it sticking up in the air.

'You look thinner', he remonstrated, at which he received a slap on the arm and a request for a kiss which he duly delivered.

'I hear it is pretty rough out there?' she asked.

'Oh it is not so bad. How are you darling?' he asked as he removed his jacket and laid it on the bed over her feet.

'I am fine, but I am afraid that we need to move rooms at St. George's soon.'

'Oh,' he replied, 'why is that?'

Katie smiled. 'Because in a few months I shall be moved to the family quarters.'

'But where you are now is fine isn't it? I mean, we have the two rooms and the other place is full of kids running about.'

'Exactly,' Katie beamed. 'And soon we shall have a kid running about.'

Billy sat where he was, looking at her quizzically for a few seconds before what she said dawned on him.

'You mean, we will have our own kid running about. Is that what you mean?' he asked incredulously.

'Yes, Lieutenant William Cortis, we shall have our own kid running about. Well, eventually,' she cried, and hugged her husband close to her.

~

The arrival of the new hurricane fighter planes and their pilots was a welcome support at the beginning of August and took much of the burden from the men who had been the island's sole air defence up until now. Ernie was able to spend more time on his reconnaissance assignments and had learned how to develop the photographs himself which he greatly enjoyed doing. When he got the chance he enjoyed taking photos of the island, the men and also scenes that showed how Malta had already been affected by the war. It was sad to see the proud ancient buildings that he had photographed only recently, now reduced to rubble. Ernie decided to make a portfolio of photos simply entitled

'Before and After the War in Malta'. Who knows, he thought, if this war ever ends, maybe he will make a complete book of the photos he took while serving here. As some of the pictures hung to dry in the dark room, he spotted some which he had taken the night he had been persuaded to accompany Anabel Mellor to her Graduation Dance, back on that first Saturday in June. He decided he must give some photos of her to Mellor. He might like to have them and it was always good to keep his Wing-Commander on side.

Later Ernie reflected that although the military and the RAF were aware of the impending threat of war, little did they all know then what the next week or so would bring. That night as the young people gaily danced and laughed, none of them knew that their neighbours just sixty miles away, would have begun a merciless onslaught of bombing on their vulnerable island. He knew what hurt and saddened the Maltese people most was the fact that they were being attacked by people who had once been their friends. Even though it was widely accepted that the Italians had not much choice in taking up arms under Mussolini's dictatorship, it was still a bitter pill for them to swallow. Numerous Maltese people were half Italian, perhaps a mother or father were from either Italy, Sardinia or Sicily and some had been educated in Italian schools. In fact, many family members were presently in Italy and now there was a huge worry about what was going to happen to these men, women and children. Would they simply be sent home or would they be interned in some Prisoner of War camp as enemy aliens? Ernie reckoned in a war situation it would sadly be the latter. If Germany marched into Italy, they could even be executed. Those Jerrys seemed to have no mercy whatsoever if the reports from France and Poland were correct.

As he looked at the photographs of Anabel and her friends from the dance, he confirmed to himself what he thought the very first time he met her. That she was definitely a very pretty girl. No wonder the guys were all jealous when he informed them that he was, to his private irritation, to accompany her to the dance. It was important that she gave good reports back to her father, so Ernie spent a good bit of time getting spruced up, shaving even more carefully than usual and even got his hair cut. After splashing out on very expensive bouquet of flowers and a large box of chocolates, he was as attentive as he thought he should be and as well-mannered as he knew he should be.

Ernie drove both Miss Mellor and her friend Miss Castelletti back to the school at a decent hour and Mellor had thanked him, saying that his daughter had notified him that she had a beautiful evening. Mellor also, to his horror, told Ernie that he was welcome to take his daughter out another time, if he so wished, which he didn't. She was a perfectly nice girl, but he had not a whit of interest in her whatsoever. She was intelligent enough and he admired the fact that she had taken up nursing in Mtarfa, but romance wise, there wasn't a hope.

He had his eyes on somebody else completely and for the first time he had an interest outside of his photography and flying. Now the only obstacle was whether he was a cat chasing a mouse that didn't want to be caught. When he visited Ted Langley he was asleep and Ernie didn't like to wake him. He was relieved however when the matron informed him that Ted was on the mend and just needed to have some rest and regain his strength before the doctors could declare him well enough to return to duty. Young Anabel was there at the time. He was happy to know that a kindly person was looking out for his friend as well as the doctors and nurses. He decided to visit again tomorrow and perhaps he would bring some of the photographs for Anabel also. He knew she would be pleased and would he hoped, tell her father of his generosity.

Tonight he would go to the bar in 'The Gut', which was in a

famous street apparently called Strait Street, much favoured by the men for its lively bars and available girls. Some of the boys were making the journey there soon by truck. He learned that night when he and the boys drank to their friend who had been killed, that the men can be quite loose-lipped with a few drinks on them. This he realised was a good way to find out some information on what they thought of him for one thing and also how they were finding the war situation. He needed to know which pilots were finding it tougher than others, because they were the ones he would need to keep an eye on. Mellor had taught him that. He advised that Ernie should know his men better than he knew anybody else. Well, to Ernie there was nobody else. He had no family and no lady friend and the welfare of his squad were of paramount importance to him.

~ *Ana* ~
9

The 15th of August was an extremely hot day and Ana baked under her uniform. The white material was not so uncomfortable, but she found the heavy blue apron a great hindrance and wished she could take it off completely. She tried to be her usually jolly self with the patients but she couldn't help feel like Cinderella. It seemed everybody else was out partying and she was here working. Katie lifted her spirits a little by asking her what she was going to wear to the festivities that night. However, before Ana could answer, Katie told her to take out a brown paper bag from under the bed. On opening it at her friend's insistence she found a beautiful sky blue summer dress trimmed with white lace edging. It was beautiful.

'Oh Katie,' she cried, flinging herself at her friend. It is beautiful. Thank you so much.'

'It kept me from going crazy in here. Catherine brought the material in for me. I was so worried she would get the wrong colour, because see, it matches your eyes. But thankfully she got it perfectly right.'

Ana was thrilled. She had planned to wear her white dress again tonight because she hadn't had time to buy anything new, but this was perfect. When she tried it on later after her shift was over, she was delighted to see that it fitted perfectly. Katie was right. It did match her eyes, and she visited the ward to show it off to her friend before leaving for the bus.

The journey from Mtarfa to Mosta wasn't very long. However when Ana arrived at the Catholic church which was in the centre of the town and known as the Dome, (or Rotunda) she could not see any sign of Jeany. She knew that the Mass had been held many hours before, and now by the time she arrived it was almost seven o'clock and already getting dark. As usual, her shift hadn't ended at four. Then she had to wash and change and go to see Katie before she left to catch a bus. As it was a feast day the buses were on a very informal basis and she was almost half an hour waiting on one.

There were thousands of people in the streets. Outside the Dome was where the main festivities took place. The air was full of the sound of brass bands and people making merry. Walking wearily around all the people, the different stalls selling food and drinks and religious objects, Ana started to become anxious that she would never find her friend. She also began to worry about how she would get home. She had been told that she was to stay in St. Julian's with Jeany's family and that both girls would travel by bus to the hospital tomorrow. Ana was quite sure that there would be no buses returning to Rabat tonight.

She didn't see any familiar faces and realised that she was beginning to feel really hungry. She walked over to a stall selling some meat pastizzi and bought one, which didn't hold very much meat inside. Ana sat on a low wall to eat whilst carefully trying not to spill anything on her new dress. Just as she took the last bite of her pie she felt somebody sit down beside her and moved over a little to allow them some space. Then she heard a familiar voice and turning around quickly found herself looking into the eyes of the handsome fisherman who had been in her thoughts daily since she met him in April.

'Hello nurse,' he said grinning widely at her, 'Do you remember me?'

She nodded dumbly that she did, her mouth still being full of the pastry which she swiftly tried to swallow.

'Yes,' she replied, finding her voice at last. 'You are Franco Vella.'

He was happy she had remembered him. Ana did not know that he had seen her the night of the dance in Sliema. Franco thought he was seeing things again when he noticed her sitting solitarily on the wall, eating her meat pie.

'Are you here alone?' he asked her, noticing as he spoke that she had begun to blush a little which was so endearing.

'At the moment I am,' Ana replied. Folding the now empty bag neatly in a square and placing it inside her handbag she continued; 'I had plans to meet my friend Jeany and her family here, but I have no idea where they could be. I have been searching for them for over an hour.'

'What is her family name?'

'Castelletti.'

'Oh, I know of them. They are a noble family. They would now be at the Casa della Marsa where their friends live on Republic Street. It is traditional that they have a banquet there with some town dignitaries, before returning back here for the firework display. I can take you there if you like, it is not far, or wait with you until they arrive.'

Ana wasn't sure which she ought to do, but she did know that she wanted to spend time with Franco. If she was in the company of Jeany and her family she knew that wouldn't be possible.

'Where is a good spot to see the fireworks?' she asked.

About ten minutes later Ana was looking out at the fireworks from the top of the Dome with Franco holding her hand. It was colder up here and Franco had put his thin blue jacket around her shoulders. Eventually she slipped her arms into the sleeves as the breeze became a bit stronger. The view was breath-taking. Below they could see the whole town of Mosta with the thousands down below, like a sea of people all dancing, singing and screaming excitedly as each firework was launched, portraying rainbows of colours which reached high into the sky. For the first time since June the only noise in the sky was that of the fireworks exploding and tonight the war could be temporarily forgotten.

When the band below stuck up a chorus of Jimmie Davis's popular song 'You are my Sunshine' Franco twirled Ana around the roof of the Dome and she decided that it was the best night of her whole life. As the stars twinkled above their heads they shared their first kiss and when the air raid siren went off neither one wanted to let go in search of a place to hide. They stayed right where they were, on top of the Dome in Mosta, on the Feast of the Assumption in 1940 while Malta was at war and the Italian bombers released their own explosives on the island. Franco drove her back to the hospital that night on his horse and cart and when Jeany arrived the next morning she chastised Ana for not turning up at the festival.

'We searched all over for you,' she remonstrated, 'why didn't you come?'

'I did. I got there about seven and it was dark and I waited and waited but I couldn't find you anywhere.' This was true, though she did feel a bit guilty for not mentioning that she chose to go off with Franco, instead of waiting for Jeany and her family to arrive at the Dome. Jeany calmed down a little when she realised that Ana had in fact turned up and had been looking for them.

'It was such a fun night. There was a fantastic firework display and a big party afterwards with bands and dancing. My parents wouldn't let me leave their side though,' she sulked. 'If you had have been there they would have let me go off to have fun.'

~

Ana couldn't stop herself from reminiscing about her night with Franco. On the way back to Mtarfa he held her hand while holding the reins with his right hand. Sometimes when he needed both hands, he simply lifted his hand from hers for a second then quickly put his hand back in hers again. Eventually she left her hand where it was as though they were joined in one and when he needed both hands, her hand joined his in the control of the reins and to her it felt very romantic. The drive from Mosta to Rabat seemed to go in a flash and when they reached the hospital they sat for some time outside talking. He spoke to her about his love of fishing and how it was a trade passed down from father to father for years. He talked about how his mother found the way of life difficult here as she was from a family involved in business. She was from Ragusa in Sicily and her father had come over to Malta to open yet another business here. She had met Franco's father while on holiday. Her father did not approve of her settling with a simple Maltese fisherman. When Franco's family helped her father during some difficulty while he was in Malta, he consented to his daughter marrying into the Vella family. Franco's father was worried about his wife. As an Italian she could perhaps be arrested as an enemy alien. However, because his father-in-law was so well connected and ran many businesses here, he hoped this would keep her from harm.

Ana confided in him about her mother's sudden death due to a heart condition and about having to leave England to join her father. She told him, which she had never told anybody, how sometimes she felt so lonely and sad that she cried herself to sleep. That she oftentimes felt as though she was caught up in somebody else's life and that she would surely wake up in her dormitory in St. Len's and this would have all been a strange dream.

'But then I would be a dream also,' Franco said as he let go of her hand which he still held and put his arm around her.

Ana looked up at him and smiled and once again he took her face in his large hands and kissed her. She was glad to be exactly here in Malta and not in England or in France where she would be, if Mussolini had not made his announcement in June. When she finally got into her bed that night, she hummed the tune of 'You are my Sunshine' to herself. Then she suddenly jumped out of bed and lifted the thin blue jacket which lay across her bed and folding it, put it under her head where she could breathe in the smell of her own Maltese fisherman.

Not too far away a fisherman whistled the same tune as he tied up his horse for the night and gave him a bucket full of water after his tiring journey. Franco Vella blessed himself as he crawled under the blanket next to two of his brothers, in the large bed with the cast iron bedstead. He said a prayer in thanksgiving to Santa Maria for answering the prayer with which he had begun his day that morning.

~ *Ernie* ~
11

Ted was more than delighted to be discharged from hospital where he had been since the war started.

'You've no idea how frustrating it was mate,' he told Ernie who had come to collect him.

'It was awful to hear those Italian bombers up above, trying to shoot down my own comrades while I was stuck in there. I thought I was going to go stir crazy I can tell you. Matron is alright, but she gave me quite a stern ticking off about apparently coming on a bit strong to one of her nurses while I was drugged up. Well, that nurse whoever she was must have got the wrong end of the stick. I would have told an Eyetie I loved him if he had been there instead.'

Ernie chortled. It was good to see Ted his old self again. The doctors had wanted him to reach a certain weight before they released him and by now he had achieved that. He had been declared fit for duty once again but the first place that he wanted to go was to a bar.

'I've been darned parched for a beer, Ernie. I know you brought in those few bottles alright, but if that matron got a sniff of beer on my breath she'd add another week on to my hospital stay and no beer is worth that I can assure you. So, where are you taking me then?'

Ernie drove to a bar in Zebbug which was on the way back to Luqa Barracks. He enjoyed watching Ted lower a beer in seconds and quickly ordered another one.

'So Ted, this nurse that you say you didn't flirt with, who was she?'

'Oh, that was Mellor's daughter. I surely picked the right nurse to make a fool of myself with didn't I? She is a good girl though, I'm sure she never told anyone or else Mellor would most definitely have been in to see me by now. I believe he is quite protective of her. She is his only daughter and all that and the wife is dead. You do know though that he has a sweetie in Sliema?'

Ernie didn't know, although he had heard rumours that his Wing-Commander was a bit of a ladies' man.

'Any idea of who it might be?' he questioned.

'I sure do. It's the woman who is the Head of that fancy boarding school his daughter went to. What do you call it? Verdala, that's it. Her name is Honeyman I believe. And word has it that he has her installed in a nice little house in Sliema too, so they can have some private time if you know what I mean?'

Ernie did indeed know what he meant. This was interesting news to him. He was sure that Ana wouldn't know anything about this and would be devastated if she did. He wondered if it was a recent thing, or if he had been seeing this Honeyman woman even before his wife had died. He got the impression that Ana and her father didn't have a very close relationship as he barely visited her or she him. Although he realised that Mellor was up to his two eyes with the war, nevertheless, if this information got out, Ana would be hurt and that would in turn hurt Mellor.

'You better keep that under your hat Ted,' he warned the other man. 'If Mellor found out you had given that information to anybody you don't know what he might do.'

'Jeez, he needs us more than we need him old boy,' Ted snorted.

'No, I am telling you Ted. You want to keep on his good side. He has the power to make or break us here, so remember that,' to which Ted nodded his head, indicating that he would.

When the men left the bar Ernie drove them back towards

Luqa Barracks where the other men welcomed their friend back to base.

'About time you got off your back mate and gave us a hand up there fighting those bombers,' Billy teased him. 'The next time a raid comes over, it's your turn!'

Ted was quite happy with that. He was looking forward to getting some target practice on those Italians, whom he had heard dropping their bombs night after night while he lay in his bed wishing he could bomb them back. Now he could, and when the air raid sounded he was already waiting, strapped into his cockpit and eager to go. On returning hours later, he felt proud that he hadn't lost his touch and therefore could hold his head up amongst the men again. The mission had been successful. Ted had hit two planes and he knew that at least one had taken a nosedive into the sea below him. Ernie was waiting for him as he landed and slapped him on the back, happy to see him back alive.

Now that there were additional pilots and planes available, the men got more sleep and Ernie was able to concentrate almost fully on his air reconnaissance missions. This in turn involved many meetings with Maynard and Mellor upon his return. Largely due to his excellent photography of the Italian fleet at Taranto, the Royal Navy was able to launch an airborne attack in November on the enemy base which was highly successful. Sadly though, military casualties were almost a daily occurrence as were the deaths of civilians. The gunners at St. Elmo came under a lot of fire and consequently there were many soldiers killed. It seemed as though the air raid siren was never silent. It didn't matter what time of day or night it was, the shelling was constant.

Ernie was completely consumed by it all. As indeed everybody was. He had no fear of death. He feared only that the enemy would prove too strong for Malta's defences and that the country might have no choice but to capitulate to the enemy. To Ernie, that was a fate much worse than death. If the Italians or Germans landed here they would most likely all be executed or put into Prisoner of War camps. He would prefer execution.

The convoy ships carrying much needed supplies to the island were taking longer and longer to get here, if they arrived at all. It was harder now to attain some goods that in the past had been plentiful. Each time Ernie passed through the different towns of Tarxien, Zurrieq or Valletta he saw that more and more shops had either been reduced to a mound of rubble or were closed up entirely. Many of the owners and their families had fled inland to the countryside and some even travelled as far as the neighbouring island of Gozo. Meals in the mess house continued to be served, but there was a noticeable lack of decent meat by November. Many of the small stalls which sold hot pastries along the streets in the towns had vanished. It was too difficult to keep them going. Every time an air raid siren went off, the owners of these stalls had to pack everything up and get themselves and their stalls into a shelter, which was basically just a slit in the bastion walls. If they left their stall behind, it would be completely raided by hungry children.

Many women who had their homes destroyed by bombs and who for one reason or another didn't want to leave Valletta, lived with their families in these slit trenches. They cooked out on the street on little stoves called 'kenur'. Children were sent to gather firewood and large pots of soup and stews were cooked on these. Oftentimes, if a siren went off the mother doing the cooking took her chances and stayed by the stove, not wanting to risk her precious pot of food being stolen. Shop-owners used limestone to scrawl 'Business as usual' on walls and on the doors of their shops and restaurants. Sometimes half of the shop would have been blown to bits, but the owners salvaged what they could. Ernie smiled when he saw a proud shopkeeper doggedly washing down his window and door frames, despite the fact that all his windows had been blown in.

Ernie had a lot of respect for the perseverance of the Maltese. Women still dressed as stylishly as they could and like the mothers who cooked their families meals in the open air, young women could be seen hanging out their freshly washed dresses to be dried for the next day. They still went to Mass, almost daily in fact and many Masses took place inside the air raid shelters.

Sadly however there were also many funerals. Ernie felt sad one day while he watched a funeral procession walk behind a coffin which was so small it must only have belonged to a child. Suddenly the siren sounded for people to take cover and most of the funeral party ran for safety to the nearest slit trenches. The coffin was left alone on the back of a cart until a young man perhaps just twenty years old or so, ran out and grabbed the coffin from the cart and took it into the trench with him. They didn't even have time to bury their dead.

One of the most daunting times was when the bombers had left and people started to silently creep out of the walls. Then the horrific sounds began when they realised that homes and businesses were gone and worst of all, the realisation that people they loved were missing. Mothers and fathers could be seen scrambling over heaps of rubble, frantically calling out their children's names. Sometimes voices could be heard underneath and anybody with two hands willingly ran over to help clear the debris away. Sadly, sometimes the voices become fainter and fainter until there was just silence. Then the wailing of mothers and fathers started. They had taken too long to reach their loved ones.

Public scenes of loss and despair were becoming all too common. Children were never allowed far from their parent's side and some mothers even took to accompanying their children to school, so they could be with them if an air raid happened. A lot of schools had been blown up and classes took place outdoors, or in shelters. On the occasional day when there was a break in the bombing, usually due to low cloud coverage, there was almost a holiday atmosphere on the island. People smiled and chatted, taking the time to do some repairs to homes and businesses. Even while they did this, there was always the concern that they would be bombed again tomorrow or even that night, but it gave them something to do. As Mellor told Ernie, while they watched as a young woman beat the dust of a mat outside what was left of her home in Sliema;

'They are a proud people.'

Ernie offered to carry the large mat back indoors for the woman when he saw her struggle with it and she smiled in gratitude.

'Why do you bother?' he asked.

She looked surprised by his question and then replied, 'If those Italians march in here and take over, I'm not having them saying that us Maltese women keep dirty houses!'

To him, that summed up the character of the people on this island very well. They were proud, they were stubborn and they endured. As a result he had great admiration for them.

~ Ana ~
10

The first time that Ana ever went into an air raid shelter was when she went to visit Franco in Sliema. She had taken the bus from Rabat which was absolutely packed to capacity. Not only were there many adults and children on the bus, there were also baskets carrying chickens and somebody even had a goat. She giggled to herself as she thought how that would never in a million years be permitted in England. The bus stopped at Birkirkara when everybody who sat in the seat on the first half of the bus where told to get off and climb onto another bus. Ana was happy about this as she was beginning to feel faint with the amount of people squeezed into a small space and the smell of the animals. She had been standing at the back of the bus and when others moved down towards the front, she finally got a seat to herself. The bus ahead moved on and the one that Ana was on followed behind. She was glad that the school crowd were on the other bus. She liked children, but these were in a rambunctious mood as they were being taken by their teachers on a day trip. In their excitement they were calling loudly to each other and singing songs at the tops of their voices. Ana didn't know how the teachers, who were just young women like herself, were able to discipline such a noisy bunch.

Suddenly the air raid siren went off and the driver gathered speed. There was an underground tunnel not far away and the driver was obviously intending to reach it for safety. Then a piercing sound was heard coming closer. To Ana's horror the bus in front turned into a ball of flames. The driver slammed to a halt and ran towards the other vehicle, as did some of the other passengers. Ana also jumped up and ran out. When she approached, she could feel the heat of the flames and was pushed back by the driver and some other men.

'There is nothing we can do,' the bus driver shouted, 'nothing.'

Ana began to scream and tried to push past, but the burly driver had a firm grip on her shoulders and she couldn't budge him.

'The children,' Ana kept screaming. 'We have to try to get to the children.'

But nobody would let her get near. The bus was completely engulfed in flames that danced into the sky with black plumes of smoke following them. Some of the passengers got off and vomited on the side of the road. Other women were crying and screaming, as they knew many of the people on board the ill-fated bus. Ana kept seeing the faces of the excited children and the beautiful young women who taught them. Just minutes before she would also have been sitting there.

Ana's legs were completely shaking. She sat down hard on the dusty road bank and cradled an older woman in her arms who was screeching the name of somebody who had been on board. Apart from the sound of crying, nobody spoke. The bus continued to burn and soon other vehicles arrived on the scene. People with horses and carts and bicycles who had heard the bomb and saw the smoke got there as fast as they could. They abandoned their transport and ran to the devastating scene to see if they could help. But it was soon obvious that there was nothing anybody could do now. All Ana kept thinking about was the parents of the children, who would soon get a visit from a priest to tell them of their loss. She thought also of Katie and her baby boy whom she absolutely worshipped and how it would be if Katie lost her son like that, on a school trip, because some horrible pilot thought it was okay to bomb a bus full of people going about their innocent daily lives.

Ana was angry and wanted to hit out at somebody. She thought of Ernie and Billy up there also dropping bombs on innocent people. For the first time, she realised the awfulness of their job. Until now she didn't think about it. She thought they were brave to fly every day to defend the island, putting their own lives at risk, but in reality they were killers. Just like the Italians. They would probably hit a bus too if they got a chance. It was horrific. It was inhuman. Ana found that she was shaking from head to toe by now. She too felt as though she might throw up but instead she began to walk towards Sliema. She had left her bag on board and as she went back to retrieve it, another fleet of planes flew over their heads, circling them like vultures. Suddenly Ana was thrown to the ground and pushed under the bus. She tried to creep back out, terrified that if they were hit she would be squashed underneath. Somebody pulled at her arms to prevent her from escaping, but she tugged herself free and ran to a stone wall and crawled behind the boulders hoping to be safe there if the bombs fell again. She heard shouting and looking around she saw an arm wave at her from a slit in the limestone wall and call out for her to run over to safety, which she did.

Just a little distance ahead there was another opening to the underground tunnel. It was a subterranean tunnel and there were several different entrances into it. Ana ducked down low and ran quickly to where the other person beckoned her.

There were only a handful of people in the tunnel that Ana could make out, for it was quite dark inside and also to her horror, it smelled awful. There were people crying here also and she soon realised to her dismay that the stench was human waste. Watching her feet as she scrambled past the others, she found a patch of dusty ground and sat down. Her legs were like jelly. An older woman sitting next to her handed her a cloth and indicated that she wipe her face. When Ana handed the cloth back, she noticed that it was filthy. She had covered the cloth in black dust or soot from having been so close to the fire. The kindly woman then took Ana's hand and began whispering. She realised the old woman was praying. Ana was unable to speak however and instead she closed her eyes, seeing once again the happy faces of the children who were now no more.

Unbeknownst to her, she had fallen asleep, for she was wakened suddenly by somebody shaking her shoulders and calling her name over and over. Opening her eyes she could only make out a shadow and then, crying out she flung her arms around the man who now held her.

'Ana, Ana,' Franco murmured, holding her against his chest, 'Thank God. I thought you were dead. I thought you were dead.'

When they exited out of the tunnel, Ana blinked as the strong sunlight hit her eyes. Up ahead the bus was now a smouldering mass of debris. Red Cross ambulances were all around it as were some military. They were trying to keep back the people who were obviously relatives and friends of those who had been killed. Women wailed and tore at the men who tried to prevent them getting any closer to the scene of death. Franco helped Ana into his cart and she shielded her eyes from the scene. Minutes later, when they had passed the devastation and were now on the road to Sliema, Franco pulled the reins to steady his horse and stopped.

'I thought you were gone,' he repeated yet again, reaching for her.

He went on to tell her that he had been waiting at their bench on the pier as agreed, when suddenly there was a commotion around him, of people screaming and shouting. It didn't take him long to find out what the ruckus was about and he said that he felt as if he went down a long black tunnel of fear. He said that he started to run wildly around asking if there was a young English woman on the bus but nobody could tell him. He immediately went to his home to get his cart but one of his brothers had taken it. Like a madman he went in search of him and practically threw his brother off the cart in his rush to get to where the accident had taken place.

He began to sob when he described the sight that awaited him on his arrival. When the knowledge hit him that if Ana was on board as expected her to be, then she was gone from him forever. He described how he simply fell to his knees in disbelief until he saw another bus parked not far along the road. Searching it, he found her black leather bag. On opening it and seeing her rosary beads which he knew she carried with her always, he began to hope that she was still alive. The driver was sitting by the roadside and confirmed that a woman fitting Ana's description was on the second bus but he did not see where she had gone. Ana lay with her head against Franco's warm chest and she could feel his heart racing fiercely. She was deeply moved by his concern for her.

'I searched everywhere. Then I thought perhaps you had tried to get to Sliema and I was turning my cart to go back, when I saw people begin to come out of the tunnels. That's when I ran inside and saw you asleep there.' Hugging her close to him he continued, 'I saw your blond hair first. There you were, lying sleeping on the floor, curled up like a baby. It was the happiest moment of my life.'

He took her to his home in Sliema. It was through one of those mysterious small doors on a long narrow street, similar to the ones Ana had passed by many times in Valletta and other towns. Franco pushed the door open and Ana was amazed by how big the inside of the house was. They stepped into a large cool room with stone walls where a tall elegant looking woman was folding linen at a table.

'Gianfranco,' she cried. 'What happened? Carlo said you nearly killed him by throwing him off the horse.'

Then she noticed the small light skinned woman behind him and she knew this was the Ana her son had talked about non-stop. She put out her arms in welcome and to her surprise the young woman ran to her and began to cry.

Later when Ana was in bed in his mother's small room, Margarita sat with her son at the long wooden table and listened when he told her of what had transpired. She was deeply shocked and saddened, for she would undoubtedly know many of the people on board the ill-fated bus and their families.

'Will this war ever end?' she asked him, knowing as she did so that he, just like everybody else, didn't know the answer. 'It is a hard time to be a mother of so many children. How do I keep them all safe? How do I know where they are every minute of the day? My knees are sore from praying. Fr Cauchi says all we can do in these times is pray and work. I told him that is all I have ever done in my life.'

Franco realised too, that now he had met Ana, his concerns were for her were just like his mothers were for her own loved ones. Already he knew that Ana was the woman that he wanted and needed to be with, always. The terror he felt thinking she might be dead was still very fresh in his memory and he shuddered at the thought of it. It would be unthinkable that she could be killed so horrifically. He thanked God that she had changed to a different bus and he knew that it was God who had a hand in saving her life. Ana was a devout prayerful woman and he had no doubt that it was her faith which had kept her alive.

~ *Ernie* ~
12

Billy was worried about his wife. She had been out of hospital for some time and back at St. George's Barracks. The baby was due in a month and he had only been able to get away to see her twice since June. Ernie had told him that Ana called to see her whenever she could get the chance and assured him that Katie was very well and very big! This made Billy laugh as he knew Katie was very fussy about her figure and he couldn't imagine her waddling around like a duck with a huge tummy.

'Are you seeing much of this Ana then?' he asked Ernie.

'No. Not really. She comes to see her father occasionally and we have been out to dinner, the three of us, a few times.'

'Ooooh. Out for dinner with the Wing-Commander and his daughter eh?' Billy said suspiciously. 'That sounds very nice and cosy. You do realize you are being set up by Mellor as a possible husband for his daughter?'

'The thought had crossed my mind,' Ernie replied truthfully. 'He has told me several times how Ana is the only child and due to inherit an estate in Yorkshire. She is a perfectly nice girl, but I have no interest.'

'So who do you have an interest in then? There must be somebody?'

'Yes there is, but I am not telling you who,' Ernie replied and left the room.

'Do you know who it is?' Billy asked Ted, as he prepared for another few hours in the sky.

'He keeps his personal life to himself,' Ted replied tersely.

'He is a bit of a loner alright,' Billy said. 'In all the years I've known him, I've never seen him receive a letter in the post or indeed write one even. I've never known him to mention anybody outside of the army and I've never heard him talk about a girl.'

'Maybe its men he likes,' shouted George Thompson from across the room, to which he received a boot thrown at his head from Billy.

'Don't let McGuill hear you say that,' he advised George. 'Or you will be on lavatory duties for a month.' However it gave him food for thought.

~

Word came just before Christmas via Ana to her father, that Billy's wife was in hospital as she had passed her due date and they expected the event any day. Billy was given some time off duty and Ernie drove him to Mtarfa where he was to stay until the baby arrived. Little Mikel was born on Christmas Eve and Billy's family arrived *en Masse* to the hospital, only to be told that their daughter-in-law was too weak for any visitors except her husband. Nevertheless they hung around the hospital until Ana agreed to carry the baby out to a corridor for just a few seconds so they could have a look at him. Billy's mother promptly burst into tears and practically snatched the baby out of Ana's arms, so anxious was she to hold her first grandchild.

'I wish that Katie would come and live with us now that she has the baby to look after,' Mrs Cortis cried.

'She may do,' Ana whispered, not wishing to wake the baby and cause a nurse or matron to come running out to the corridor. 'I will talk to her.' She also agreed that Katie would be better in St. Julian's where she would be surrounded by Billy's loving family and there were fewer bombs than at the Barracks. Eventually it was Billy who talked her into going to his family home when Christmas was over. By now Katie was exhausted as baby Mikel was a hungry baby and she got very little sleep.

'Just for a little while then,' she consented. 'But I do intend to go back to the Barracks as soon as the weather picks up a bit. Catherine says it is quite cold there at the moment and I don't want Mikel to catch a chill.'

Billy was relieved and when he handed his wife and baby over to the charge of his mother he kissed them both and said he would try to get to St. Julian's as soon as he could. His mother had told them that the Castelletti family had kindly bought a perambulator as a gift and that it was filled with baby clothes and blankets. Katie was astounded at the generosity, but Billy was not so pleased.

'We can afford to buy our own things for the baby,' he insisted.

However, when he saw how thrilled Katie was with the gifts and he was told of the Castelletti family's delight at his becoming a father, he acquiesced. They were very fond of Billy and his parents. On the first Sunday in January 1941 baby Mikel was baptized at St. Julian's parish church. Hours later his father returned to Luqa Barracks with his friend Ernie who had stood as Godfather with Ana acting as Godmother and the two men took to the sky again. The German Luftwaffe had arrived in Sicily and their aim was to intensify its air attack on Malta together with the Italian *Regia Aeronautica*. Every pilot and plane was needed.

As Katie and her new baby slept they were unaware that the small harbour town of St. Julian's was being shelled around them and that Billy and Ernie were both up there trying to protect them all from harm.

~ *Ernie* ~
13

Less than a week later on 10th January, Ernie and some of the other the men were having a drink in Caffé Cortina on Republic Square, which was one of their regular haunts in Valletta, when they were told about the attack on a convoy. 'Operation Excess' which was en route to Grand Harbour with much needed supplies had apparently been ruthlessly attacked by Italian bombers as it sailed in the Mediterranean. The Fulmar fleet which launched from the decks of The Illustrious cargo ship, was thankfully able to drive them away. Their relief was short-lived however. Much to the dismay of the Naval escort for the convoy, the bombers which arrived just after midday were not the Italian fleet. There were about 24 German Ju 87 and Ju 88 dive-bombers. This was the first knowledge of the arrival of the German Air Force in the Mediterranean. The Illustrious was severely damaged as a result of 6-direct bomb hits causing fires which also disabled her steering gear. H.M.S. Warspiie also sustained slight damage from a near miss. During this attack one Fulmar and one Swordfish were shot down, their crews being saved, and two enemy aircraft were shot down by gunfire.

At approximately 1.30 in the afternoon an unsuccessful attack was made on the Illustrious by high level bombers. Then again while the ship tried to cope with the damage and see to its wounded men, from 4pm to 5pm another attack by about 30 aircraft was made on the ship by the German bombers. During this attack planes from the Fulmars fleet which were from the Illustrious, just having re-fuelled at Malta, successfully shot down six or seven Ju 87 or 88's dive-bombers and damaged several others. Heavy bombs of about 1,000 lb were used in all these attacks. The brave Illustrious covered by the Battle Fleet, finally arrived at Malta at about 9pm after yet another but final unsuccessful attack had been made on her by torpedo bombers, just outside the entrance to Grand Harbour. Eleven of her Swordfish and five Fulmars were destroyed by fire.

The German dive-bombers were relentless in their shelling, so intent was the enemy on completely sabotaging the convoy to Malta. By the time the Illustrious limped into Grand Harbour it had huge casualties. Eighty-three men had been killed, sixty were seriously wounded and forty were slightly wounded, including several officers. As the ship sailed into harbour it was met by thousands of people cheering who had been waiting patiently for its appearance on the shore. When Ernie, Ted and Billy arrived with about fourteen other men, they were met by an eerie silence. The onlookers watched in disbelief as the wreckage berthed at Parlatorio Wharf.

'The poor girl looks like she took a terrible thrashing,' Ernie said sombrely as he made his way down to the water's edge. He was shocked at what he saw. Men lay dead on the deck, many looked burnt beyond recognition. Some men sat with their heads down, feet hanging over the edge of the ship and a lot of them had roughly made bandages around their heads, arms and legs. Already several priests, summoned on the appearance of the Illustrious into the harbour had got on board and were administering to the men, both the dead and the living. Their murmurs could be heard by the bystanders who stood on the shore as they tried to offer prayers and reassurances. Ambulances had begun to arrive. Ernie and the men were asked by a stunned looking crewman to help move the injured men into the waiting ambulances and when that was done to remove the bodies of the dead. As Ernie and the others carried the bodies from the ship, the people still standing silently at the harbour's edge blessed themselves as they passed by. Many of them wept openly for the loss of so many lives. They were aware that these brave men had died valiantly trying to get supplies to the islanders, who were in dire need of them. Ernie felt sickened to his stomach. He tried not to look at the faces of the dead men that he carefully tried to lift, but he found it impossible not to. He saw blackened faces with horrific burns, bodies with pieces missing, many of them just young boys really. He knew the images would never leave him. The scent of burnt flesh was nauseating and he already, to his shame, had vomited over the edge into the water below. Ted was crying. Tears streaked down his face which was now covered in grime and dust.

'I hate this wretched war,' he swore. 'What the hell is it all for anyway? Tell me that.'

But Ernie couldn't answer him. Tonight he didn't know the answers to that himself.

The dead were last to be carried off the ship. One of the young men whom he had helped into an ambulance had pathetically screamed and begged Ernie to find his arm...... there were many body parts and the men looked bewildered at each other not knowing whether to remove them or not? Nobody had been trained in this. Suddenly Ernie felt a tug at his arm and turning around he looked into those familiar piercing blue eyes. It was Ana. She had been on duty when Matron ordered that all but two of the nurses were immediately to accompany the ambulances to Grand Harbour. She had seen him and the other men as they stared in horror around them and she quietly approached him.

'I have been told to ask you and your men that the dead and any remains, are to be put into the back of the ambulances when they return from the hospital. They are to be buried at sea.'

Just then Mellor approached.

'I wish you didn't have to see this Anabel. It is not exactly something that a young girl should witness, but here you are and I suppose you have a job to do, so I suggest you get on with it. I will take over ordering my own men from here.'

To this rebuttal Ana's face reddened and she simply replied 'Yes Father,' and walked briskly in the direction of one of the ambulances where another young nurse beckoned her.

Ernie thought that Mellor was a bit unkind and gruff with the girl. If anything, he would have expected that he give her some words of encouragement and support instead of appearing annoyed. He always got on well with the Wing-Commander, but he knew that Mellor could be harsh when he wanted to be. However Ana was his one and only daughter and he seemed to offer no kindness to her whatsoever. He didn't understand him at all.

Mellor gathered the men around him and gave instructions as to exactly what was required of them. It was literally a case of all hands on deck, regardless of rank. The dockyard crew needed to get on board as soon as possible to begin repairs without delay. They couldn't do so with bodies still on board. Ernie reckoned that they had their work cut out for them and he wondered if it was even possible to repair this damaged wreck at all. Huge gaping holes peppered the ship. Mangled lumps of steel were strewn across the decks and nearly all the compartments that Ernie had been into were almost obliterated and were now just burnt and blackened shells. Despite their attempts to remove remains, the ship also contained parts of limbs scattered across the ship. Blood was splattered on the wooden decks and the men slipped on it as they dragged the dead. It resembled a scene from 'Dante's Inferno' and Ernie knew that so far this was the worst devastation he had experienced in his military career.

When the men finally got back to base nobody was much in the mood for talking. Ted took out some bottles of grappa which he passed around the men, who gratefully poured the liquid liberally into tin mugs. When Ernie refused a cup of the strong liquor Ted told him that he would never sleep if he didn't have some. He reminded him that those same German bombers would probably be back tomorrow. So Ernie lifted his cup and with his friend he drank to the dead they had just helped to bury.

~

Over the next few days all the men were quite subdued. Many had difficulty trying to sleep after the sights they had witnessed on board the Illustrious. As Billy Cortis said,

'We might be all trained to kill, but none of us are trained in dealing with death.'

Ted seemed to be more sombre than the rest and Ernie noticed he had taken to going off by himself a lot more than usual. The next time he noticed his friend slip out he followed him. He couldn't see him at first. It was already quite dark even though it was just after six o'clock and the sky was lit up with many twinkling stars that promised another frosty morning. As he struck a match and held a cigarette to his lips he heard a snuffling sound coming from the direction were the rubble collected from that day's shelling had been piled up. There he found Ted and to Ernie's disbelief, loud choking sobs came from where he sat huddled against the pile of stone. Ernie instinctively ran over and threw his arms around his friend. After a couple of seconds when he felt Ted try to shrug him off he kept a firm grip on him and simply said;

'As my mother, God rest her, used to say, 'better out than in.' So let it out mate!' at which Ted noisily did.

'I wasn't cut out for this lark. I just wasn't. The old man said the RAF would make a man out of me but it clearly hasn't worked,' Ted cried, as he accepted the cigarette from Ernie and continued, 'I hate every last thing about it. I hate this sodding uniform, I hate having to take orders, but most of all I hate cursed fighting. Imagine a soldier and a fighter pilot who hates to fight. It's a flaming joke. I hate to kill someone. I'd rather take a hit myself than attack. If Maynard got wind of it, I'd be out on my ear and sometimes I wish that's what would happen. But then I think of going home to my father and facing him and I couldn't bear the disgrace. It would kill my mother too and I couldn't bear to hurt her. What a horrid mess.'

Ernie looked down at Ted's long fingers. His hands were like a girl's, long and slender and lily white. He felt an overwhelming desire to hold that hand, to feel if it was as soft as it looked. The hand shook as it held the cigarette and he longed to still the shaking with the strength of his own hand. He had always known that Ted was a gentle sort. He was quieter than the rest of the men also. Some of them called him a 'sissy' or 'mama's boy' because of his reluctance to do any of the other activities that his comrades enjoyed. Ted never seemed to want to get off with the women they met in the bars, or get involved in the rough and tumble friendly fights when the men challenged each other's combat skills to pass the time. He was more likely to be found off somewhere reading a book or writing letters to his mother than hanging out with the other chaps.

His height kept him from getting much jeering from the men as he was even taller than Ernie who was six foot four. However where Ernie was muscled and strong, Ted looked as if a breath of wind would knock him over. He was extremely slim and fair with blond hair which he hated having to cut tight. He was a good looking man. As Ernie looked at the long fair lashes tinged with tears he couldn't help but reach out and touch his friend's face, brushing the tears away as he did so. Expecting a rebuff or worse, he was both surprised and pleased when Ted grasped his hand. Without saying anything they sat there, holding hands, thighs pressed closely to each other and silently blew their cigarette smoke out into the frosty air.

Ernie felt a sense of peace he hadn't experienced in so many years. The last time he could remember feeling so safe was when as a child, he had been home alone with his mother. She would rock him on her knee as he stared into the fire, looking for the pictures that she said would be there if he looked hard enough. He would then describe any shapes that he could see and she would make up a story about them. At those times Ernie had felt the same peace that he was now experiencing. Suddenly he leapt to his feet, just as he had done back then, when he would hear his father and brother's footsteps outside.

'Somebody is coming,' he whispered to Ted and they watched as men vacated the canteen and headed towards the sleeping areas. They both knew to be found together in such a way would be catastrophic.

~ Ana ~
11

After the horrific incident of the Illustrious Jeany surprised Ana by telling her she was moving to a different hospital in Valletta.

'My mother was appalled to hear that I was tending to the wounded men. She said it was immoral for an unmarried woman to be so physically close to men, even though they were dying and she insisted that I stop nursing immediately. The only way I could get her to let me stay was if I agreed to nurse children only, but Matron won't let me do so here. She said that if she is seen to move nurses around from ward to ward because their parents wanted it, she would lose all respect in the hospital. She managed to get me into the children's hospital in Valletta though and I have to start there on Monday. I had a job to get my mother to allow me even to go there because Valletta is such a dangerous place to be right now. I eventually talked her into it by agreeing to live at St. Ursula's Convent when I'm off duty. It is a cloistered convent so no men can get in there. Honestly, you would think I had no mind of my own.'

Ana was saddened by this news. Jeany was the only one of the graduates from Verdala who was still in Mtarfa. The other girls had left one by one because either their families had left the island on the outbreak of war, or their parents demanded they leave as they believed it too dangerous to continue nursing in a military hospital which could be bombed at any time.

'Oh Jeany, I will miss you terribly,' she cried to her friend.

'I know. I will miss you too, but we will keep in touch and we can still go dancing at The Regent if we both have the same weekends off. Come and visit me when you go to Valletta. If you can tear yourself away from your fisherman that is,' she winked.

However it wasn't until Easter that Ana saw her friend again.

The year had gone quickly and so much had happened since they danced at the hotel in Sliema last March. It was a wonder it was even still standing as it was so close to the harbour. She had seen Katie a lot though and was Godmother to little Mikel whom she absolutely adored. Billy was seldom home so she visited St. George's Barracks whenever she could. She and Franco had taken Katie and the baby out several times on different day trips. Motherhood suited Katie. She had filled out a bit from the skinny young girl she had been and she had an air of pride about her now that she was a mother. However, she still loved to hear all about Ana's romance with Franco and the young women talked about little else when they were alone together.

'You know him about a year now don't you?' Katie asked as she handed Ana a cup of tea.

'Yes, but it wasn't until the Feast day of Our Lady that we kissed and started dating remember. You know, he told me that he saw me the night of my Graduation Dance. I had gone over to the harbour to sit by myself and he saw me on his way back into shore in his boat. He could tell me exactly what I was wearing. He said he thought I was a mermaid,' she giggled.

'You were with Ernie that night weren't you? I thought something might happen between you two. You made a handsome couple. Gosh, I remember my Billy got so drunk that night and I was so ill, remember? I didn't know then that I was pregnant.'

'Oh Ernie is nice alright, but he didn't seem the least bit interested in me. My father keeps making him chaperon me to different events and it's getting harder and harder to get out of them. Franco doesn't like it and Ernie clearly does it just to please my father.'

'Billy says that he has never seen Ernie with a girl. He said his only love is flying. Still, he is a handsome man. It's surprising somebody hasn't snapped him up.'

'My father is expecting me to go with him to the Easter dance, but I've told him I already have a date so now he said he is going to the dance also so he can meet whoever I bring.'

'Oh, make sure and come back to tell me all about it. I'd love to go dancing but Billy is on duty and it wouldn't do for me to go without him. Anyway, I've already offered to sit with Catherine's brood as she and Fred are going.'

Ana promised to visit soon and give her all the details. She was very excited about the dance, it was actually her first one with Franco. Any time there was an event run by the RAF wives, her father made her go with Ernest McGuill. This was the first time Franco would accompany her on an official occasion. She looked forward to showing him off to her father and dancing the night away with her beau. They hadn't danced together since the night they were on the roof of the church at Mosta. Ever since that night Ana had a soft spot for this church and often went there for Mass with Franco on her Sundays off.

~

'I am so sorry Franco for how my father treated you,' Ana said regretfully. 'He was abominable and I am so ashamed.'

'It's not your fault imħabba tiegħi, he was probably disappointed that you didn't attend the dance with the officer he had chosen for you.'

'But the way he looked at you, it was disgraceful.'

Laurence Mellor had indeed not hidden his disdain at his only daughter's choice of partner for the dance. This man was clearly of a peasant family and he was both surprised and appalled at his daughter's interest in him. Ana had been brought up as a lady and the man before him was clearly no gentleman. After making enquiries, he discovered that his suspicions were well-founded. This young man belonged to a family that Mellor believed were unsuitable for his daughter to associate with.

'They are a good family sir,' Pedro, his trusted driver assured him. 'The mother is of good Italian stock and the father is well respected in Sliema.'

'But he is a fisherman, is that correct?' Laurence questioned further.

'Yes. Young Gianfranco is a good fisherman and a good man also. Your daughter would be respected I am sure,' Pedro continued, not liking to be interrogated about people who he knew as friends. He didn't however reveal that his own family and the Vella family were neighbours.

This information only made Laurence Mellor more convinced that the lowly fisherman was no match for his daughter. As soon as this war was over he had plans to return her to her home in Britain. He had already decided that Officer McGuill would be a fitting husband for Ana and somebody who would also be capable of running his estate in Yorkshire. The extensive estate he had acquired on his marriage to Christabel was nothing but a burden. He had no interest in it and he looked forward very much to retiring in Malta, where the climate was favourable and his rank gained him respect. He also planned to marry Miss Honeyman when this infernal war finally ended. This, Mellor believed would be in the near future. Travelling around Europe on the income from his estate with an attractive woman at his side was something he eagerly anticipated.

His daughter getting caught up with a ruffian like Franco Vella was not part of his plan and Wing-Commander Mellor always liked to plan ahead. That's how he got the position he held today. No, Franco Vella had to go and he would ensure that he wherever he went would be well away from his daughter and the heir to his estate.

~ Ana ~
12

Ana didn't have much time to dwell on the details of the war from a political standpoint. She was too busy dealing with it on a different level. Every day she was busy in the wards trying to save those who had been injured by the war in some way, or in trying to get time to see Franco or her friends Katie and Jeany. Sometimes she tried to get to St. George's Barracks only to have to turn back because of heavy shelling from the air. Other times she was forced to spend the night in air raid shelters either on her way to St. Julian's or Valletta or Sliema.

The air raid shelters terrified her. She was never able to get used to the claustrophobic tunnels or rooms that were just caves carved out of rock in the bastion walls. Every time she heard an air raid siren go off, no matter if she was in the hospital or on the road or out shopping, her heart would race. Even hours later, she would still feel its vibrations ricocheting through her body. Sometimes when she sat in the shelters she felt an overpowering wave of panic encapsulate her and she tried on these occasions to run outside for air, but was always pulled back by some kindly person just trying to save her from being blown to pieces. The fact of being so close to so many people and sometimes hoards of men terrified her. It was ironic that outside, she was always taught to be ladylike and chaste and yet in the middle of the night if she was stuck in one of these tunnels or shelters she often had to relieve herself with men nearby. Women took turns to shield each other while they used the bowl or bucket reserved for these purposes, but it was impossible to have any privacy in such close proximity to others. She had heard that the original plan was for men and women to have different shelters, but this just wasn't feasible. When an air raid came it was a matter of diving into the nearest safe place possible. Sometimes, especially in Valletta when she went to visit Jeany, she would be in a shelter for hours, sometimes alone, with men who were just out of the bars and full of drink. During these nights she just hid herself under her nurse's cloak and prayed for the raid to be over.

For this reason she rarely got to visit Jeany, as her friend never returned to Mtarfa once she had moved to Valletta. Franco usually made the journey on his cart to pick Ana up. Then they would just travel about together and spend the time talking in the cart which Franco would park up somewhere. For them dating did not include dinner dates and dances and visits to the cinema. They simply saw each other when they could. Often one of them was unable to turn up at the designated place because of an air raid, or sometimes Ana had to work late if a large number of casualties came in at once.

Franco's mother Margarita invited Ana to their home for Christmas but she was unable to get out of the hospital until four o'clock. She was touched however, to discover when she finally arrived at the Vella home, that they had waited for her before having their Christmas meal and even had a gift with which to surprise her. It was a white lace collar which his mother had crocheted for Ana's Christmas dress, which was really a cut-down of an evening gown. She had no presents to bring as she had not been anywhere to get some, but she did have one small gift for Franco. It was a box of pencils and some paper which she bought from one of the office girls in the hospital. She knew he loved to draw and in return he gave her a small ring.

'It is not the kind of ring I would prefer to give you,' Franco said as he nervously placed it into her palm. 'It was my mother's, but her fingers have swollen now over the years and she suggested I have it, for you.'

Ana was both astonished and deeply moved. The thin gold

band nestled in her hand and she stroked the tiny encrusted rubies embedded into it.

'Oh, Franco I love it,' she cried and threw her arms around his neck.

'It is a promise ring,' Franco continued anxiously. 'You know that I am asking you to keep yourself for me and one day be my wife?'

Ana looked into his dark hopeful eyes and whispered that yes, she would keep herself for him. As she had been doing since the first time she met him. He was the only man for her and to know that he felt the same way meant everything in the world to her.

'Of course,' was her simple reply and she laughed out loud as Franco picked her up and swung her around the large cosy kitchen.

On hearing his whoops of delight Margarita came running in, closely followed by her brood of children of all ages. Her questioned look at her son caused him to affirm that Ana had agreed to be his and that some day in the future she would be Mrs Anabel Vella. His father Nikola came into the room then. Ana had not yet met him as he was always out working when she called. It was almost impossible now for him and Franco to make a living from fishing, so they got work trying to rebuild homes and bridges and roads which had been damaged in the raids. However, the Christmas celebrations had kept him home today and he warmly hugged Ana and welcomed her into their family.

'You are as pretty as he said you were,' he exclaimed loudly, followed by; 'I don't know what you see in him though,' which caused more laughter all around.

The Christmas meal was a sumptuous affair and Ana didn't know how Margarita managed to feed so many. There were eleven people seated at the long wooden table and there were many dishes of different types of food, rice and potatoes, vegetables that had been baked in the oven and seasoned with delicious oils and herbs. There were also platters of salted meat and fish piled high. After the meal there was a variety of cakes and dried fruits and Ana could barely move with all she had eaten. Afterwards the family all wrapped up warmly to go down to the new church of San Girgor il-Kbir (St. Gregory, the Great) in Sliema where the very first procession of the 'Presepju' (crib) was taking place. Four Benedictine priests proudly carried a beautifully carved wooden crib through the streets and Sliema was honoured to have Bishop Mauro Caruana lead the procession. The new church had been founded by him, a Benedictine monk as it was his long cherished dream to have a friary in Malta. Inside the crib the elaborately decorated figurines called 'Pasturi' represented figures such as the baby Jesus, Mary and Joseph, shepherds and angels.

As Ana walked alongside Franco and his extended family carrying their lighted lanterns, she felt a wonderful sense of belonging. She felt loved and cherished among the Vella family and when Franco linked her arm in his proudly, she felt that she was at home. That this is where she fitted in and she never wanted to be anywhere else than this war-torn island with the man and people that she loved.

~

Ana had an arrangement to meet her father on New Year's Day. He had invited her to spend Christmas Day with him at a dinner being given by the wife of one of his colleagues. She declined, saying that she only had a short time off work and would be given some days off in the New Year. Laurence was quite sure that she had plans which included the Vella person. When he questioned her about it, he couldn't hide his contempt that she was still involved with the lowly fisherman.

'He is a good man Father,' Ana said defensively. 'You don't even know him. So how can you say anything bad about him?'

'Anabel, you must realise dear that this war will be over at some stage, hopefully in the near future. You will then be returning to Yorkshire and this nursing lark and running about with the natives will all be a thing of the past. You have responsibilities as my daughter and I shall expect you to take them up when you return there.'

'Return,' Ana cried, 'I don't ever want to return to Britain. I am happy here. I have a job I love, I have good friends and I have Franco. He has asked me to marry him and I said that I would.'

At her father's horrified expression, she explained; 'Not yet of course. But I am promised to him and I intend to keep that promise. I love him.'

'Love!' her father said scornfully, 'what do you know about love?'

'I know it's what I feel for Franco. I know it's what Mother felt for you and you felt for her...'

Her father interrupted her by retorting,

'What your mother had for me? Don't you know you stupid girl that she had nothing for me? Where do you think she was the time she died? She wasn't out shopping like you think! She was in the home of her lover!'

Ana reeled, she couldn't believe it.

'It's not true' she whimpered, 'Mother missed you always. She hated you being away all the time.'

'Oh Anabel, grow up. She didn't miss me, any more than I missed her. Ours was an arranged marriage. She was always a flighty thing and her father needed somebody stable to look after her and his estate when he'd gone. I was the son of his best friend and a willing candidate. We married for conformity. How do you think I moved up the ranks so quickly? God, you have a lot to learn about life yet my girl.'

Ana was weeping by now and longed for her father to put his arms around her and tell her that what he said wasn't true. But instead he threw her a more hurtful jibe than anything he had said before.

'We always did our own thing, but then you came along,' he laughed cruelly, 'despite her delicate heart condition. But she couldn't even get that right and give me a son. Just get out,' he shouted. 'I don't want to see you again until you have got rid of that nobody.'

Stung by his words Ana raced out of the building that housed the RAF and her father's operations room. Franco was waiting outside. He had taken her on his cart to visit her father at the War Rooms at Lascaris in Valletta where Mellor was now based. He was leaning back against the cart, cigarette in hand, as he chatted with a few men when Ana came running out of Headquarters. She was crying. Throwing his cigarette on the ground he ran towards her.

'Ana, Ana, what happened? Is your father alright?' he asked worriedly, thinking Laurence Mellor must have been killed or something.

She jumped up on the cart and through trembling hands which covered her face she asked him to take her away from where they were.

It was minutes later while they were on the road to Sliema, with Franco casting anxious glances at Ana the whole time that she suddenly began to cry loudly. He pulled his cart to the side of the road so he could hold her.

'What is it love? Please tell me.'

So she told him all that had transpired between herself and her father. It was all that Franco could do, not to turn around and punch this self-righteous bully right in the nose for the pain he had just caused the girl he loved. Ana was inconsolable. Not for the first time since she arrived in Malta she wished Kitty was here. Because he had to go out with his father on a job, Franco drove her to Katie's in St. George's Barracks where she spent that night and the following one.

~

'I hate him,' she cried to her dear friend, 'I hate him so much. I never want to see him again as long as I live.'

Katie hugged her friend and they talked long into the night until eventually Ana fell asleep. The next day the two women spent the day doing household chores. Katie was expecting her second baby and she and Ana chatted as they made adjustments to some dresses which no longer fitted Katie.

'I hate destroying the pattern on this dress,' Katie moaned. 'Now that I've cut it, the red poppies are all off centre.'

'It's a beautiful dress,' Ana agreed. 'The poppies with the yellow background are so cheery looking. But we'll have to let it out. You can't get into it the way it is.'

'I am like an elephant.' Katie laughed, patting her large stomach. 'I was never this big with Mikel. I am almost embarrassed for Billy to see me.'

Ana laughed with her and admitted that yes, her friend certainly was big, but she also looked beautiful.

'You know, we could ask Billy to get us one of those parachutes. Then we could just put two arm holes in and make a dress out of it for you,' she joked, ducking her head as Katie threw her shoe at her.

When Franco came to collect Ana the following day he was happy to see that she was in much better spirits and eager to get back to the hospital.

'Spending time with Katie made me realise what is important,' she told him as he left her back at Mtarfa hospital. 'It's family and good friends and you.'

~ *Ana* ~
13

What horrified Ana the most about the effects of the war in Malta was the fact that people were now actually starving. Her wards were full of people who presented with what turned out to be malnutrition. Jeany had told her about children in her hospital who had almost nothing to wear. Ana had donated almost all of her once huge wardrobe to the hospital where her friend worked. She didn't feel the slightest bit grieved to know that her expensive dresses and coats were being cut down to make outfits for the orphaned children. By now even her uniform had shrunken down to just a plain pinafore. Matron's strict rules regarding their dressage on the wards went out the window when aprons were beginning to be used to bandage the wounded.

'In a war situation like this,' Matron explained, 'patients still always come first. If you can't get hold of a bandage and something you are wearing will suffice, use it.'

Daily food rations were also curtailed. The nurses no longer got cart blanche in the canteen and were simply served up whatever was available. Ana sometimes even went to bed after a long day of nursing with an empty stomach. The convoy of food supplies to Malta in February was unable to get through and this caused terrible hardship to the people. The one that did make it through in March from Alexandria was depleted by the time the Red Cross people were able to get anything for the hospital as so great was the need in Valletta and the Three Cities. Ana's main source of food came from the Vella family. She visited there whenever she could, but even when she did she felt guilty taking meals from Margarita, worried that she was depriving her own family.

'Don't worry love,' Franco's mother assured her, 'because I

have such a large family, I am entitled to ample rations. Also the men still get some fish and many of my family no longer live at home, so we have plenty to go around.'

However Ana couldn't help but notice that neither Margarita nor Nikola ate very much at meal times, saying that they usually ate together first as there was no room at the table. She knew this wasn't true and noticed that they both looked thinner than usual. When she confided this to Franco he said that he had also had the same thoughts. After their chat he told his parents that as their eldest son he would eat with them in future. This way he could ensure that they ate properly.

~

At the beginning of April, Ana and Franco were at Mosta church. It was one of their special places after the night of the 15th of August last year, where they had shared their first kiss. Ana was kneeling in prayer when she heard a tremendous whining noise. The next thing she knew, Franco threw her on the ground under a seat.

'What is it?' she screamed in panic.

'It's a bomb,' Franco cried. 'A bomb just came through the roof.'

People were screaming and crying all around her but miraculously nobody was injured or killed and some people even stayed on in the church. Ana was too terrified. They spent that night in an air raid shelter close by. The shelter was empty and this fact, together with Ana's fear that she might die without ever knowing of Franco's physical love for her, prompted their relationship to become even closer than it had before. She told Katie about this recent development. She felt that Jeany would be horrified, but Katie at least was a married woman.

'Oh Ana, go to Confession if you are so worried about it,' Katie told her friend after listening to Ana's worries about sin and eternal damnation. 'You are engaged. There is a war on. I'm sure God makes allowances for that.'

Ana knew that Katie was worried about the baby coming. She worried a lot too about Billy. The air raids were almost daily now and so many were being killed.

'Thank God we are safe here at the Barracks,' Katie said. 'It is so full here now though with all the RAF families from the Three Cities and Valletta moving in. I am the only one so far that hasn't had to give up one of my rooms for them, but I'm sure it is only a matter of time. Though, the company might be good.'

~

On Saturday the 25th April in 1942, Katie was baking bread in the kitchen of her little house. Flour was getting harder to get hold of and she had mixed it with some oatmeal, hoping to make it stretch out the dough a bit. Also it might make it more nourishing for Mikel who was growing fast. At seven in the morning, most people were still in bed undeterred by the roar of stukas flying overhead. The bombers were on their way again to Valletta or Sliema to cause more destruction and death. Perhaps they hoped to catch a ship arriving to port with ammunition that they could destroy before it even touched land.

Those lucky enough to be still in their beds turned over hoping to get some more sleep. Others who like Katie had already started their day were outside looking up. They noticed that planes seemed to be approaching much closer than usual and the engines sounded much louder. Katie threw a cloth over the dough and picking up her son's jumper she stepped outside, her body heavy with the second child making it difficult to run. 'Mikel,' she called out to the skinny dark haired boy. The toddler was holding fast to the hand of an older girl who kept an eye on him whenever Katie was busy or needed to rest. Oblivious to the shouts of his mother to get inside quickly, Mikel crouched, too absorbed in the antics of a baby lizard darting between the pots of flowers to heed her anxious calls.

The blast blew Katie through the open window of a neighbouring house. Little Mikel and his minder knew nothing after the thousand pound bomb was followed by forty-six minutes of relentless pounding of missiles. Dust and debris flew through the air. Panicked people could be seen running on the street looking for shelter or children not accounted for. Then silence. That night the English camp stood empty. Ninety-nine of its residents now slept on the stone floor of St. Andrew's underground tunnel half an hour away from their former homes. During the ten hours of shelling, just a couple of people were killed. The enemy had picked a new target.

~ Ana ~
14

'It's all hands on deck,' Matron told her hurriedly, 'there is an influx of patients now but thankfully no injuries that seem life threatening.'

When Ana arrived at the huge casualty department she was met by a sight which should have been familiar by now, but one to which she never learned to become immune. The room was filled with crying, hysterical people, reaching out to her for help and reassurance. She expertly weaved her way through them until she reached the Staff Nurse in charge to await instruction.

'Take the younger ones down to the children's ward first,' Sister Elizabeth ordered. 'Then come back up here and start a triage.'

On her return, Ana met several orderlies pushing trollies with sheets that were draped obviously over bodies. These she knew were no longer people she could help and averted her eyes as she let them pass. However, out of the corner of her eye she noticed a fragment of material which hung over the side of one of the trollies. It was a yellow dress, with red poppies and she recognised it immediately.

Fear clutched at her chest as she asked 'Who is that?' of the man pushing the trolley.

When he didn't answer and walked on down the corridor, she ran after him.

'Tonio, please stop.' And he did.

Ana lifted the sheet and screamed in horror. It was Katie, and lying next to her was her little boy Mikel.

~

By the time Billy had left with Ernie, Ana had been awake for almost twenty-seven hours. When Franco eventually made it to Mtarfa she was exhausted and too tired to even cry. He bundled her into his cart and took her straight to Sliema to his mother and together they sat with her as she lay unspeaking on his parent's bed until eventually she fell asleep. During the night Franco awoke to her crying out for Mikel and ran into the room where she clung to him until finally falling asleep once more. The next morning, as the sun shone bright through the windows of the large family home, Ana sat with Franco and his family while his mother washed her blood spattered pinafore in a tub on the kitchen table. She insisted that she needed to get to work and despite his protestations Franco took her, clothed as she was in a dress of his mothers' which reached down to her toes.

At the hospital Matron took one look at her and ordered her to bed. But sleep would not come. She kept thinking of little Mikel and the baby that never got to be born and most of all she thought of Katie. Ana remembered how excited her friend was when they had met on the ship on their way to Malta, where Katie was to begin a new life with Billy. That seemed a lifetime away and yet it was just over two years ago. Little did they both know then what lay in store for them! They had no idea that they were entering into a place that would be under siege, where bombs would rain down on their heads from dawn till dusk, where they would be hungry and see their loved ones killed. Ana felt like she wanted to lie there on her small single bed forever, but something inside her made her get up, get washed and present herself for duty at four o'clock as usual. She could do nothing for Katie or Mikel now. But hopefully she could help others. Her wards were full of people who needed her and she wanted more than anything to be there for them.

The next time she saw Billy it was at the little hospital church where they held a funeral service. Ana and Ernie stood by him and the Cortis family as Billy watched the burial of his loved ones in the adjoining cemetery. There was nobody there from Katie's side, except for Ana. Her family would receive a telegram like the countless others who did so and would continue to do so during this horrific war. Afterwards, Billy went back to Luqa airfield with Ernie and Ana went back to work. The days and months afterwards passed in a blur of work, in survival, in hunger and blissfully when possible, in sleep.

~ *Ernie* ~
13

The arrival of twenty-three Hurricanes in April and a further forty-three in June greatly helped the pilots who had been courageously trying to fend off the never-ending air attack by the Luftwaffe and the Regia Aeronautica. Then in March 1942, Ernie was delighted to be given charge of a new Spitfire for his reconnaissance missions and also another recon pilot. This meant that instead of his flying a solo reconnaissance plane on missions he could be accompanied by another one. He and the new pilot named Jack Gregson could share the workload and each could get some much needed sleep and free time. The HMS *Ark Royal* had been sunk in November by a German U-boat and in February the convoy from Alexandria was forced to turn back, without delivering crucial supplies to the people who were by now almost starving in Malta. So it was now more critical than ever that Ernie was able to keep an eye on what the Axis were planning and doing. Altogether a total of thirty-one Spitfires were delivered to Malta in March, which had been flown from the HMS *Eagle*.

In April Ernie, and everybody else on the island, were both honoured and pleased when news came that the George Cross had been awarded to Malta by King George VI. In a letter dated 15 April 1942 to the island's Governor Lieutenant-General Sir William Dobbie, the King had written:

"...so as to "bear witness to the heroism and devotion of its people during the Great Siege it underwent in the early parts of World War II."

This was a most welcome boost to the morale of the people who had suffered terribly and so far had lost so much in the siege. Ernie was still needed in air combat as there were never enough pilots available. He tried to ensure that he was always in the air at the same time as Ted. He was only too well aware of his dearest friend and lover's hatred of conflict and was dismayed at the times when Ted retreated when really he should have been contesting his rival.

'You are going to get your stupid blasted head blown off,' Ernie roared at him.

'Good. Then at least I won't have to listen to you bellowing it off,' Ted retorted, throwing himself down on the sand dune behind him. Even in April the sun was now quite hot and the military liked to spend any leisure time they had on the beautiful sandy beaches at Rabat. Ernie was livid. Just an hour ago he had watched Ted once again retreat to Ta-Kali airfield when he came under attack and the other pilots were beginning to question his competence.

'He's like a girl up there,' Billy yelled. 'Have you seen him? The first sign of an enemy plane and he turns tail and gets the hell out of there. What kind of use is that to us trying to save our own necks, never mind the lives of people on this island? You are going to have to have a word with him Ernie. The lads are baying for his blood and I don't blame them. That's the truth.'

Ernie lay beside Ted and lightly brushed his arm with his fingertips. They always had to be careful of somebody spotting their intimate moments together. However, for Ernie at least, this added to the thrill and joy of it all. The stolen moments and knowledge that every wondrous moment that occurred between them was forbidden, not to mind illegal, just made it more exciting and special. He was happier than he had been in many long years. He also saw a difference in Ted. He seemed more self-assured and confident, except when he was in the air. However when the men challenged him about his ineptitude, he held his own and shouted them down just as much as they shouted at him. But it couldn't continue.

'Look Ted,' Ernie said, raising himself up on his elbow and gently scraping back a lock of golden hair that was stubbornly growing across Ted's forehead, despite his constant cutting, 'I will have your back okay? If you take out just one or two of those Eyeties or Jerrys, the chaps will leave you alone.'

'I'm scared Ernie,' his friend admitted. 'I know it's shameful but that's how it is. I don't want to die and I don't want the murder of somebody else on my conscience either. I keep hearing my father's voice in my head telling me that 'beasts' like me go to hell for eternity. I don't want to go to hell.'

'Rubbish,' Ernie shouted, grabbing Ted by the shoulders. 'It's all a load of rubbish. If there is a God, did he want my mother to suffer under a brute of a husband when she was the most angelic soul ever lived? Did he want all these innocent people caught up in a war they had no choice to be in, to be killed and maimed and starve? Why would he want you, or me to burn for eternity because we love each other?'

'It's not the love that's wrong though, it's the act of love,' Ted replied miserably.

Ernie was about to give his opinion on that statement when the sound of loud voices and singing announced the arrival of a gang of younger soldiers and their girls on to the beach.

'Look, think about it Ted, alright. I can't hold the men off you much longer. Billy has warned me and so now I am warning you.'

Ted cast his eyes down, lips pouting like a child and Ernie longed to embrace him, but couldn't for fear of being seen. Instead they walked towards the noisy crowd and sat with them for a little while, having a beer and pretending to flirt with the pretty young girls they had in their company.

When they got back to base they were met by a sombre mood in the officer's mess.

'What's up?' Ernie enquired nervously, wondering if anybody had cottoned on to his and Ted's unlawful relationship.

'It's Billy Cortis,' replied the new pilot Jack. 'His wife and kid have just been killed in the Barracks at St. George's.'

Ernie was stunned and gathering his senses he ran out the door immediately in search of his mate, when the men informed him that Billy had gone to Mtarfa. It took some time to find a spare truck that he could take and with Ted alongside him he drove hastily, until quite quickly he reached the hospital. Running through the mass of corridors he stopped in his tracks when he met the tear stained face of Anabel Mellor. He remembered that she was a very close friend of Katie, Billy's wife.

'He is in there,' she whispered, obviously trying to hold back tears while she pointed to the door which had Hospital Morgue written above it. 'They are all in there.'

Billy was beside himself with grief. Ernie could tell by his swollen eyes that he had been crying a lot. His heart went out to him.

'Billy...' Ernie moved towards his devastated friend, 'I don't know what...'

'Don't say anything. There's nothing anyone can say.' Billy pushed past him. 'But there is something I can do.'

After he had buried his family in Mtarfa cemetery, all that the grief-stricken man wanted to do was get into the air and kill as many enemies as he could.

'I don't need any time off,' he insisted. 'Time off to go mad? Just get me into a damn plane and I'll show those bastards what for. They have killed my wife and my babies. I don't care anymore about myself. I just want to do what I can to make sure that other Maltese people don't have to go through what I just have in this futile war.'

With another supply of Spitfires to the island in May, the air battle was now in Malta's favour. Ensuring the safe passage of convoys to the island kept Ernie and his men busy. A convoy sailing from Alexandria was forced to turn back due to the Italian Navy showing their presence. Another convoy from Gibraltar also endured heavy bombardment. Fortunately two merchant ships managed to reach Grand Harbour with supplies, saving the island inhabitants from imminent starvation. On 15th August 'Operation Pedestal' successfully brought more supplies, although the convoy lost nine merchant ships, one aircraft carrier and two cruisers. When word of the terrible battle it endured en route to Valletta spread, the locals named it a miracle, especially as it happened on the Feast of the Assumption.

'It *was* a blinking miracle,' Ted laughed when he heard about what was being said. 'It was a miracle we weren't all killed.'

Ernie was still worried about Ted's flying in combat. Only for the fact that he had saved his neck several times, Ted wouldn't be here. He was beginning to wish that his friend could get a non-life threatening injury, just so he could be kept on ground for a while. At least till these heavy air battles were done with. Billy on the other hand was ruthless. He took his grief and anger out in the sky and Ernie worried about him for the opposite reasons. He had no fear in him whatsoever and if there was a miracle on this island, it was that Billy Cortis was still alive. He would dive into a swarm of enemy aircraft, guns blazing and swoop back out again unscathed. It was almost as if he wanted to die. Mellor had kindly visited Billy after the death of his wife and little Mikel. Billy told Ernie that the Wing-Commander had offered his condolences.

'Yes, he's a good enough sort,' Ernie said, 'but you would never take him for a family man. He's quite hard on his own daughter.'

'Yes, Katie was always telling me that,' Billy replied, 'she said that he doesn't approve of the fellow that Ana is seeing. There was some awful row between them after Christmas. Katie said Ana was in a terrible state and Franco was quite worried about her. He took her to our place to stay for a day or two.'

'Yes. She's a good kid, but Mellor is hell bent on getting that fellow away from her. I've met Franco Vella a few times with Anabel.'

'I have a few times too and he is a decent man. They are promised to each other now you know. That was one of the reasons for the row. Anyway, at least you know you won't have to take her out anymore eh!'

Ernie nodded his head, affirming that he was glad about that. However, that wasn't what Mellor had told him. He seemed to be annoyed with Ernie. He accused him of letting her slip through his fingers and lose her to the fisherman.

'If you had kept a better eye on her like I asked you to, she wouldn't be caught up with this lout,' Mellor had bawled at him.

Ernie was quite annoyed to be the brunt of the older man's anger but not wanting to further enrage him he acquiesced and said that all was not lost. They weren't married yet.

'You know, the RAF like their Commandants to be family men,' Mellor told him pointedly. 'And when this war is over, have you thought about what you will do?'

Ernie had, a lot. He was well aware also of what he was being advised, but there was Ted now and whatever his plans were in the future, they included him. However, even Ernie was appalled at what Mellor engineered for Franco.

'He is an Italian. I found that out after I did a bit of research on the family. The mother is from Ragusa in Sicily and he was the only one of her litter to be born there. So he is an enemy alien and therefore he should be arrested,' Mellor informed Ernie gleefully, 'and by God, arrested he will be if I have anything to do with it.'

~ *Ana* ~
15

When Matron called her into her office in November, Ana knew it wasn't to admonish her for any problem with her work, for it was exemplary. Nobody worked harder than her or with as much passion for her nursing as Ana. When Matron suggested that she run some medical tests on her, Ana looked up puzzled and was about to question why when Matron cut in.

'Don't ask me any questions now Nurse Mellor,' Matron said, matter-of-factly. 'In a week or so, you may ask. I am quite within my rights to check on the health of my staff, especially during these times.'

She was pregnant. The symptoms that had gone unnoticed by Ana had not gone unnoticed by Matron.

'So, I presume that Mr Vella is the father,' Matron asked, or rather stated as Ana sat shocked in the small ante-room almost ten days later.

'Yes Matron,' Ana answered. Though she could barely talk, given her astonishment at Matron's revelation.

'An unmarried pregnant nurse has no place on my ward. You do understand that?' Matron said, though not without a hint of sympathy.

'We are promised to be married Matron,' Ana replied quietly.

'Then the sooner the better is my advice.'

~

Franco was ecstatic.

'Then we get married right away,' he cried excitedly. 'We don't need to wait.'

Ana agreed, not just because she was pregnant, but because

she wanted Franco to be close to her as much as possible. They decided not to tell anybody until Christmas was over. Then they wanted to get married immediately in the New Year. The doctor Ana had seen in the hospital told her that the baby would be due sometime in July. Franco said that they would have to live at his brother's house in Sliema until they could get a place of their own, but at least they could be together and be a family. That was all that Ana wanted, Franco and a family of her own. She hoped to live out her days on the island she now felt was her home and prayed that someday soon Malta would be at peace.

~ *Franco* ~
1

By the time Franco moored his boat in the harbour at St. Julian's he was absolutely frozen. He had been out since dawn on that cold December morning and was happy with his catch of lampuka and young swordfish.

'This will keep the family going over Christmas,' he thought happily as he dragged the heavy nets behind him onto the shore.

This Christmas was going to be the best ever. He and Ana were informally engaged now and his uncle Fr. Cauchi had eagerly agreed to marry them in the new church in Sliema as soon as possible in the New Year. If Franco had his way they would be married before Christmas, but his uncle said they first needed to have Laurence Mellor's consent as Ana was not yet twenty-one years old. Ana was sure once she told her father of her pregnancy that he would give it, albeit begrudgingly. She decided that instead of spending Christmas with the Vella family where she would much prefer to be, she would spend it this year with her father and his colleagues and break the news to him then.

'Anyway,' she reminded Franco. 'In May I shall be twenty-one and if he doesn't give his consent before then, we will still be able to be married before the baby arrives in July.'

So despite his concerns regarding Ana's father, Franco was happy. He was in love and he had a new baby to look forward to. He whistled cheerily to himself as he tramped across the flotsam thrown up by the day's tide. Looking up he waved when he saw a group of men gathered on the pier. He recognised some of the soldiers and called out,

'Are you lot looking for something for your evening meal?'

He was a bit worried that he might be in trouble yet again for disobeying the rules of no fishing, but the local fishermen largely disregarded this and the soldiers also turned a blind eye as they were quite happy to accept some of the catch for their own use. They were sick of the canned meat that was served up in the Barracks daily.

When the soldiers began to approach him with their guns raised, Franco still wasn't too concerned. At least not until his brother Pawlu started shouting, 'Run Franco, run.'

Franco stood still where he was and a feeling of fear gripped him. As the soldiers grew closer some of his fishermen friends ran closer and were shouting at the soldiers that Franco had done nothing wrong. He had no lights on his boat and he was always back before it grew dark. Franco yelled out to Sergeant Richard or Ricky whom he knew well,

'Hey, what's up Ricky?' The man he had taken out on his boat a few times murmured something to the others and walked over to him.

'I'm sorry my friend, but you are under arrest.'

'Why?' Franco let go of the nets which he was still holding.

'Where were you born?' Ricky asked.

And Franco knew then that his mother's fears had been realised, for he was an Italian, even though he had only lived in Italy for a few short weeks. He had been born in Sicily, in his grandmother's house in Ragusa, where his mother had gone to give birth and be nursed by her own family. This simple fact made him an enemy alien in his own country where he had lived for twenty-five years. Although his fellow fishermen put up a protest as the soldiers accompanied Franco into the waiting truck, he went without any argument for he knew it was no use. After shouting at Pawlu and the others to take the catch home to his mother and tell her what happened, he climbed into the truck and sat in between Ricky and another soldier who still had his gun pointed towards him.

'Put that away,' Ricky shouted.

Turning to Franco he told him that they had been given orders to arrest him as an enemy alien and take him to Grand Harbour and a ship that was bound for Egypt.

At this Franco jumped up in his seat aghast, 'Egypt? Why am I being sent to Egypt?'

Ricky shook his head, 'Don't ask me Franco.'

Franco almost felt like crying by now but willed himself not to. This was much more serious than he had originally thought. He assumed that at the worst he would be held as a POW at the Barracks in Malta, maybe until the war ended or even sent to a prison somewhere in Italy. He would never have dreamt that he would be sent to Egypt.

All he could think about was Ana. He had arranged to meet her at their usual spot in St. Julian's where there was a little park overlooking the sea. He knew that soon she would be sitting there waiting for him, wrapped warmly in her heavy woollen coat which she had taken from England. It had fur around the hood and the cuffs and he used to tell her that she looked like a Russian princess in it. He imagined her sitting there, tapping her feet as she did when she got impatient and constantly checking her wrist-watch. He knew that she would wait a long time for him and might even go down to the harbour to see if his boat had come in or ask his friends if they had seen him. This worried him even more, knowing that they would tell her about his arrest. He felt sick at the thoughts of his mother's reaction also when she heard, as she was already in poor health. Franco began to realise what his arrest would mean to a lot of people.

On reaching the harbour he prepared himself to be taken to some military personnel in the War Offices or some similar place to be interviewed. He had heard that was what happened. You would be asked to produce your birth certificate or a passport which Franco obviously didn't have on his person. He was curious to know how his Italian birth had been discovered. To his knowledge nobody had made any enquiries and nobody apart from his parents and their own families knew that he had in fact been born in Sicily. It was not something that he ever mentioned as he had been there such a short time. Then horror overcame him as he realised that they could also have arrested his mother.

Ricky had left him in the charge of a naval officer. This man was unknown to Franco and he was aware that all the other man knew was that Franco was a prisoner of war. Although he was treated with decorum, it was obvious that he wasn't as sympathetic to Franco's plight as the other soldiers who arrested him had been. His concerns about his mother and Ana were foremost in Franco's mind as he was led into the large hold of the ship. Entering inside he was struck firstly by the darkness of the area. There was an odious smell of male sweat and waste and when his eyes became accustomed to the dimness, he could make out a group of men who were huddled together playing cards. Towards the rear there were other men lying on the ground who looked asleep and a few were sitting up and leaning against the wall of the ship's hold. Everybody turned to look at him.

After the huge steel door was locked behind him Franco picked out a spot close to where he stood and sat down and nodded his head to the other men who were all staring at him. He realised he was the only one in civilian clothes. The rest were all in the Italian army uniform. It was a uniform he already had learned to despise. These were the men who had been bombing his island relentlessly for the last two and a half years and instinctively he felt hatred towards them. He thought of the bus full of children killed and his fear that Ana had been among them. He remembered the bodies he and his father had pulled out of houses that the Italians and Germans had shelled. He clenched his fists at his side. He was surrounded by the enemy.

About an hour later the door of the hold was opened shining a shaft of light into what was now Franco's prison. His name was called and with pounding heart he stood up and walked towards the men standing at the door. Hoping to God that there had been some mistake and that he could go home, he was filled with relief when he recognised the blue eyes of Laurence Mellor peering in at him. He made to move towards him and was pushed back by the naval officer whom he had met previously.

'Yes,' Mellor said nodding his head. 'That's the man.'

Franco once again tried to reach him and was forced back. He called out to the father of his fiancée hoping for help, but when he saw the look of grim satisfaction on Mellor's face before the door was closed, he knew immediately who was responsible for his arrest. Franco sank on the floor in disbelief. He knew his fate was sealed.

2

Egypt was horrendous. It was hot, but Franco was used to the heat of the sun. He wasn't however used to the sand and the thirst and the lack of water to drink, or food to eat. He hadn't been able to wash himself in weeks and his lips were cracked and sore. He knew he had lice also as his head itched terribly, as did his skin. Christmas day was spent on the ship and he felt guilty knowing that his arrest had probably ruined this festivity for his whole family, especially Ana who should have been looking forward to their wedding. Worst of all Franco was lonelier than he had ever been in his life. After the first couple of days in the hold he gave in to the tears that up until then he had fought back. After yet another barrage of jokes and abuse at his expense by the other men, he curled on the thin mattress on the floor and facing the wall he stuffed his hand into his mouth as sobs wracked his body.

The men seemed to hate him as much as he hated them, but there were twenty-three of them and only one of him. They were from several different regions in Italy. Although the diverse accents caused confusion at times amongst the men, they all shared the same language. Franco had a spattering of Italian picked up from his mother but he wasn't fluent and he found it difficult to follow the men when they spoke. However it wasn't hard to understand that the points in his direction accompanied by laughter and coarse hand movements were not out of friendliness. After yet another accident involving his blanket somehow being soaked in the toilet bowl, he squared up to the man named Toni only to be pushed down to the ground by several hands, which were only too willing to be used in violence towards him if necessary.

He missed Malta and his parents and siblings, but most of all he missed Ana. She would know by now that he had been arrested. He guessed that she would go to her father to find out what he knew and he also knew that Mellor would lie. His only hope was that his mother had not been arrested and God forbid taken as a POW too. He tried to pray but found that although the words were going round on his tongue, his mind was always on Ana and the position they were both in now. The only thing that he held on to was the belief that once she told Mellor about the baby, he would surely get Franco back to marry her. He wouldn't want the scandal of his daughter being an unmarried mother. Keeping up good appearances to his colleagues was too important to him. This knowledge was all that kept him from going crazy.

~

All of the men were relieved when they were told of their imminent departure from Egypt. That was until they discovered where their next destination was to be.

'Where the hell are the Orkney Islands?' Giuseppe asked the Sergeant in charge.

'Scotland, well off the coast of Scotland anyway, far north,' he replied and laughing at the irate looking Italian in front of him continued, 'Don't worry. It won't be so hot there and there won't be a shortage of water for you lot either.'

Franco couldn't believe his ears. Scotland! That was thousands of miles away. Although he was relieved to be leaving the Egyptian desert which by now he hated the sight of, he would rather be there than in Scotland. At least it was closer to home. To him Scotland and England were the other end of the world.

'They want us to work at building barricades in the sea,' he overhead Giuseppe and the men say.

Franco didn't care about work. If anything he preferred to finally have something to do. The days passed interminably in Egypt and the men had long since got bored of card games and football. He missed the sea. When he discovered that they were going to an island he was glad, hoping that maybe he would get to fish. Even just to see the ocean would lift his spirits immeasurably. Like on the journey to Egypt, many of the men were seasick. However this time the voyage was a lot longer and it looked as though the Italian platoon sergeant was not going to make it. Franco could tell that he was severely dehydrated and the men were frantic about him.

'He's been with us from the beginning,' Giuseppe explained, 'and he didn't even have to go with us to the Orkneys but he said he wasn't leaving us. He's been keeping all of us going with the drills and stuff and I really don't know how the men are going to continue without him.'

Franco already could tell that this man was respected by the others. It was he who would call a halt to their teasing of the Maltese prisoner at times and Franco also noticed how the sergeant, named Carlo, seemed to know when one of the men was on a thin thread of sanity and would find him some task or other to keep both his mind and body busy. He could understand therefore the concerns of Giuseppe and the others. However all the men were quite ill themselves at this point. The only one who thrived on board was Franco as he was accustomed all his life to sailing in all kinds of conditions. None of the other men were fishermen or even lived near the coast which was hard to believe. They all came from either mountain towns or inland cities.

So it was Franco who played doctor and nurse to Carlo and the other prisoners. He donated his water supply to the sicker among them and as his English was excellent he was able to argue and plead with the officers on board for medical aid and supplies for the ill men.

By the time they reached the Orkney Islands on a wild and wet February evening the animosity between him and the Italians was gone. However Sergeant Carlo was still quite ill. When he was carried onshore he was whisked away in a Red Cross ambulance immediately after having been checked over. All of the men were deloused on their arrival and given medical examinations before being shown to their living quarters. These were simple Nissen huts complete with bunks and the exhausted men gladly fell into them.

'I don't know what makes me feel worse,' Guisseppe murmured in the bunk opposite Franco, 'the fact that I am bloody delighted to be here or the fact that I never want to go home if it means travelling back on that ship.'

Franco didn't agree with him however. He would gladly go back on that ship if it meant going back to Malta and Ana and all the people that he loved. As he lay on his own bunk, he pulled out the sheets of paper, folded and refolded many times where he had done pencil drawings of his fiancée. He knew that he would never forget her face and her smile but he wished he had a blue pencil to colour in her eyes. When the men saw him drawing they begged him to do caricatures of them which he did obligingly, glad of anything to pass the time. He also drew them pictures of gargoyle faces on the bodies of Mussolini and Hitler, who to his surprise they all hated passionately. He was amazed to learn that not one single one of the men had joined the army voluntarily and none of them agreed with the Fascist views of either Dictator.

'Mussolini said it was our personal choice if we wanted to serve our country, but those who refused discovered that their homes or businesses or farms were mysteriously burned during the night. People stopped being served in some shops or cafes and generally we were bullied into it. We joined in the end because it was safer for our families and homes if we did so. Or at least that's what we were led to believe,' Giuseppe told him.

Fabrizio and Lorenzo agreed, with Fabrizio adding that he knew of man whose sisters were threatened with rape if he did not join up, so he did do the very next morning.

'To us the Maltese are our friends, our neighbours,' Fabrizio said, 'none of us wanted to do the things that we were ordered. But also Franco, none of the men here ever flew a plane or were even in Malta before we got arrested, so we are not responsible for anything bad which happened to your country.'

Franco nodded his head in acceptance. 'Yes, I understand that now,' he agreed.

3

Franco never mentioned Ana's name the whole time he was a prisoner on the cold and windy Orkney Islands. Each one of the men had their own heartaches to deal with. Eventually they were allowed to write letters home and Franco often found himself writing several letters in one day for the men who were illiterate. The first letter he received from Malta was from his mother in her beautiful script. Just touching the letter than she had sent made him feel a little closer to home. He could tell that she was trying to keep his spirits up as she didn't mention anything about his arrest or what agonies she went through herself afterwards. He was relieved to finally know that she had not been arrested also as he had worried about that since becoming a POW. Instead she spoke of how his siblings were doing and how much fish his father had caught. If she mentioned the war he didn't know, as some of her letter had been blacked out, by censorship. She also didn't mention Ana which he thought strange and immediately sent another letter back asking once again, as he did in his first one, if she had seen her.

By this stage he knew Ana would have given birth and the fact that his mother never mentioned anything about a baby or Ana made him believe that she didn't know about a grandchild or that if she did, there was must be bad news that she was keeping from him. He thought he would go mad from frustration of not being able to get satisfactory answers to all the questions he bombarded his mother with. He began to be convinced that Ana was dead. If she was alive he knew that she would be in touch with his family and would have written to him. He sent letters to Mtarfa but didn't receive any reply. Then his father wrote to him, which was unusual as his writing skills were not very good and indeed his handwriting was more like that the scrawl of a young child. He asked Franco to please stop tormenting his mother with questions. He said that she blamed herself for his deportation and that right now she needed to know just that he was well, that he was eating enough and not pining for something out of his reach.

So Franco did as he was asked. His letters to his mother from then on were all about how he had taught the Italian men how to fish and the funny escapades they had in doing so. He drew her pictures of the landscape in Orkney and of the progression of a little chapel that he and the other men were building on the island from just two Nissen huts. He wrote that he was doing some of the art work of the chapel and sent her pictures of the angels he had drawn around the Madonna and child. However, he did not draw the ones he sent to her exactly the same, because the face of the angel in the chapel was the face of Ana with her beautiful blue eyes.

Sergeant Carlo was back with them by now and his health was slowly improving, though he had lost a lot of weight. However his appearance buoyed his men up a lot and they eagerly complied with his orders of exercise drills. He even made them stand in line each morning so he could inspect them. Franco knew the real reason for this was to keep a sense of routine and order in the camp, as the men seemed to need it. Keeping busy was what got them through the day. Before Franco and his men arrived, a German U-boat had got through a gap in the defences of Holm Sound in October of 1939 and in doing so was able to sink the *Royal Oak* battleship anchored of Scapa, killing eight-hundred men. The Navy were therefore forced to leave Orkney until all gaps were secure. This involved building massive barriers from stone and concrete onto the sea-bed from island to island, stretching for nearly two miles. The POWs were assigned to the back-breaking work of building what became known as the 'Churchill Barriers'. Their task was made even more difficult by the weather conditions they endured. From as early as September right up until April it seemed to be always winter on the Orkneys. It rained almost every day and the cold north wind never seemed to cease blowing. During the peak of winter, icy conditions made their work treacherous and coupled with food shortages and the lack of adequate clothing it was difficult for the men to keep going.

Although Franco was by now on good terms with the other POWs, he still felt very much the outsider. He was the only one not a soldier and also Maltese, as he considered himself to be. He spent long stretches of time by himself and this was when he drew the pictures on the walls of the little chapel. Painting was not something he was good at, so he merely drew the outline in thick pencil and the other men filled them in. When it grew dark he lit candles to work by, but the whole time he drew, his mind was on Ana. On one occasion he became quite upset while drawing the face of a baby in the arms of an angel, as he thought about the child that Ana was expecting. Not knowing if he was a father or if something had happened to Ana whilst she was pregnant gnawed at his heart every day. He fully believed that if she was alive, she would make contact with him somehow. But she hadn't and this fact worried him.

~

On 9th September 1944 Franco and the other POWs finally left the Orkney Islands. One of the men, Chiocchetti, stayed behind to finish work on the little chapel, as he wished to complete the font he was in the process of making. Franco however wouldn't have let anything stand in his way of getting back to Malta and looking for his fiancée.

The ship took him with the other men to the bay of Naples and that was where they said their goodbyes. Giuseppe however insisted that Franco accompany him to his home at the city of Potenza, in the Basilicata region of Southern Italy. At first Franco refused the kind invitation, citing that he didn't wish to intrude on his friend's homecoming as a reason, but he just wanted to get to Malta as quickly as possible. However, when Giuseppe reminded him that Potenza was on the way towards the port at Civitavecchi where he could get a ferry to Sicily and then on to Malta, he took him up on his offer. Otherwise he would have to make the journey alone and at least this way he would be guaranteed a bed for the night.

It was very sad saying goodbye to the men who had become his friends over the last twenty or so months that they had spent on the Orkneys. Some swapped addresses and there were many promises to meet up again, but Franco wondered if they ever really would. It was a long journey to Potenza cadging lifts along the way and by the time they arrived at the Piazza Pagano in the centre of city they were both exhausted.

'*Mio Dio,*' said Giuseppe, as he took in the rubble of what were once beautiful historical buildings. 'I can barely recognise my own town.'

Turning a corner just off the piazza he pointed to a beautiful church that was still standing.

'At last, there is something to prove to me that I am in the right city. That is 'la Chiesa di San Noraco', where I was married and my children were baptized.'

The older man's mood was jubilant by now as he neared home and he practically dragged Franco down a wide street as he loudly shouted out the name of his wife and family. People came out of doors and hung over balconies to see what the commotion was and several of them, on recognising their friend and neighbour, came running out to embrace him. Franco felt quite awkward, and leaned quietly against a doorway whilst he watched his friend being swept along to a house opposite by a crowd of people all calling out and some crying. But he was not to be left alone, as just before Giuseppe entered into the building which was obviously his home, he let out a roar to Franco and beckoned for him to join him.

'*Questo è il mio buon amico,* Franco,' (this is my good friend, Franco) he shouted to the others and Franco found himself pushed into the room where his friend was now standing in the arms of his wife, with his children wrapped round his legs.

The scene caused him great happiness for Giuseppe but also made him yearn even more to get home to Ana and his own family. There was a feast that night and both men ate hungrily and drank merrily. The next morning early Giuseppe himself drove Franco in a battered old truck as far the port in Calabria, where he waited with him to catch the ferry to Sicily and then on to Malta.

'I can write to you, now that you have taught me how,' Giuseppe said hugging his friend close.

He pressed a straw bag into Franco's hand which contained some bread, cheese and wine that his wife had packed for his trip and stood at the pier as Franco disappeared into the mouth of the ferry. 'If we meet again, I hope it is not on Orkney,' he shouted after him. But Franco didn't answer. Returning to Malta and finding Ana and his child was foremost in his mind.

~ *Ernie*~
14

Ernie heard about Franco's subsequent arrest from Billy. Apparently Ana had called to the Barracks to enquire if he had heard anything about Franco. Ernie hadn't. He also claimed that he knew nothing and said he would try to find out. However what he had suspected proved to be correct when a delighted Mellor verified that he'd had the young man arrested as an enemy alien. Franco was now on a ship en route to Egypt. Ernie was flabbergasted, but he didn't dare show the resentment and revulsion he felt toward his superior who appeared extremely happy that his plan had worked.

'Does Miss Mellor know yet?' he asked.

'Oh indeed she does,' Mellor replied unkindly. 'I was told she was here looking for me, so she will no doubt be back to see if I know anything. And let me tell you McGuill,' he said, shaking a finger at the tall man in front of him, 'you know nothing. Do you hear me? If I hear one word from you to Anabel about this, then its goodbye to your career, understand?'

Ernie did tell somebody however. He told Ted, who wasn't as surprised as Ernie thought he would be.

'Those people, it's all about appearances Ernie. I live in a family like that too you know. They don't care how people feel, only what other people just like them, think of them. I tell you, I am not going back to that life. Not for anything.'

~

On January 21st Tripoli fell to the Allied Forces. This caused great celebrations among the people of Malta, no more so than the military, including Ernie and his men.

It seemed like the whole island was out to celebrate and there was partying, drinking and dancing all night. Alcohol of all kinds and food were unearthed from hidden hoards and fireworks were launched into the sky. This could be the beginning of the end and everybody was in a mood to party. Christmas had been a quiet enough affair that year for most, but this was news that brought people out of the shelters and caves that by this time were the only homes of the majority of the coastal population. Even Billy was celebrating.

'Any news of those bastards getting their come-uppance is damned good news to me,' he shouted loudly, as he took another swig from his almost empty whiskey bottle.

Ernie and Ted and the others were also well inebriated by now. Ernie still wasn't used to alcohol and just one or two glasses of grappa or whiskey, or even just one beer would make him wobbly on his feet. The men all left Caffé Cortina to join the throng of people out on St. George's Square in Valletta who were dancing along to a band which had been set up on a make-shift stage. By midnight Ernie was euphoric. He had drunk a cocktail of drinks, whiskey, vodka, grappa, beer, ouzo….. and he began to be more openly affectionate towards Ted. Luckily for them both, Ted was much more able to hold his liquor and steered Ernie towards the harbour where it was quieter. He hoped that maybe he could persuade his lover to douse himself in the cold sea to sober up a little.

'Ted, Ted, my beautiful boy. Don't you know how much I love you?' Ernie yelled at him, as Ted tried to coax the tall well-muscled man onto the beach. By this stage Ernie was missing a boot and although Ted was the tallest, he had difficult in keeping him upright. Then Ernie flopped down on the pier amongst a bundle of nets and lay against the side of an old boat.

'Sit with me Ted, come on sit down.'

So Ted did. Ernie lit a cigarette and passed it to Ted, then lit another one for himself.

'I love you, you know,' Ernie repeated, spraying spittle onto Ted's face. Then he suddenly grabbed hold of Ted and kissed him full on the mouth. When he let go, the two men lay back together against the boat and Ted raised the cigarette to his mouth. Then out of nowhere, a voice hissed;

'So this is where you two love-birds went!'

Ernie didn't move his head. Ted didn't think Ernie even heard the voice of the man who loomed large behind them. Turning around he didn't have to look to see who the voice belonged to. He knew exactly who it was. It was Wing-Commander Laurence Mellor and he looked like the cat that had got the cream.

PART II
~ Ireland ~
2001

1

Ana had never been on an aeroplane before. Any time she had travelled in her younger days, or later on her trips to England, it had always been by boat. The only reason she eventually agreed to take this trip to Malta was because Jessy had paid for their fare. She wouldn't have her grand-daughter disappointed or wasting hard earned money because of her. She thought Jessy was working extra hours in the library to save for leaving home and the thoughts of it had kept her awake on many nights. Lying in her single bed downstairs in the housekeeper's apartments she shared with Jessy, she listened to the priest's footsteps as they pottered about above. Fr. Sean was obviously trying to silently help himself to yet more chocolate bars. She could tell just by the creak of the floorboards that he was standing right in front of the food larder in the huge kitchen just over her head. She smiled to herself, because she was small and couldn't reach the top cupboard; Fr. Sean thought she didn't know where he kept his stash of goodies. However Ana knew that the empty chocolate wrappers she found in the mornings were not left by a mouse. Who did he think replaced the stash when he had finished it? Obviously it was Ana, carefully climbing onto a stool to do so.

Usually a great sleeper, these last few weeks she found herself waking with a start, her heart quickening and then found it impossible to go back to sleep. Everyone was advising her to cease her job of twenty-three years. She knew the priests kept her on solely out of a sense of responsibility because she had nowhere else to go. The fact that she was a great cook was an added bonus and nobody knew the ins and outs of the parish as well as Ana. So she happily stayed where she was and the two priests residing in the parochial house were happy to have her there. Having the young village woman coming in to do the heavy work was a blessing she didn't like to admit to. She was glad Jessy wasn't moving out, but now she had other reasons to keep awake. When she opened the package at the surprise meal Jessy had cooked for her birthday, she expected just another lovely handmade card and maybe a nice cardigan or something. When she saw the flight tickets to Malta with the card she couldn't hide her shock.

'But I can't go to Malta,' she cried, her face immediately turning pale. 'The priests couldn't possibly spare me!'

Jessy laughed and hugging her grandmother said, 'It is alright and you can go, and we are going, and the priests know all about it. Sure Fr. Sean is going too. For once I am spoiling you.'

Later after many cups of tea and laments about squandering money and coming up with every excuse she could think of under the sun for not going, Ana began to feel the first real stirrings of anxiety, as reality dawned on her and she knew that there was no way out. She was going to Malta whether she liked it or not and the latter was how she honestly felt. At the same time she couldn't let Jessy have any idea about her real feelings surrounding the upcoming pilgrimage to see Pope John Paul II, on his second visit to Malta.

'Can you believe I'm going to meet the Pope?' she declared to Nora for the twentieth time that evening as they pored over the brochures Jessy had given her.

Jessy had left the ladies to chat in their cosy basement sitting room while she cleared up after the birthday meal. The other guests, neighbours and old village friends of Ana's had already left except for Nora. Ana called her 'the thorn in her side', who wouldn't leave a place until everyone else already had, so she could talk about them all after they'd gone. The other woman sniffed and throwing a cursory look at the brochure on the table reminded Ana that she wasn't exactly 'meeting' His Holiness. She would just be in with a crowd of other people seeing him on a stage, and from a great distance, mind you.

'No, Ana replied, 'Jessy said that if it killed her, she would get me to meet him so that's enough for me.'

Ana knew there wasn't a chance of meeting the Pope but she wanted to annoy Nora for just another while. She'd never been given a pilgrimage to Malta to see the Pope as a birthday gift and her neighbour could keep the fancy ornaments her sons brought her home on Mother's Day and Christmas. For she, Ana McGuill, was going to Malta and Jessy was going with her and if it killed her she wouldn't let it be known that the thoughts of it scared her half to death.

~

Malta, May 2001

'Gosh Gran, but the heat here would kill you, so it would.'

Jessy could feel the sweat sticky under her arms and she wished she had worn a sleeveless dress. She was convinced she had bingo wings, even at the young age of twenty-one. She had never been a skinny girl, 'well rounded' as her Gran called her, thanks to her good home cooking. However she certainly had no bingo wings and right now she couldn't care less as she yearned to whip the sticky dress of her completely.

'I thought you said it'd be cooler here in May?' she panted, as she tried to manoeuvre the two trollied suitcases up the steep cobbled hill to the convent.

'Well, never cast a clout till May is out,' replied Ana, stoically trying to hide the fact that the heat nearly had her wiped out too.

She was grateful for the sensible walking shoes she had worn, but the support tights she had on under her skirt had sweat running down the inside of them and in the name of all, why did she wear a girdle? Vanity, that was why. She wanted to show off that this grandmother could hold on to her figure and you never knew who one might meet in Malta. She was stopped suddenly in her tracks, almost tripping over the pink matching suitcases in front of her, by her grand-daughter squealing excitedly and pointing over the high limestone wall which almost reached their heads.

'Gran, would you look at that view.'

Ana shaded her eyes as she leaned out over the wall and gasped. Below her and as far as her eyes could see was the splendour of Valletta. She could see the majestic St. Elmo's fort jutting out into the sea with all the little fishing boats like white dots on the blue water far beyond. The white glare of the sun beating down on the city made it look almost surreal, as though it was a mirage and she felt a pull in her heart. She had returned.

2

Salvatore squinted his eyes against the evening sun while he watched the young and the not so young women trudge up the steep hill to St. Ursula's Convent.

'Oh heavens,' he muttered to himself, 'I would like to know who that little bird is.'

He was enthralled as he watched the girl swaying seductively in her light red dress as she climbed the hill ahead. When his father yelled for him to come in from the doorway where he had disappeared for yet another cigarette, he decided to find a reason to call to the convent later if he could, to get to know more about the beautiful girl.

'You spend far more time out there ogling the women than you ever do in here helping me,' his father swiped the back of his head before handing him a large earthenware jug full of their best olive oil. 'Take that up to the convent. Lucija, or Sr Lucija I should say, has run out again.'

To his surprise his youngest son eagerly snatched the jug from his father's hands and was gone out the door as quick as lightening. Scratching his head, he watched Salvatore throw his leg over his moped having carefully placing the jug in the baker's basket in front before speeding off up the hill.

'Well that's a first. I was expecting his usual twenty excuses. It's probably just another reason not to be in here helping me.'

With a deep sigh he went back to his stove where he spent almost his whole day, if not his whole life. He longed for the day when Salvatore would take over completely, but he thought that day would have come long ago. His son's reluctance to work, to take over the business despite his father's age and to find a wife, were a constant source of argument between them. At not much more than Salvatore's age he was already married with children and was working in his wife's family restaurant to support them. The arrival of Salvatore when he was over fifty years old was a surprise to everybody and he felt that his son had been spoiled far too much. It was so much harder nowadays to make a decent living for families and he didn't expect to still be working at his ripe old age. Granted he was in good health and barely looked sixty, thanks to his love of exercise, but he was much too old to be still cooking, even if he loved it and his younger brothers did most of the work nowadays. The exciting visit by His Holiness in just a few days time had already brought much needed business to the small island and he had never been so busy.

Thoughts of his father were far from Salvatore's mind as he drove maniacally up the hill almost driving over several of the feral cats that were plentiful around the city. He could already see Sr. Lucija waiting for him outside the heavy oak door. She had been watering the plants in the courtyard when she heard the familiar sound of his moped.

'Hello my Salvu,' she cried happily, using the family pet name for him as she reached up to hug him. Giving him a perfunctory kiss on both cheeks she asked 'How is your Papa?'

Sr. Lucija was his father's youngest sister and had belonged to the convent since her entry as a novice. Her birth name of Rigalla which means 'gift from God' was given to her by the nurses who worked in the hospital where she was born. Salvatore was the son of her favourite older brother, who was twenty five years or older than her and with whom she had lived until becoming a novice in Sr. Ursula's convent. She had a soft spot for Salvatore and he adored his aunt. Now towering over her, he bent down and whispered in her ear;

'I wonder who you have staying here tonight.'

Sr. Lucija laughed and slapped her young nephew's arm. Lifting the jug from his strong arms she replied; 'It didn't take you long to find out for yourself!'

The pretty dark haired young woman named Jessy and her delightful grandmother Ana were already settling into their rooms and were now currently changing for evening prayers and a meal. Sr. Lucija couldn't believe that they had walked the steep hill instead of getting a taxi, until Ana explained she had been told by a fellow pilgrim that the convent was 'only up the road'.

~

Jessy looked over at Ana and felt the usual rush of love for the slender elderly lady who was hunched over the wooden church bench beside her. The pearl rosary beads which once belonged to Ana's childhood nurse and never far from her hands were familiarly entwined in her arthritic fingers. It was only really now as she was getting older that Jessy started to appreciate her Gran and all she had done for her. Even though sometimes she still got so frustrated and angry with her old fashioned ways, she knew that anything Ana said or did was only ever out of love. Her strict religious values were a constant source of frustration however. At times she could completely understand her own mother's desperate desire to get out of the confines of a strict Catholic upbringing in the seventies and run away to live a more exciting and bohemian kind of life somewhere else. Just then a different kind of a shadow from the window caught her eye. She thought at first it was a nun in her white habit, then realised it was a man and he was the most handsome man that Jessy had ever seen.

3

Ana looked transfixed. Today they were in the beautiful fortified city of Valletta. On arriving at the walled entrance into the city, Ana had stopped still in her tracks. She shook her head, marvelling at the city once again returned to its former glory and exclaimed:

'You know when you dream about a place for so long, when you see it, you don't really believe you are actually seeing it. Do you know what I mean? Jessy, Jessy are you listening to me at all young lady?' Ana poked Jessy in the back with her fan and the girl turned around.

'I am listening to you, and I know exactly what you mean.'

She did too... She never dreamt that the man she would fall in love with would actually be so beautiful, just so unbelievably beautiful. She would never have used that word to describe a man before, but there was no other word to describe Salvatore, nephew of Sr. Lucija and the person that Jessy had never stopped thinking of since she had first set eyes on him two days ago. Jessy wasn't aware that she actually gasped out loud in that tiny church when she first saw Salvatore, or that Ana thought she was having an apparition when she saw the girl turn pale and actually sway as she stared at the window in front at the man who was looking back. Jessy felt herself as though her own heart had one of its funny missed beats. She felt thumped in the chest and she didn't know yet, that at that moment Salvatore was feeling exactly the same way.

~

'Will you put your cardigan on dear?'

Ana didn't want Jessy going outside on her own but she

guessed it was to have a secret cigarette so she relented. Did the girl really think her Gran didn't know she was smoking? Ana smiled to herself remembering how at Jessy's age she had often slipped out somewhere for a longed-for cigarette. Those in glass houses... Jessy shrugged her arms into the white cardigan and pulled away as Ana tried to do up the buttons.

'Will you leave me be,' she cried impatiently.

While descending the stone steps which led from their tiny veranda onto the cobbled courtyard she felt a bit guilty for snapping. Poor Ana was only doing what she does best which is keeping Jessy warm and safe. But she thought she would burst if she didn't get outside to see if she could find that man, the thoughts of who had been in her head all through their evening meal.

Ana would surely put on a few pounds on this pilgrimage she thought, as she wandered through the cream and brown tiled courtyard which wound its way around the convent. Her grandmother had tucked into the pasta that she was served for dinner assuring the nuns that it was her favourite, when Jessy had never seen her cook it in her life. The only thing Ana ever cooked at home was potatoes as it was all that the priests would eat. She had nearly a full bowl of olives eaten before the meal and when the nun placed a bowl of squid in front of her sprinkled with lemon, Ana had almost purred. Jessy also had devoured the meal, revelling in the strange flavours and textures and was hardly able to eat enough of all the different dishes on the table. Even still her mouth watered at the memory of the hot tomato sauce, the surprise at the spiciness on the tongue, which she was told on asking, was red chilli that was mixed into the tomatoes with something called 'anchovy'. Apparently it was a type of small fish. She really wanted to get that recipe before she went home. Though where she could buy the somewhat exotic ingredients in her small village she didn't know. Jessy giggled to herself thinking that both she and Ana would both need extra seats on the way back if they kept eating like that. Although Ana was well known for her culinary skills, the priests liked the simple home cooked meals of meat, potatoes and vegetables, a fry for breakfast and ham and tomatoes for the evening meal. She couldn't imagine Sean, Father Sean that is, ever eating a squid.

Finding a spot that looked quite secluded Ana breathed in the sweet smell of the flowers dampened by the gardener's hose as she felt around inside her dress for the hidden cigarette. Then she spotted him. He was still standing outside the same window of the small convent church and he was watching her approach. He stared at her with eyes that looked like they were black as coal and even from where she stood, she could see the length of his dark lashes and his thick black brows like curtains framing that beautiful face. She took in the dark curls on his head and she knew she had fallen in love right there and then.

Salvatore never dreamt that he would not be able to talk to her. Imagining what he would say when he got the chance, the fact that she would not be Maltese never for a second crossed his mind. She looked just like a local girl. So when he asked 'Do you need a light?' and she replied to him in English, he was taken aback and unable to make any sort of reply. Then she made the first move over to where he stood. He had been watching the small veranda since the two women retired to their rooms after the evening meal in the hope of catching a glimpse of her. As he watered the pots of plants and flowers lovingly tended by his aunt and the other nuns, he was trying to think of ways he could meet her. Suddenly he heard somebody descend the steps and seeing it was the girl, he dropped the hose quickly and hid by the Church wall.

'Do you speak English?' the girl asked him.

He felt angry. He felt stupid and uncouth and uneducated. His father always said that he would regret leaving school so early.

Well never had he regretted it more than now. He had studied English at school like everybody did, but hearing her suddenly come out with what was still a foreign language to him, made him completely tongue tied. He understood what she said alright, but although his English was excellent, his accent wasn't exactly perfect, so the teachers had reminded him constantly at school. Fearing her mockery, he shook his head and began to stomp off when the girl boldly ran past and stood in front of him saying in badly pronounced Maltese.

'Skuzani, iI-Malti tieghi hjazing?' ('I'm sorry, my Maltese is bad?') Her dark brown eyes were looking directly into his, eyes that were full of hope and vulnerability and suddenly he felt that everything would all be alright.

~

He had really long legs. This was what she was looking at. The beautiful man was leaning against the wall beside her and both of them were drawing silently on cigarettes. She could feel her shoulder touching his arm and it felt warm, even through the white shirt he wore. She was too nervous to look up at him. Instead Jessy kept her head down, looking at the frayed black jeans he wore and the long toes that peeped out from under his dusty sandals. You'd never see the fellows at home wear sandals she thought. They are always in wellies or runners. Then after what seemed like an eternity he finally spoke.

'What is your name?' he asked her.

'Jessy.'

He repeated it. 'Jeshy, Jesshyy... it's like a boy's name?'

'It is short for Jessica.' He nodded his head. This was more acceptable apparently.

'My name is Salvatore. I live down there.' He pointed down towards the hill that she and Ana had trudged up just a few short hours ago.

It was her turn to nod now. 'Malta is beautiful,' she replied, waving her arm over the view of Valletta city below them, now lit up in the dark of the evening. 'It is amazing.'

'You are beautiful also,' he answered quietly and she looked up at him.

4

The first time Jessy had been kissed was by her best friend Tina's older cousin, who also happened to be the local milkman. She had seen him on his rounds, but never thought much about him as a possible boyfriend. She knew that Ana thought he was a bit 'common'. He always looked scruffy, with a cigarette usually hanging out of his mouth and he wasn't even all that good looking. She knew immediately when she saw her friend's face that Tina had arranged for Gerry to 'just happen' to turn up outside the local shop as they were leaving. When he offered to walk them home Jessy dug Tina in the ribs saying 'I'm not going out with him you know.'

She did though, well at least she kissed him in the doorway of the parish hall on the way home and she didn't enjoy it one bit. First of all he kept his chewing gum in his mouth the whole time and he tasted of stale smoke. Then he stuck his tongue inside her mouth which she found revolting and then, horror of horrors, he tried to feel her breast through her jacket. That was the last straw and she mumbled something about being late home and ran the whole way. She was sure when she landed breathlessly into the house that her Gran would know as soon as she saw her that she had been kissed by a boy. However Ana had simply looked up from her crochet and retorted that she could have baked the bread in the length of time it had taken Jessy to come back from the shop. She saw him around the village a few times afterwards, but the mortification she felt every time she thought of him roughly grabbing her breast the way he did, made her cheeks burn each time she heard his milk van on the road and she studiously ignored him every time he waved hello at her. You wouldn't call Gerry a boyfriend though. He wasn't anyone she went on dates with or anything like that. He was just a kiss. She had been dying to know what it was like to kiss a boy and if that was the height of it, then she was in no rush to try it again.

The pickings in her small village were very small when it came to finding romance. Almost all of the young men around emigrated nearly as soon as the Leaving Cert was over. Often before even finding out their results, they were gone. If they didn't go abroad then they usually had uncles or some sort of family in Dublin or over in England who could fix them up with some type of work. Sadly though, the vast majority of the young men went as far as the States, or Australia to make a living. The ones that stayed only ever did so because they had to work on the family farm and that meant that you never saw them, unless they were driving a tractor through the village, going from one field to another. They were always in old working clothes and smelled of silage. They were also the ones, regardless of their looks, who wouldn't marry till their parents died, then would marry in haste whatever local girl was available and have a gang of kids to keep the farm going. She was in no rush for somebody like that or for a life like that.

Jessy had better things in mind for herself. She didn't really know yet what she wanted to do but she felt inside that she was just biding her time for something exciting to happen. She already was regarded as being different because she was an orphan brought up by her grandmother. Because they lived in the parochial house where Ana was housekeeper to the local priests, she got preferential treatment in school. *'She'll tell the priest on you,'* was always the cry of her classmates if somebody annoyed her and even the teachers were a bit in awe of her and hesitant to correct her if needed.

Because of her home life, Jessy's small eccentricities were seen as a result of living with her Gran and for this, Jessy was grateful. She somehow always felt on the outside of the other girls her age, never quite fitting in with the fashion or past-times that everybody else had. If baggy jeans were the fashion, Jessy wore straight leg jeans. If her friends ran about in flat suede boots then Jessy tottered about in her high heels. She got away with it because it was thought that poor Ana couldn't afford to buy the new things that came out, or because she had no big sister or a young mum to advise her on what to wear. But Jessy just liked different things to the others.

A serious bout of pneumonia as a child when she spent six weeks in bed began Jessy's love affair with books. It was a relationship that consumed her day and night since. Because of her home-life and the fact that the highlight of her week was going to the local Legion of Mary meeting, Jessy lived an extremely innocent lifestyle, but this was compensated for by her love of reading. Reading was what opened the world to her and encouraged her love of languages and thirst for travel to all the places she visited in her books. She often turned down trips with friends because she preferred to curl up in bed with a new book and dive into a world far away from her own. Ana often complained about the things that would happen to her eyes or worried about Jessy giving herself headaches. However she was also content to know that once Jessy was enthralled in a book that she could get on and do her own jobs without having to feel guilty about the child being on her own. So every birthday and Christmas Jessy, to her delight, would receive a huge assortment of reading material, many ordered via the priests as they were able to obtain books not found in the local shops. Books teaching foreign languages, cookery books from Italy and France and her favourite, books on the Second World War. There was nothing that Jessy wouldn't read and she would devour them hungrily as though they were nourishment for her very soul.

There was one boy that she liked though, liked a lot. Conor Mahon. He was much the same as the other boys in her school. He lived on a farm and played football in the local GAA team but unlike his classmates, after the Leaving Cert he went to College. None of the local lads ever went to College, unless it was the agricultural college. But Conor did and in doing so he immediately went up a notch in Jessy's estimation. She had always liked him and they had gone to both primary and secondary schools together in the neighbouring town. He had a slightly older Mum than the others. Like Ana she wore older ladies clothes and had grey hair that she got set every week in 'Olives' which was the one and only hairdresser in the village. Conor's mum and Ana were firm friends and Ana thought that he was ideal for Jessy.

'He has a good future in front of him,' Ana would say, 'he won't end up on the farm.'

Saying this she hoped would make Jessy sit up and take notice, as she knew that ending up on a farm was something her Jessy didn't want, but a young man with education and a good profession was. The fact that Conor was a local man and the son of her good friend Joyce was an added bonus. It was times like this she wished the old tradition of match-making was still up and running because if it was, she'd pair the two of them up and have them down the aisle, before she ended her days.

Kissing Salvatore was much better than kissing Gerry. His lips were so soft and if there was a taste of smoke she didn't notice because she had smoked too. He didn't try to put his tongue into her mouth or grab her breast. He leaned down to her height and taking her face in his hands he simply kissed her, just for a few seconds before whispering, 'Like Malta, you also are amazing.'

5

'I will have words with Patricia when I see her,' Ana implored as Jessy zipped up the back of her dress.

'Gosh Gran, these girdles really work. This dress was harder to zip up before you put it on.'

'Excuse me young lady,' Ana replied. 'Are you saying that I'm fat?'

'Not a bit Gran,' Jessy laughed, 'I'd say Patricia did that on purpose you know. She was spitting feathers that you were going to stay in the convent and she had to stay in the hostel.'

'Yes I am aware of that,' Ana replied.

'I have to laugh at people going on pilgrimage and some of them would take the eye out of your head and come back for your eyelashes, given half a chance.' Jessy giggled as she thought of the palaver at the luggage carousel after they got through passport control in Luqa, Malta's one and only International airport. Some of the older women and men who had piously prayed on the plane with Fr. Sean in preparation for their pilgrimage in Malta, were swearing at each other as the scramble for luggage began.

'Did you hear Sean?' Jessy asked putting on her parish priests Armagh accent, *'Practice your Christian charity now folks, help thy neighbour'* and then he nearly yanked the head of Patricia when he spotted his own case coming round.'

'It's *Father* Sean to you young lady, don't be so irreverent,' Ana retorted as she fished in her toiletry bag for her heart tablets. Between the heat and the walk up that hill she was very out of breath. Though somehow she knew inside that there were other reasons for her heart misbehaving today and she doubted that it was anything that a pill would help.

Jessy found the sun so terribly hot. It wasn't like the sun at home. This burned your skin immediately on going outside, like when you stood too close to the range. Ana said that it got much hotter in June and July but that August and September were unbearable.

'You were here that long?' Jessy asked incredulously as she applied yet more sun-cream to her arms. 'I thought you just came for a week's holiday or something.'

This was news. Ana had never spoken about her time in Malta. Jessy had only found out that she was there by accident. It was stamped on the back of a dog-eared ancient passport that Jessy found among some of her mother's things that her Gran kept in a suitcase of old memorabilia. Ana had brushed it off saying that she had gone there ages ago and that she'd forgotten all about it. However Jessy had heard Joyce and Ana talk about it not too long ago and from the way her Gran talked lovingly of 'those brave Maltese people', she got the opinion that Malta was somewhere Ana might like to re-visit. She had been thinking about taking Ana to Lourdes as a surprise for her birthday. When the priests began talking about the Pope going on a pilgrimage to Malta in May and Fr. Sean said he was going as spiritual director with a group, she decided there and then that that was where she would take her instead. She knew that Ana had greatly regretted not seeing the Pope on his trip to Ireland in 1979. That was the year that she, Jessy, was born and also the year that her mother had died.

The first plan of action was to find out whether or not her Gran had an up-to-date passport. The last time that she remembered Ana leaving the country was to go to Yorkshire last summer where she went once a year to visit old friends. Ana was from Yorkshire and although Jessy travelled with her there many times, her grandmother seemed to prefer to go alone. She knew there would be a passport about somewhere, so while Gran was out at the Monday night novena with Joyce, she guiltily rifled through the bedside locker where Ana kept important paperwork. Thankfully the British passport was easily found sitting on top of a consortium of photos, letters and about a hundred different holy prayer cards. Good, the passport was in date for another eight years. Placing it back in the overflowing drawer, Jessy spotted the old brown leather photo album that held the treasured pictures of her mother, Maria. Tentatively she opened the well-worn book and flicked through the photos she often pored over as a young girl. Her mother was stunning. Gran told her everybody used to say that Maria had her father's dark curly hair, but the brown eyes and deep tanned skin were a constant wonder to her. Neither of her grandparents had brown eyes either. Both were blue, but who knew how genes worked. It's not as though Ireland was blessed with year round sun. How did her mother come to be so tan? The photo showed long thick black hair cascading around her shoulders and Jessy ran her finger over the image, feeling the usual sadness in her heart that she had never met her. She also had thick black hair and brown eyes and she had sallow skin too, but not as dark as her mothers. Having said that, whenever Ireland did get a bit of sun occasionally Jessy would turn brown as a walnut much to the envy of her friends.

'If I had your colouring Jessica McGuill, I'd run around Aghameen village stark naked in the summer,' her friend Tina used to complain to her. 'I'm lying out here this last week and I'm red as a beetroot. You look like you've just come home from Spain.'

Jessy did like the fact she had skin that Gran said attracted the sun, but wouldn't admit this to her friend who was already jealous of her hair.

'It's because of all the good fruit you eat,' Ana would tell her, 'you are full of vitamin B or C or whatever and it draws the sun to you.'

'Well my mother must have eaten it by the crate,' was Jessy's reply, 'because she was like an Indian.'

Ana pursed her lips and carried on taking washing from the line which was strung from one tree to another at the back of the parochial house.

'Put some cream on yourself and don't lie out there too long,' were her departing words as she slowly walked back into the house, washing basket under her arm.

'Aw, you've annoyed her now, going on about your mother,' Tina remonstrated.

'I did not,' replied Jessy defensively, 'she loves to talk about her.'

'Yes, looked like it alright,' retorted Tina, lying back down on the tartan picnic rug they had laid out on the lawn.

'Come on, we better get up.' Jessy started to pick up the books and CD player which had been entertaining them all afternoon. 'The priests will be back from their retreat before tea-time and we're not allowed to be sunbathing out here.'

Tina chuckled, 'I'd love to see their faces.'

Not being allowed to sunbathe in the garden of the parochial house which was home to herself and Ana, was just one of the many rules she had to abide by. She had pretended all her life that she didn't mind being an orphan, having no brothers or sisters or even cousins to play with. It wasn't much fun living with an old woman and being surrounded by priests all the time, praying the rosary every night and wearing scapulas that scratched her skin under her vest.

Even having to wear a vest over her bra was bad enough. She disliked feeling she was the odd one out in school and in the village, never being asked out to the pictures or discos and having to always come home early. Also, nobody would dream of posting Valentine cards to the parochial house or be seen calling there for fear people would think there was a problem at home.

These things she really minded but pretended not to. Gran had been housekeeper here all of Jessy's life and the basement apartment was her home. They had their own front door and a little garden at the back where none of the priests ever set foot. It was quite large and really cosy. The only drawback was that the rooms at the front had barely any light coming in and Gran had to keep the lights on even during the day. Nevertheless the bedrooms to the back were bright and airy and Ana often lamented that the place had been built back to front.

'Wouldn't it make more sense to have the bedrooms darker, instead of having the sun streaming in at six in the morning to waken us up? It's very silly,' Gran could often be heard complaining.

Jessy sat in one of the bedrooms now and the sun was indeed coming through the windows on this sunny March afternoon. As she placed the passport and photo album back into the drawer, she suddenly realized that she didn't have a passport of her own. She was so worried about getting her Gran's sorted out that she forgot about one for herself.

'I need my birth certificate again Gran. Is it in your drawer?' Jessy asked Ana, as she set the table in the dining room for the priest's tea.

'No. I put it up in the case with your mother's things,' Ana replied. 'Why do you need it?'

'I want to open a Credit Union account, they asked for it.'

Jessy crossed her fingers on telling a lie. Well, it wasn't really a lie as such as she was indeed intending to open a Credit Union account, but to date nobody had asked her for her passport.

'Why did you put it up there anyway?'

'Because I'm going to get one of those filing cabinet things from Fr. Sean when they get the new built-in one and so I started to get documents together. Everything going into the filing cabinet is in that case. It will contain everything that belongs to you and your mother. That way you can access what you need easily yourself. I'm going to keep all the paperwork that belongs to me in my drawer. '

This was interesting to Jessy. She was only ever permitted to go through that case under the watchful eye of her grandmother. Now it seemed she was getting freedom to delve into it unsupervised. The only things she had ever seen were photos and some of her mother's old song lyrics. Her mother had been very musical and had wanted to become a famous singer some day. Some of the songs were quite strange to Jessy though. It was all very 'hippy' stuff, not something that Jessy would ever want to listen to at all.

6

Trying to get away from Ana to see Salvatore was more difficult than she had thought. She had seen him three times so far and they were here two days already, but the last few times she tried to get away Ana had found something for her to do. After they kissed that first evening she had to run away almost immediately when she heard Ana call out to her.

'I was worried you'd get lost,' her Gran said when she arrived breathless into their room after sprinting up the steps to their veranda. 'You've no sense of direction like myself, and I want to close up this door. All the mosquitoes are getting in and I don't want to get bitten or you either for that matter. Aren't you exhausted? I know I am. We've been up since four this morning.'

Jessy smiled as she noticed that Ana had boxes of tea-bags piled up beside the kettle and cups on the little kitchenette shelf. Her Gran always took her own tea-bags everywhere she went. She felt she would never be able to sleep, being so wound up. Jessy could still taste Salvatore's lips on hers and the faint hint of garlic on his breath. Or was it she that smelt of garlic after all those delicious dishes she'd eaten? She hoped she hadn't put him off if she had. Nevertheless sleep came quickly. She too was dog-tired after a long eventful day and before she knew it, she awoke to the sun shining through the windows and could hear Ana already up in the bathroom. Breakfast was a feast. The nuns here were fantastic cooks. Jessy wondered if they would allow her to watch them prepare dinner in their kitchen later that evening. Cooking was another passion of hers besides reading and she was eager to learn some basic Maltese dishes before she went home. Although whether the priests would eat any of it was doubtful. As usual though, Ana was way ahead of her.

'Jessy, Sr. Lucija said you can go into the kitchens any time you like, isn't that right Sister?' she enquired of the friendly faced nun in front of her.

'Yes, of course. We would be delighted to have any help and your grandmother tells me that you are a marvelous cook.'

Jessy blushed, taking compliments was never her forte. 'Well I just enjoy it that's all,' she explained, 'I wouldn't get in the way or anything. I'd just like to see how you cooked some of those dishes you served us last night. They were fabulous.'

'Certainly, I would enjoy that,' Sr. Lucija replied, 'and perhaps you could show me also some of your own home-cooking. I believe you are very good at baking bread and…. what were those other things called Mrs McGuill?'

'Ana dear, call me Ana. She is brilliant at the scones. She has a lovely soft touch with her baking.'

'Ana with one 'n' of course, isn't that right Gran?' Jessy broke in. 'Gran is always fussy about how her name is spelt. It's actually Anabel.'

Jessy's laughter was cut short by the noise of shattering glass on the flag-stone floor. St. Lucija bent to pick up the broken pieces of the jug which she had let slip through her fingers.

'Let me help Sister,' Jessy began to gather the broken crockery into her hands but to her surprise Sr. Lucija had already left the kitchen.

~

Baking bread and scones wasn't exactly the type of cuisine Jessy had hoped to do. She did enough of that at home, but she would be happy to show this nice nun how it was done. The bread on the table here was gorgeous even if it was a bit hard. Jessy had eaten a fair amount of it already. She longed to ask Sr. Lucija about Salvatore but she knew that would cause no end of questions from her Gran. If she got any inkling that Jessy had an eye on him she'd put a stop to it before she even got started. She had already warned her about 'holiday romances' on the aeroplane, much to Jessy's embarrassment.

'I'm only putting you wise darling,' Ana whispered, not wanting to be heard by anybody else, 'I was young once too you know and these Maltese men can be very good-looking and much too charming for their own good. Just try and be careful. You are here to see the Pope remember, not the local boys.'

Jessy was well aware that anything to do with Salvatore had to be kept to herself.

The second time they met was early the next day. Conscious of the fact that she might see him, Jessy took extra care getting dressed that morning. She left her long curly dark hair to hang loose. It was too warm in the bedroom to use her hairdryer and she decided to let it just dry naturally in the sun. Carefully brushing some mascara on to her already dark eyelashes she then added some lipstick which highlighted her full lips. She wore the new white cotton dress which flowed gently over her hips to her knees and low heeled gold strappy sandals. Jessy wasn't aware of it, but she looked just like a native Maltese girl. Although she was dressed modestly, the dress fitted the contours of her body like a glove, which for a young woman was quite curvaceous. When Salvatore spotted her in the dining hall at breakfast, helping one of the older nuns to lay cutlery on the table, he thought she looked like a goddess. As she leaned over the table her dress rose a little showing toned tanned legs, but unlike yesterday when he had just lustful thoughts, this morning he felt more protective of her. She didn't seem to realize how beautiful she was. He suddenly felt quite jealous, thinking of what the other young local men would be dreaming of if they met her. When he had kissed her last night, she did not move to closer to him like a more experienced girl would. In fact she didn't touch him at all, apart from with her lips. This gladdened him. He wouldn't like to think that kissing young men was something she was expert at.

Patiently waiting until breakfast was over with, Jessy once again helping the nuns to clear away the dishes, Salvatore rapped the window as she passed by on the way to her room. Immediately she smiled and waved at him and he beckoned to her to come outside. Quickly looking around, Jessy opened the side door leading out to the sunlit courtyard, where to her delight he hastily grabbed her hand, steering her towards the little wall where they met yesterday and which was out of anybody's sight.

'l'*Għodwa t-tajba*,' she whispered to him and he laughed at her pronunciation.

'Lod –wa t-tay-ba. This is how you say it.'

Jessy repeated the words after him and to his surprise she got it perfect the first time.

'*Bongu*, is enough to say. l'*Ghodwa t-tabja* is quite formal. It is like if you say, 'A very good morning' instead of just 'good morning.'

She nodded her head, 'Will you teach me some other words please? I would really love to learn to speak Maltese a little before I go home.'

'Home, where is home?' he asked her.

Already he hated the place that she would return to and take her away from him.

'I live in Ireland.'

'Ah, Ireland. It is a good place I hear,' nodding his head in approval.

From his history and geography lessons at school he knew a little about Ireland as it was so close to England. He knew they also achieved freedom from Britain and were a proud people who were eager to hold on to their traditions like the Maltese were.

'How long will you be in Malta?'

'Just two weeks. We came to see the Pope. I bought the tickets for my grandmother for her birthday present. Tomorrow morning we are going to the airport at Luqa to see the Pope arriving. Then Gran wants us to go to Valletta, to the Presidential Palace where he is going to meet President Guido DeMarco. She insists on following his every move while he is here, but I guess that is why we came, so I can't complain.'

'Ah, yes I will be going there also tomorrow. They say that if you go over beforehand and pay a local kid they will sit in a good spot for you to keep a place until you get back,' Salvatore laughed. 'We Maltese always were good at making a living from nothing.'

'Yes, we heard that too. Ana thinks it's a great idea. She was worried we'd be way at the back and she'd see nothing.'

'Ana?' he questioned, crinkling his forehead which she thought was really cute.

'My Grandmother, that's her name,' she answered.

'Ah okay. Is your mother here too?'

Jessy shook her head. 'No, my mother is dead.'

Salvatore was silent for a moment then quietly replied, 'Mine is too.'

This little confidence made both of them feel closer to the other. He yearned to kiss her again, but doing that in the darkness was easier. It took more courage to do so in broad daylight. He still held on to her hand since he had grabbed it as she came out and he rubbed his thumb along the back of her hand in circular motions. For a little while neither of them spoke. They both just watched his thumb, then his fingers touch her hand, then he began to move up her arm. Although it was warm, she felt goose-bumps rise on her skin and shivered a little bit.

'Are you are cold?' Salvatore asked her.

She shook her head in reply, not wanting to speak just yet. He placed his left arm around her shoulders and pulled her in closer to him.

'Would you like to walk a little?'

'Yes,' she replied quietly and he guided her along the orchard with his arm still around her shoulder, dipping his head under the branches of the huge trees.

'Oh, what are they?' Jessy pointed to the side of the orchard they had just entered, to a group of trees that looked like a species of cactus.

'Ah, those are prickly pears,' answered Salvatore, 'Here, have one,' and pulling one off with his hand he handed it to her.

'Oooh, it's spiky,' Jessy said, gingerly holding it by one thorn, in between her thumb and index finger. Laughing again, Salvatore took it from her and expertly peeled the fruit, tearing it into small pieces. Dropping its skin on the ground he stopped walking and faced her;

'Close your eyes,' he ordered.

Jessy did as she was asked and upon his second request she opened her mouth to receive the sweet fruit. 'It's sweet,' Jessy said conscious that juice was running down her chin. 'Am I supposed to eat the pip things?'

'Yes, you can, or spit them out.'

She didn't fancy spitting in front of him so she chewed on the hard little seeds. Then Salvatore once again lifted her face to his, but this time to wipe her chin with the tips of his fingers.

'Now, you have had your first prickly pear,' he whispered to her, and then he kissed her.

7

Salvatore had kindly offered to give Jessy and her grandmother a lift the next day to save them the trip by bus. The journey to Luqa was not far, but because of his Holiness' imminent arrival there would be double traffic on the roads.

'Gran would want to know how I met you, and then afterwards she would do everything in her power to make sure I didn't see you again,' Jessy told him.

'Why would she do this?' Salvatore asked, 'My aunt would tell her I am of good character.'

'It wouldn't matter Salvu, (as he told her to call him), because she is always worried about me being hurt by a man. She is just trying to look out for me.'

Salvatore could understand this, especially with Jessy's obvious beauty. He was sure he was not the first young man to notice her. However, trying to keep their 'friendship' a secret was difficult. He was confident Lucija would tell Ana that he was a good person, who never had a bad reputation with ladies. But they had such a short time together. It was unthinkable that Jessy would be gone from him in less than eleven days.

'Maybe I will see you in Valletta tomorrow?' he asked.

'Won't I see you tonight?' Jessy asked nervously.

'Yes of course, if we can.'

Together they walked with Salvatore's arm still proprietarily around her shoulder until they came to the orchard's gate and they let go of each other.

'You go in first,' he advised her. 'I know that today you are working with Lucija in the kitchen. Why do you want to do that while you are on holiday?'

'Oh, but I love to cook,' she explained, 'It is my favourite thing to do after reading.'

'You read and then you cook?' he asked, with a glint in his eye. She nudged him playfully with her elbow.

'Silly. I want Sr. Lucija to teach me some of the local Maltese recipes. Today she has time. Cooking is my *other* favourite interest. I enjoy it.'

'*Hekk tajjeb*,' (That's good), he replied, 'Because I love to eat!'

~

That evening after prayers in the little convent church Jessy again told Ana that she wanted to go out for a walk. She had thoroughly enjoyed her few hours in the kitchen with Sr. Lucija.

'My, you are a natural,' Sr. Lucija had exclaimed as she watched Jessy expertly throw together a dish with just minimal direction. It was as though the girl knew instinctively which ingredients went together. This was even more admirable considering that Jessy had said nearly all the food on the wooden preparation table was new to her.

'We just don't have this type of food at home. At least not where I live,' Jessy explained. 'I think I will be packing my suitcase full of food before I go back.'

She showed the nun how to bake scones, brown bread and boxty, which were potato cakes famous in her home county. Jessy informed Sr. Lucija that she didn't usually go by recipe, but wrote one down all the same so that the nuns could make them another time.

'I shall put the scones out with the evening meal tonight,' Sr Lucija offered, 'and in the morning we will have boxty for breakfast!'

They did indeed have boxty for breakfast as promised and it went down a treat with everybody. To Jessy's amusement she was told by another nun that Sr. Lucija had sent a basket of her baking down to her brother's home to try out. This meant to

Jessy's delight that Salvu would be eating food that she had baked herself for his breakfast. She wondered if he would know where it came from.

~

He did know, because his father never stopped talking about it.

'This is the bread I want,' he cried several times that morning, stuffing yet another thick slice of the brown bread into his mouth as he went on, his mouth full to capacity, 'It is different and different is good in a restaurant. It is soft. Those buns...' he pointed to the scones in the basket his sister left with him this morning, 'They are not buns and they are not bread. They are bun-bread,' he laughed at his own little joke. 'I want to buy these. I will put them in my display cabinet today and if they sell then I want to hire the person who makes them in here. Whoever made these is a good baker and I know good bakers are hard to find. It is a woman, I can tell. And she is a woman who knows how to bake.'

Salvatore smiled to himself.

When he met Jessy last night she was beaming after her cooking session with his aunt.

'It was wonderful,' she told him excitedly. 'She let me do whatever I wanted. She laid out all this food on the table and asked me what I thought we should make. I didn't even know what half the stuff was. I just picked everything up and smelled and tasted some of it and I just kind of went with that, with what I thought would go well together. It was great. There were little teeny tiny prawns and I mixed them with the those little green things.... capers, and some fresh herbs and I cut one of the *dedeci*, the fish that taste like cod down the side and stuffed everything inside and grilled it. Then I made a tomato sauce with parsley and garlic and.......'

Salvatore kissed her to keep her quiet, 'I get the story. You cooked and it made you happy. Now I want to taste something too,' and he leaned his mouth down towards hers.

They were able to spend more time together that evening as Ana said she wanted an early night before their six o'clock start in the morning. Jessy promised her Gran that she would be back before ten and would be really quiet. She just wanted to wander around the gardens on her own and find some of the herbs and other fruits and vegetables that Sr. Lucija grew there.

That evening Jessy and Salvatore left the confines of the Convent grounds for the first time. Giggling nervously she settled herself on the back of Salvatore's dilapidated old moped. When he shouted back that he had no brakes, Jessy quickly grabbed on to his waist as he drove speedily down the hill towards Valletta. Just minutes later he brought the moped to a rather sudden halt outside a rustic looking restaurant. Jessy hoped he had not decided to treat her to a meal for she had just eaten a huge one less than an hour before.

'This is my home,' he gestured proudly towards the building which had the words, *'L'artiste'* over the door. Within seconds an older version of Salvatore rushed out of the restaurant's glass front door.

'Fejn kont?' (Where have you been?) The man threw his hands in the air, before stopping short when he spotted Jessy gingerly stepping down from the moped. Her legs were shaking and she wasn't sure if was because of the scary ride she had just taken, or from nerves because she was now at the home of Salvatore. She presumed that this man was his father, given the fact that they looked so alike.

'English please,' Salvatore requested of his father, laughing. 'My girlfriend still has a lot of Maltese to learn, which I am trying to teach her.'

Jessy blushed. This was the first time she had heard him refer to her as his girlfriend. This was just their fourth time to meet, but the term made her heart swell and she was very happy that he had. The older man immediately took both her hands in his, shaking her arms vigorously as he did so.

'Come in, come in,' he offered, throwing open the glass door from which he had just come through, 'Salvatore, you surprise me more every day.'

8

Jessy entered a bright airy room, with huge windows overlooking the city of Valletta from where could be seen the harbour lights glittering below. To her delight she saw that the restaurant's white washed walls were festooned with photographs and beautiful paintings. Some photos were in black and white and others were in colour. The subjects of the photographs were all of people, presumably guests of the restaurants over the years, tucking into food. Some of them had been caught with dangling threads of spaghetti being forked into their mouths, others laughing while they pulled a huge lobster apart with their hands. Some of the photos, mainly the black and white ones, were obviously from the war.

There were scenes of devastation, buildings in rubble, with images of barefoot children, still smiling for the photographer amongst the ruins of what could possibly have been their homes. Most of the pictures were of soldiers. Silently walking along the white washed wall Jessy gazed at them, unaware that she was being closely watched by the two men she had left standing at the door. The paintings were incredible. The pictures, all mostly oil painted but some pencil drawn, were quite breathtaking. There were simple scenes of fishermen tending their nets or casting them out into the sea and wrinkled faces of older seamen, each line in their face lovingly sketched.

'Oh these are beautiful,' she whispered, reaching up to touch one of the paintings which were not protected by glass. They looked like they were so old that they might disintegrate in front of her eyes.

'*Iva*,' Salvatore's father agreed, nodding his head proudly. 'These photographs and pictures are the history of my country.'

'Did you take any of the photos?' she asked.

'Me? No. No. Not me,' he answered. 'I found them.'

With that he ran behind a high wooden counter top and disappeared into a back room where he re-entered in seconds carrying a carafe of wine.

'We must toast to this occasion,' he cried. 'The first girl my son brings home must not go without celebration.'

Salvatore shut the door of the restaurant, first looking behind for his father's approval.

He obviously did approve for he shouted; 'Yes, yes. No more customers tonight. Instead we have a very important customer which we must entertain,' and Jessy was poured a rather large glass of deep red wine. As the two men toasted to her health, she took a sip and coughed as the strong liquid burned her tongue with its potency.

The men laughed. 'You are not used to Maltese wine?' Salvatore asked her.

'I am not used to any wine,' she answered smiling, wiping away the drops which glistened on her lips.

'Another first,' Salvatore beamed at her.

At his father's inquisitive look, he explained that Jessy had earlier just tasted her first prickly pear.

'Ah it is lucky for the young who have still many firsts to experience,' his father replied with a sigh.

Jessy watched father and son as they talked, noticing how alike they were. They were tall with beautiful dark eyes and both men spoke dramatically with their hands, their gestures seeming to take over the whole room as they talked. Just then out of the corner of her eye she noticed the display of local food which was decoratively laid out on shelves. Rows of jars with red and white checked cotton lids, were lined up under the counter-top. Little cards selotaped to the front of the jars described their contents, written roughly in black pencil. Some of the jars had lids made of white lace and Jessy wondered if the nuns had supplied these.

There was also a fish tank inserted into the counter where she could see crabs and lobsters moving about inside. Then Jessy spotted another shelf containing a selection of breads and to her surprise she noticed some of her own baking.

She pointed to the shelves. 'Did you like my scones?' she asked.

The older man jumped to his feet '*Your* scones. You baked these?'

Jessy laughed and admitted that yes, she did.

'I don't believe it,' he cried, slapping his son on the back of the head. 'Why don't you tell me this, you fool.'

'Because then it would not be a surprise like now,' Salvatore answered laughing.

His father pulled his chair around the table closer to where Jessy sat.

'Tell me how,' he demanded. 'How do you make the brown bread so soft like that? My brown bread is all seeds and hard. How do you do this potato bread? All day I am boiling potatoes but they do not come out the same way as you do it.'

Now it was Jessy's turn to laugh. 'Did you grate the potatoes first?' she asked him.

'Grate, what is grate?' looking up at his son he once again started throwing his hands in the air. 'Tell me Salvu now what is grate?'

But this seemed to baffle Salvatore also. Jessy got up and went towards the door leading to the kitchen, 'May I?' she asked.

'*Iva, Iva, Iva,*' she was ushered into the kitchen by the excited man and he began to spin around telling her to 'Do what you want, do what you want.'

Still laughing she quickly scanned the spotlessly clean kitchen until her eyes rested on what she was looking for.

'This,' she pointed, lifting it off the hook on the wall. 'This is a grater.'

Salvatore took it out of her hand and told her it was the same in Maltese, but she pronounced it differently.

'What do you want to do with the grater?' his father quizzed.

'For the potatoes, or patata.'

'French fries?' he asked, confused.

'No, first to make the potato bread, or boxty as we call it, you must grate the raw potatoes. Then you put them inside a cloth,' she picked up a tea-towel that hung over what looked like a clothesline strung over the end of the kitchen on which cloths were draped.

'You squeeze out the water...'

'No, it's no good. You must show me. Show me now,' and already the older man began running around the kitchen pulling out potatoes and a bowl and knives.

Salvatore took control. 'Pop, come on. Jessy doesn't want to cook now.'

'Ah, so now you tell me she has a name. Welcome Jessy. Now, do you want to cook?'

Jessy was already tying a man's huge apron around her waist.

~

'Fantastic,' as he wiped his mouth with a napkin, he grabbed Jessy by the shoulders and kissed her on the cheek.

'Hey Pop, that's my girl,' Salvatore remonstrated, but he did so with a big grin. He liked to see that his father obviously approved of Jessy.

'This is my new cook,' was his father's reply.

Jessy looked aghast at Salvatore.

'Don't be silly Pop. She is only here for two weeks. She will have to go home soon, isn't that right Jessy?'

'Yes,' Jessy sadly agreed.

'Do you cook at home?' Pop asked.

'Yes. I cook for the priests.'

'Priests, what priests?'

This also was news to Salvatore who cut in before she could answer his father.

'You are a cook for the priests?' he asked her.

'No. I work in a library. But it also has a small café and I cook there sometimes. I just help my Gran with the cooking, though she is a brilliant chef. She is the housekeeper for the priests at home. We live in the parochial house.'

'Ah ok.' Salvatore felt bad that he didn't even know what she worked at. They had spent so little time together so far. He resolved to get to know everything he could about this Jessy who he called his girlfriend.

~

Later as they walked hand in hand along the water's edge he questioned her relentlessly about her life at home.

'I want to know everything,' he said.

She told him some simple facts. What age she was for example, he did not even know that. He informed her also that he was twenty-five which was four years older than her.

'What about what you want for your life Jessy? What do you want to do? Are you happy to just live in your small village?'

'No,' she shook her head resolutely. 'I want to see the world. I want to go to all the places in my books.'

'Is this your first time in a different country?'

'Yes,' she replied, 'and what about you?'

'Oh, I go to Sicily a lot. That is a different country. But it is just sixty miles away so I cannot really say it is foreign travel. For me it is expected that I take over the family restaurant. It belonged to my mother's family, but Pop took it over when she died. I don't want to work there all my life. I want to find my own career. Not be forced into one.'

Jessy could understand that. 'What would you do then?' she probed.

'I don't know. I don't know what I would like to do, that is my problem,' Salvatore sighed. 'Pop gets crazy with me sometimes. He wants me to take over from him. He doesn't look his age and he still gets up at six every morning. But I know he is tired now. I don't like to see him work so hard and I do help as much as I can, but if he would only let me cook it would be better. I couldn't believe he let you work in his kitchen. He only lets me or his brothers in, nobody else. Not even to clean it.'

'Well you clean it very well,' Jessy assured him. 'Do you like to cook?'

'Oh yes, as much as you I think, but Pop finds fault with every way I do things. I just stopped doing it when he is around. I like to try other foods that he doesn't have on his menu. I like to cook international food, Indian for instance, or Chinese food, but my father got annoyed when I suggested it. He says that this restaurant has only served Italian and Maltese dishes for years and if I want to cook Asian or Indian food I can go to St. Julian's.'

'St. Julian's?' she queried.

'Yes, it is where most of the tourists go, for the night-life. They have lots of Indian and Chinese restaurants there.'

'Has your father ever eaten that type of food?' Jessy asked, putting her arm around Salvatore's waist as they walked when he did the same. 'I love it too although we don't have any restaurants in my village apart from the library café.'

'Oh, I will cook for you then,' he promised. 'You shall have a feast. One night I will cook Indian. Another night I will cook Chinese.'

'Where will you cook it though?' she questioned.

'Hmmm. That is a good question. Pop will smell the spices a mile away. I wonder if Sr. Lucija will let me cook in her kitchen.

I will ask her.'

'So you would like to cook, be a chef. Is that what you want to do with your life?' she enquired of him.

'No, not at all,' Salvatore exclaimed, 'I want to paint.'

'Oh, you paint also like your father?' Jessy asked.

'My father doesn't paint,' he laughed, 'the only thing he can use a paint brush for is coating his pastries. He is a brilliant pencil artist though, he can draw anything.'

'So, the paintings inside, they are yours?' Jessy gasped incredulously.

'Yes. They are all mine.'

'They are fantastic. Oh Salvu, you must show them to people.'

'But I do,' he responded, 'they are seen daily by many people as my father insists on covering the walls with them. He says it saves on having to repaint every year!'

'No, I mean in a gallery. You could be famous.'

But before Salvatore could reply Jessy suddenly let out a cry of alarm. 'It's after eleven o'clock. My grandmother will go mad with worry. I have to go,' and she immediately turned around to walk back in the direction in which they came.

'Don't worry. I will get you back quicker.' Salvatore put his hand out for a taxi which was parked beside where they stood.

In the back of the car they held hands once again and when she opened the door to get out he got out of the other side, handing the taxi driver some money before telling him he would walk back.

They kissed briefly at the convent door. Jessy stood on her tippy toes with her arms circling his shoulders and kissed him quickly on the lips.

'I had a wonderful night,' she whispered, and ran up the stone steps once again.

9

To Jessy's relief Ana was fast asleep when she quietly crept into their room. Unknown to her, Ana had taken a sleeping pill. She was worried about waking during the night, as she was wont to do these last few weeks. She knew that the plans they had made to go to Luqa airport to see the Pope arrive and then follow him to back to Valletta would tire her. They all had to be awake very early in the morning to be at Luqa in plenty of time. Because of this she wanted to be sure of a good night's sleep. Ana couldn't wait to see the Holy Father. His pilgrimage to Ireland in 1979 had been overshadowed because of Maria's death in the same month. Now Jessy had made it possible for her to be part of an audience with the Pope on his second visit to Malta. The roads to Luqa would be thronged tomorrow and Ana knew they would have an early start.

~

Wednesday morning the 8th May did indeed begin early for the two women. They were awakened by one of the nuns knocking at their bedroom door. Already they could hear plenty of activity around and Jessy laughed heartily as Ana jumped out of the bed like a child on Christmas morning.

'The Pope,' Ana cried. 'We've to see the Pope.'

Jessy was still laughing as she reminded her Gran that the Pope hadn't even arrived in Malta yet. In fact, he was still probably only wakening up himself wherever he was. There was a great air of excitement at the breakfast table that morning. The nuns from the convent were having an audience with His Holiness. Their joyful faces showed how much they looked forward to it. Sr. Lucija was beside herself.

'It is such an honour for all of us,' she explained. 'We will be in the palace when the Pope arrives and he is going to pray with us and bless us.'

Ana wanted to ask her if the Pope would bless the old rosary beads which she had for years, but she didn't have the nerve to ask the nuns if this would be possible. As soon as breakfast was over a minibus pulled up outside and Ana was first on the bus, seated in front and impatiently tapping her foot as she waited for her grand-daughter to come back from wherever she was. 'She's having another cigarette no doubt,' she fumed. 'If I miss the Pope again because of her, I will choke her,' she guiltily thought to herself.

Jessy was not far away however. She was once again in the orchard being kissed good morning by Salvatore who had come to see her before their journey to Luqa.

'I like the smell of your hair,' he murmured into the top of her head, 'it smells like peaches.'

'That is because my shampoo is called Peaches & Pears,' Jessy replied.

'Prickly pears?' he asked, smiling at her and then kissed her mouth before she could answer.

'I must go. If I hold up the bus Gran will go crazy at me.'

'I will look out for you at the Palace later,' Salvatore shouted after her as she ran towards the courtyard where the bus driver was revving its engine, intent on leaving without her, despite Ana's protestations.

Ana didn't go crazy at her, which was worse than if she had. Jessy knew her Gran well enough to know that when her lips are pursed like that and she is silent, that you are in more trouble than you want to know about. She slid quickly into her seat and as the bus drove off she was relieved when the nuns started to pray the rosary, so Ana couldn't give her the tongue-lashing she knew might be coming. There were thousands at the airport awaiting the arrival of the Pope's plane. Neither Ana nor Jessy expected there to be so many people. Were there even this many people living on the island? The bus had to park quite a way from the terminal, but a little car thing like a trolley with an engine, was waiting to pick Ana up to save her the walk. Two of the elderly nuns also got in. There was no room for Jessy. She assured her Gran that she would stay with the group and proceeded to walk with the others towards the huge crowds ahead.

The sun was very hot and Ana was glad she had worn a sun hat. She always got a migraine if she didn't cover her head. She kept her eyes peeled for Jessy. She knew that her granddaughter got lost everywhere she went and she could feel her heart giving little warning jolts of pain when she thought about Jessy getting lost among so many people. Even though the girl was an adult now, Ana always still thought of her as a child and could never relax when Jessy wasn't by her side. After a long wait she suddenly felt a pull on her arm and Jessy was there.

'It took me ages to find you. There must be a million people here.'

'I doubt a million love, but I'm glad you are standing where you are. I was getting worried.'

Jessy hugged her Gran and told her that the Pope was due to land in just ten minutes time at two o'clock. Soon the crowd began to roar as the plane came into sight and Jessy laughed to hear her Gran scream as loud as everyone else as it landed on the runway.

'It's him Jessy, it's him,' she cried, shaking her granddaughter's arm up and down in her excitement. It seemed to take an eternity before they could see anything though and then suddenly they were able to see Pope John Paul II on a huge television screen. He was apparently kissing a bowl of Maltese soil that was presented to him by two children. Then they could hear his voice coming through a microphone as he addressed the crowd:

"With heartfelt gratitude to God, I stand on Maltese soil for the second time. The Jubilee Pilgrimage which I am making on the Two Thousandth Anniversary of the Birth of Jesus Christ has brought me to Malta. After visiting some of the places especially connected with the history of salvation, at Sinai, in the Holy Land, and now in Athens and Damascus, my pilgrimage in the footsteps of Saint Paul brings me to you."......

Jessy looked over at her Gran, noticing as she did that she was crying. She wasn't alarmed though. She knew that this was a dream of her grandmother's and that Ana was simply happy to be here. Suddenly Jessy felt a sharp stabbing pain and screamed as she realised that somebody had rammed a high stiletto heel through her foot.

"Aaaghh,' she yelled, 'my foot, my foot.'

Within seconds Gran had her seated on the ground while she pulled off Jessy's sandal to investigate. Suddenly Ana swayed and was grabbed just in time by the people standing around them. Someone who had a small fold-up stool put the elderly lady sitting on it, while instructing Ana to keep her head down and breathe in and out.

'It's okay,' Jessy explained to the concerned faces about her, while she limped around her Gran, trying to get her to drink some water from the bottle.

'She always faints at the sight of blood.'

Jessy's foot was indeed pouring blood from a deep puncture. She calmly took her handkerchief out of her rucksack and wrapped it around her foot, while keeping a close eye on Ana.

'How are you feeling?' she enquired of her grandmother.

When Ana didn't answer she knelt down and was shocked to see the ashen complexion on her grand-mother's face.

'I'm fine love, just fine. I'm thinking of strawberry jam. Help me up.'

Jessy did as she was asked and wasn't surprised when her Gran shrugged off Jessy's attempt to put an arm around her. She was stubborn as a mule sometimes and never admitted when she felt ill.

'I'm grand love. It was just the blood. How is your foot?' she asked, trying to keep her voice steady and hold on to her senses. This was not a simple fainting attack, she knew that. This time it was the sharp pain in her heart that made her keel over. She decided that when she got home she would go to see Dr. Hogan. She had been putting it off long enough.

When the nuns heard about Ana's little episode on the way back to Valletta they were horrified.

'Oh goodness, we must take you to a doctor immediately,' they cried. 'The surgery is closed today because of the streets being cleared for security, but we can take you to the hospital.'

Characteristically, Ana wouldn't hear of it.

'I'm not missing His Holiness again,' she said emphatically.

'But you have just seen him Gran,' retorted Jessy, trying to keep the exasperation from her voice.

'Not for Mass I didn't. He is saying Mass tomorrow in Floriana and doing the beatification of those saints and I am going to be there. If I go to the hospital they will keep me in because of my age and I will be well vexed if that happens. I'm telling you, it was the blood that got to me as usual.'

When Jessy explained to the nuns how the sight of blood always made her grandmother faint, or at least feel faint, they calmed down a little. Nevertheless they never left her side until they reached Valletta. There they carefully placed Ana in the care of some Red Cross people. One of the staff kindly promised to accompany her while she and Jessy went for something to eat. While Jessy and Ana sat outside the restaurant in the town square opposite St. John's Cathedral, Sr. Lucija came running over to them.

'Did you forget something Sister?' asked Ana, surprised to see the nun back so soon.

'No. You are to come with me,' the nun replied, hastily getting Ana to her feet and beckoning to the driver of a car that she just alighted from seconds ago.

'I'm not going to the hospital. I feel fine now, don't I Jessy,' Ana insisted, motioning to her grand-daughter with her eyes to assure the nun that yes, her Gran was feeling much better.

'You are going to meet His Holiness with us,' whispered Sr. Lucija, 'now quickly because we haven't much time.'

Jessy threw their belongings which scattered the table hastily into bags and followed the two women into the back of a sleek black car, driven by a very distinguished looking gentleman in front.

'What's going on?' she asked the nun sitting on the far side beside her Gran, who looked like she was going to faint again.

'I was asking Bishop Cauchi, who is a relative of my family, to offer prayers for your grandmother because I was worried about her and he told me to bring her to the Palace. He said she couldn't stand in the crowds with so many people if she is ill. He said that she is a testament to her faith and she is to be with us when His Holiness gives us his special blessing.'

Ana immediately took out her cosmetic bag and a hairbrush and started freshening herself up. For once she was speechless. She checked that she had her treasured rosary beads in her handbag and then beamed at Jessy.

'Nora will be so jealous when I tell her,' she whispered into her grand-daughter's ear and the two women held on to each other giggling with mirth, until they reached the magnificent palace gates and were ushered inside.

10

Jessy had never seen anything so opulent in her life. As the women were shown inside a massive hallway which was adorned with elaborate paintings even on the ceilings, they were met by uniformed men. They were escorted into another sumptuous room where the floor was luxuriously carpeted in a deep soft red covering. The walls and curtains were also swathed in red and high on the walls were more magnificent paintings.

'Wow, it's incredible,' Jessy whispered in wonderment. 'I've never seen anything like it.'

Ana nodded her head. 'It's good to see this room so well repaired.'

Jessy gaped at her, 'Have you been here before?' she asked astonished.

'Yes,' he grandmother replied, 'a long time ago.'

Jessy was rendered speechless, but before she could even utter a reply the huge doors were opened, and flanked by an assembly of richly robed priests entered Pope John Paul II. Jessy felt her Gran take hold of her arm in a fierce grip.

~

Ana felt as though His Holiness could see right inside to her very soul with eyes that were just five years older than her own. His livered spotted hands grasped hers as he murmured words of prayer over her head. Then taking Kitty's pearl rosary beads from her hands he blessed them before gently placing them back into her outstretched palm.

'If I die now, I will die happy,' Ana quietly voiced to her granddaughter as they were once again guided down the long hallway, towards the waiting car outside.

Back at the convent that night it was unanimously agreed by the guests that it was much too late to expect the nuns to cook anything for them. However everybody also agreed that they were very hungry. Jessy took the initiative and suggested that they go out together as a group for dinner and they readily acceded to her idea. She knew just the place to take them. She fully expected Ana to want to go to bed as it had been a long day, but Ana was full of energy, buoyed up from her unbelievable experiences of the day. She was also very hungry and never turned down an opportunity to eat.

It wasn't a long walk down the hill, though Ana hoped that they wouldn't have to climb back up, as she had done that once already and wasn't eager to repeat the journey. In no time at all they entered the lively restaurant where a handsome young man showed them to a large table which was able to seat the whole group. Taking a place opposite the window and facing her granddaughter, Ana couldn't help but notice that the waiter seemed to know Jessy and speculated if this could be the reason for her little night-time walks. She resolved to have a word or two with this young lady on their return that night. The menu was very tantalizing and Ana was eagerly anticipating the meal to come. Ordering the seafood platter, she also accepted a glass of cold white wine and with the others, joined in the toast to *I-Papa.*

Obviously after the excitement of the day's events, the topic of conversation was about Ana and Jessy's audience with the Pope. There was some envy on behalf of the others, especially the Italian journalist Ricardo who was staying at the convent also and who had hoped to get an inside story for the Catholic newspaper he wrote for. He couldn't believe that they didn't even take a photograph, but Jessy informed him that they had to leave their bags outside in the car before even entering the palace for security reasons. Jessy was happy to be back in the dimly lit restaurant with Salvatore hovering around her. She had not been able to warn him of their arrival, so when she went first into the restaurant on the pretence of checking that there was space for the others, she caught his attention as he served at a table and he came rushing over to greet her.

'I have my grandmother and I think nine other people outside who want to eat. Do you have room?' she asked.

'*Iva*, yes of course, for you we will make room,' he answered eagerly.

'My grandmother knows nothing about you, remember,' Jessy warned him, 'so don't try to steal a kiss of me okay,' and she wagged her finger at him.

'Can I have a quick one now instead?' he asked and bent down to give her a brief kiss before she went back out the door to beckon the group who were patiently waiting outside to come in.

~

Ana was very happy. Today she had met Pope John Paul II and as she told her grand-daughter, if she died now, she would do so contentedly. As the rest of the group were busy chatting and drinking wine, Ana gazed out the window. From her seat she could see down into Grand Harbour. Although it was dark, Fort St. Elmo was lit up as was the whole harbour below. She wondered what had happened to all the people she had loved on this island. Where was the man who had never been far from her thoughts for over fifty years? Where were the girls she had been to school with, the nurses she trained beside and lived with through those terrible war years? She remembered vividly the horror of the war. It was impossible now to imagine battleships moored where there was now a pretty marina, or the frightening sound of the siren warning of yet another air raid.

Sadly Ana knew the fate of some of the friends she had loved in her time here during the war. Looking over at her granddaughter she smiled to herself as she realised that when she was Jessy's age, she had been here in this country of sunshine and sadness, of laughter and loss and love. Thanks to her granddaughter she was now back in Malta. Although she had been shocked and excited when she realised she was to return to the island, Ana was happy now that she had come. The place she had tried to forget for years was still familiar and just as beautiful.

She noticed again how the tall waiter hung about Jessy a lot. She would have to find out more about this young man, for he definitely seemed to have some sort of friendship with her cherished grand-daughter. Realising that if she wanted the sleeping pill to work, she would have to take one now if she wanted to get a good night's sleep. She didn't want Jessy seeing her take a tablet, so excusing herself and lifting her handbag off the floor she made her way to the ladies room. Enquiring from the waiter where it was, she slowly walked down the long room which was beautifully decorated in paintings.

As she waited outside the door marked '*Nisa*' for 'Women' she lifted her glasses from the chain that hung around her neck to get a better look at the wall art. Her eyesight was still good for distance but not so good for reading and seeing something close up. With her glasses properly positioned on her nose she looked up, and after a couple of seconds she put a hand out on the chair opposite to steady herself as she wobbled a little on her feet. Immediately strong arms held her upright and she turned to see the young waiter at her side.

'Are you alright there Madam?' he asked her. Then he grinned and said with a smile that looked very familiar, 'Have you had some of our local wine?'

She pointed at the photos on the wall in front of her.

'Where did you get those?' she asked breathlessly.

'My father found them, after the war.' Salvatore replied.

'May I ask who your father was?' Ana queried nervously.

'But of course,' he answered. 'My father is Franco Vella. Gianfranco Vella.'

11

Jessy was a bit upset that Ana wanted her to go straight home with the group after the meal. She had wanted to spend some time alone with Salvatore, but her grandmother insisted that they needed a good night's sleep before the busy day in Floriana tomorrow. Even when Jessy promised to be in bed before 11pm, Ana wouldn't hear of it. Salvatore ordered a taxi to take the older members of the group up the steep hill to the convent, but when Jessy suggested that she walk with the others her Gran had resolutely disagreed. So, any plans for meeting Salvatore were out of the question.

As a result she was quite grumpy with Ana when both ladies retired to their rooms and didn't even notice that her grandmother was very quiet in herself. She assumed that she knew Jessy was annoyed with her and that was her reason for not having the usual chatter tonight as they prepared for bed. As Jessy lay looking out the balcony window from her bed she pondered on sneaking out after Ana had gone to sleep, but against her will sleep won the battle and she was out for the count in minutes after the hectic day. Not so for Ana. She thought she would never sleep soundly again after the shock of this evening. Her high spirits were brought to an abrupt low when she realised who the owner of the restaurant was and she felt sure she was still in shock with the information she had just discovered.

When the waiter Salvatore confirmed her suspicions on seeing the photos, she slowly walked the length of the wall, scrutinizing every carefully-placed photograph. There was no doubt about it. These were her late husband Ernie's photos. She had been with him when he took some of them. She scanned the wall and as she thought, she was in two of them. It felt like a blow to the stomach when she spotted the pretty blonde haired girl smiling innocently at the camera. In one photo she has her arms around two women, namely Katie Cortis and Jeany Castelletti. In another photo she is standing in a comedic pose, as though about to dive from the harbour into the sea, although of course that would have been forbidden then. She looked with envy at the long thin legs and tiny waist. How times had changed her.

In some other photos Ernie was there, with his arm outstretched in front as if giving directions to the person on the other side of the camera on how to operate it correctly. He was very protective of his cameras. And then there were also many photos of Billy Cortis and Ted Langley. Higher up on the wall were pencil drawings and she recognised these instantly. These were Franco's drawings and again there was just one of her. He had drawn her many times, so she couldn't help but wonder where the other sketches were. Did he still have them? In this particular sketch which she vividly remembered him drawing, she was in his fishing boat in Sliema. They weren't allowed to sail the boat owing to the restrictions, but Franco said that he wanted to have a picture of her in it. He said that when they were hopefully once again allowed to fish in their own seas, he would keep her drawing as a good luck mascot, just like the painted eye on his boat. In this sketch she is wearing a white dress and in her hair is a red ribbon which tied up her long hair. She remembered that the ribbon was red, but Franco had simply shaded it darker than her dress, signifying she supposed the difference of the colour. The drawing did not extend to her feet, but she recalled that she had worn white strappy *plimsolls* and that by the time she had got back to Mtarfa that evening she was quite dusty and dirty, but happy.

She had none of the photos or drawings that she had just seen on the walls of the restaurant. In her hasty departure from Malta after the war she had left behind a lot of stuff which would not fit in the shipping case. Although she looked for these mementos which she thought she had stored carefully away in her suitcase, they were not with her belongings when she unpacked. This upset her. Seeing all of these memories tonight with her own eyes brought her back to a time and place she had tried to put behind her for so many years. It felt like opening up a 'Pandora's box' and now that she had done so, she could not shut it again. After asking if Franco was in the building and being informed that he had just left to meet with friends tonight, she was partially relieved and also partially saddened.

~

The next morning both women were quieter than usual. Ana, because of the revelations made known to her the night before and Jessy because she wondered when she would see Salvatore again. She knew he was going to Floriana today with his father. Until now his father, who was a devout Catholic, hadn't been to see the Pope at Luqa airport or in Valletta because he was working. On Wednesday nights he left his precious kitchen to the care of Pawlu, one of his brothers, while he met up with old friends when they talked of long gone days, played cards and generally grumbled about lives and wives. However, today Salvatore and Franco were going to Floriana with everybody else on the island for Pope John Paul II's celebration of Holy Mass.

After breakfast everybody from St. Ursula's convent were going *en masse* to Floriana. Ana was looking forward to it, but her heart was elsewhere. She had about only about two or three hours sleep at the most and felt exhausted. Jessy's attempts to chat over breakfast only received yes or no answers from her grandmother. By the time they boarded the minibus on the short journey to Floriana neither woman was in very great humour.

Ana could not stop thinking about Franco. Until now she

didn't know if he was still alive or if he had died. The last time she heard his name had been in the fifties, when she had met Billy Cortis and he mentioned that Franco had returned to Malta after the war and quickly afterwards married a Sicilian woman. This knowledge, even many years later, caused her much suffering at the time and although his name never left the confines of her heart, she refused to think about him. To do so caused too much pain and only made her life more difficult than it already was. However, despite her best intentions it only took a simple memory, like a smell or a taste of particular food, or a face in a crowd to take her back to those times to rekindle that feeling of love and loss. She didn't listen to any music from that era, or talk about the war or even speak about having been in Malta. To know that he was alive, and living just a brief walk away from where she had been sleeping for the last few days was unbelievable. Naturally on discovering that she was to return to Malta thoughts of Franco were foremost in her mind once again. However, she was so busy trying not to think about him, she succeeded to the extent that discovering he was so close came much more of a shock.

As their mini-bus passed his restaurant on the way out of Valletta, Ana craned her neck to see if she could catch a glimpse of him, but like most businesses in Valletta that day his too was closed. She noticed also that Jessy was gazing eagerly out of the same window at the restaurant which was perched precariously at the edge of the hill looking over the harbour. Ana wondered with anxiety what the situation was with Jessy and Salvatore. She could guess exactly what the situation was. Somehow during her time away from her grandmother, Jessy had one way or another taken up a friendship of some sort with the young man and this knowledge worried Ana very much. She could not allow history to repeat itself. She had so far managed to keep Jessy away from the pain that men could cause and she most certainly did not want her to fall in love with a Maltese man. Ana knew first-hand what that could involve.

When they arrived in Floriana and the scramble for good seats began, neither Ana nor Jessy had time to think about anything other than ensuring they didn't lose each other. This was extremely difficult in the crowds at The Granaries, where His Holiness would soon arrive to celebrate Mass. Jessy spent her whole time looking out for Salvatore who she knew was here, but it was like looking for a needle in a haystack. She scanned the crowds for a tall dark haired man, but there were many who fitted that description.

Ana on the other hand was also searching for a tall dark haired man in fisherman's clothes of the 1940's until she realised that of course that was ridiculous. Just as it would be, if he was looking for a young twenty year old Ana in a nurse's uniform with long blond hair and skinny waist. Actually, he didn't see her in uniform, except once and that was long after uniform was of any importance. By that stage a roughly sewn or drawn red cross somewhere on her person was enough to signify that she was a nurse. When the war was at full throttle their strict uniform rules were ignored as the emergency of war took over protocol and they simply did what they could in whatever state of dress they were at the time.

Now when Ana looked at the Red Cross ambulances and staff which were situated plentifully around The Granaries, she wondered how they would react if they had air raid sirens going off and bombs landing on them continuously, and having no bandages or medication of any kind. She missed her nursing, as she had missed it for over fifty years, but she didn't miss the war. When Ana asked her grand-daughter if she would mind going in search of some water Jessy eagerly took up the opportunity of an escape so she could go in search of Salvatore. They had packed some water for the trip as the sun was at its peak, but they had drunk it all already.

Jessy didn't know how people coped with the heat here in the height of summer. To her, it was unbearable already. She was still trying to come to terms with some things she had discovered about her grandmother since they arrived. She believed Ana had simply been here on holiday when she was younger. Now it seems as though she had been in Malta for quite some time. Suddenly she felt arms encircle her waist from behind and she swung around to see Salvatore's handsome face grinning at her.

'Darling, I was looking everywhere for you. How are you?' he asked, as he planted a kiss on her lips.

'It is so good to see you Salvu,' she cried excitedly, hugging him back and noticing as she did so that his father stood right behind him.

'Mr Vella,' she said, politely 'I did not see you there, how are you?' she asked and Franco laughed happily as he saw with his own eyes what he already surmised, that these two young people were in love.

'Me? I am the better to see you Jessy,' he replied, and also hugged her.

'I have to get water for my grandmother, we have run out,' Jessy explained.

'Oh, don't worry. Show me where you are seated and we will bring so much water you could swim in it,' Franco replied merrily.

They pushed their way through the crowds until they came to where Ana sat modestly in her deckchair kindly supplied by the Red Cross team. Sr. Lucija was taking special care of her and ensured she had a comfortable seat. As Jessy approached her grandmother, calling her name as she did so to let her know she was back, Ana turned around in her chair and her face flushed. She knew him instantly.

Franco noticed the eyes first of all. Her piercing blue eyes seemed to be even more noticeable now with age. They stared at one another for what seemed like eternity and then Salvatore spoke.

'Mrs McGuill, this is my father, Gianfranco Vella,' and he pushed his father in front of the older woman.

They were looking at each other, both with a mixture of surprise and shock and pleasure for what seemed ages, until eventually Ana spoke.

'Franco. It has been a long, long time.'

Jessy and Salvatore looked at each other in wonderment. Salvatore spoke first.

'You know each other?' he asked.

After several seconds his father replied;

'Yes. We do.'

He leaned down to the seat and grasped Ana's hands in his and he said;

'Leave us.' And they did.

12

Neither Ana nor Franco got to hear the Pope say Mass that day. Without speaking or asking where she was going, Ana simply allowed Franco to take her arm and within a few minutes she was seated in an old white car of some sort and they were driving out of the Granaries and out of Floriana. Not until they were on the road back towards Valletta did Franco suddenly pull over to the side of a road. Switching off the engine, he turned and faced the woman sitting next to him, whom he had thought about for many, many years.

'You...' he made to speak and before he got to finish his sentence, Ana suddenly turned rapidly around in her seat and with eyes blazing she cried out.

'You left me!' and to his astonishment she began to cry.

For some seconds Franco simply sat and stared at her. Tentatively he put his arms around her and held her as she wept into his new blue blazer, which he had bought especially to see His Holiness. When her sobs seemed to have subsided, Franco began to quietly speak into the top of her soft white hair while he still held her.

'I had no choice, they took me.'

'Who took you?'

'The soldiers, the British soldiers. They arrested me, as an enemy alien. I actually knew the men, they were no older than me and they wouldn't let me talk to anybody. I was thrown into the hold of a ship and when they let me out I was in Egypt.'

'Egypt! Who... why, I don't understand?'

'I know you won't like me to tell you this but I discovered later Ana that it was your father. He had me arrested.'

Ana remained silent. She was trying to push down the huge scream that was building up inside her throat.

'My father, I know he didn't approve of you, but surely he couldn't do that to me.'

'He did, love.'

Ana flinched when she heard him call her 'love'. He said it so easily, just like he used to do many years ago.

'He found out that I was born in Ragusa in Sicily, so I am Italian. Therefore I was an enemy alien. It was the perfect way to get me away from you.'

'You were in Egypt all that time?'

'No. I was only there for a short time. There was a boat going to back to England and it was organised for me and some others to be on it.'

'Where did they take you?'

'They took us to the Orkney Islands and we stayed there until the end of the war. When I came back I looked for you. Jeany told me you had married that Ernie fellow. She said you and she had a row and because of that, she didn't know what became of you. I couldn't believe it. I couldn't believe you married him.'

'Like you Franco, I had no choice.'

Ana tried to stretch her legs out, they were beginning to feel cramped and Franco noticing this asked if she would like to get out for a minute or drive on until they found a place to stop and talk. She replied that it was too dangerous to walk on the side of a busy motorway, and that she was alright. She would like to drive, please. They approached Valletta quite soon and impulsively Ana said she would like to go on to Sliema. Franco looked over at her. They had not spoken again until now and he knew that she was digesting what he had just revealed to her. As they passed by Valletta and made the coastal journey towards Sliema, Ana began to talk.

'Matron told me that I could no longer nurse if I was an unmarried mother to be.'

At this remark, Franco swiftly turned his head.

'Mind the road Franco,' she chastised him. 'You were always careless on the roads.'

'So you married him so you could continue nursing. Is that what you are telling me?'

'I don't want to talk about it Franco.'

Instinctively Franco pulled in front of the harbour where his little boat used to be moored. He still had a boat here and as he looked out at the sea, he watched it bob up and down, like a cork in a pail in water.

'Whether you want to or not Ana, we have much to talk about. Do you want to get out?'

She indicated that she did and he ran around to the passenger side and smiled to himself as she tossed her head at his offer of help to get out. She was always so stubborn. She did however once again accept his arm and they slowly walked over to where some little benches were parked in front of the sea. The place was deserted for once. Everybody but them was in Floriana.

'Do you remember we broke up the benches that used to be here for firewood?' Ana asked him as she ran her hand along the cool iron of the seat which had replaced the wooden bench.

'Yes. I wonder is that why they now are made of iron? So nobody can burn them?' Franco replied. He did not release her arm as they sat side by side and he patted it as he said that there was something she should know.

'Not yet,' Ana replied. 'Not yet. For now I want to just sit here, like we used to.'

Franco pointed out his boat to her and she gasped when she could see that her name was painted in blue on the side of the boat.

'I never forgot you,' he told her and this time it was him who wept.

13

It somehow felt as though they were breaking and entering. The shutters were down on the door and like Sliema, Valletta was almost empty. When Franco turned the key and showed Ana inside, he didn't even put on a light or pull the blinds from the windows. He was worried that somebody would think the restaurant was open and start banging on the door. Instead he took some candles and when they were lit he told Ana he would be a few minutes. He then returned with a platter of some cold meats, fish, bread and cheese and also a bottle of white wine.

'I think first we will eat and drink and then we will talk,' he suggested and Ana agreed.

They spoke first about their lives as they were now. Ana told him about her long serving job as a priest's housekeeper. He was amazed that she had never continued with her nursing. Ana found it strange that he was now a chef and restaurant owner. She always imagined that if Franco was alive, that he would be somewhere out sailing in the sea, taking in his nets and maybe even having a fleet of fishing trawlers by now. He explained how his wife's family owned the restaurant and that bit by bit he took over more and more responsibility until finally he had taken it over completely. In the early days he mostly fished, but it wasn't enough to keep a family and although he still went out on his boat it was becoming more and more difficult to find the time.

Ana told him about her daughter Maria dying and that Jessica was the love of her life. He smiled when he spoke about how fond he was of Jessy already and what a wonderful young lady she was. They spoke about Salvatore and Jessy's relationship and both agreed that despite their reservations, perhaps they should leave well enough alone. Then when the bottle of wine was almost finished Franco followed Ana's eyes as she gazed along the wall at the old photographs there.

'This is how I found out where you were and your relationship to Salvatore,' she explained. 'When I saw the photographs it all fell into place. Where did you get them?'

'I went to the Barracks where Jeany said you had been living after you got married. A woman there named Catherine told me that you had left in a hurry and that she had some of your belongings. These photos were among them.'

Again, Franco left her for a few minutes and when he returned he had a suitcase which he placed on the table beside them. Opening it up to Ana's utter amazement he pulled out her blue dress. The one that Katie had made for her and once again she cried.

'I loved Katie so much. I can't believe you have this.'

As he held the lid of the suitcase open Ana rifled inside, finding the pencil drawings he had drawn of her, her nursing manuals, some hair ribbons and other small items.

'I know why you rowed with Jeany,' he declared.

Ana sat down again, still clutching the blue dress.

'She said some horrible things and I couldn't forgive her.'

'She spoke the truth.'

Ana glowered. 'What do you mean by that?' she demanded.

'She was correct when she said your baby didn't die. It lived, Ana. It was taken to the hospital at Valletta and from there was sent to Gozo.'

Ana put up her hand. 'Enough. I won't hear any more of this. It is outrageous.' She began to get out of her seat until Franco came around and lifted her face up to his.

'You must hear.'

Ana sat down once again and said, 'You better get another bottle of wine.'

'The baby was a girl. When she was taken to Valletta hospital Jeany was on duty. She took care of the baby herself. She said she was about seven or eight pounds and was quite healthy. They named the baby Rigalla. Jeany took the baby to the convent where she was living. That is the same place where you are staying now. She knew the nuns from there had a convent on Gozo for unmarried mothers and abandoned babies and after the war Rigalla was sent there. That is where I found her.'

'But, it doesn't make sense,' Ana exclaimed. 'How did you find her? Why do you think she was our baby?'

'I went to the hospital in Valletta to look for Jeany. I knew she would know where you were. She told me she heard you had been sent to Mtarfa hospital. That you were very ill after giving birth and that your baby had died. She went to visit you but you didn't wake up the whole time she was there. When she spoke to the Matron she enquired about the baby and was told that it had died and that Ernie and Ted had buried it before they brought you in. Jeany realised then that it was your baby that had been brought to her hospital. She knew because it was the same night that you had given birth. She said the baby was wrapped in a blue jacket. Inside the pocket was fishing twine and pencils. She realised it was my jacket. The one that you always wore and when she asked you about it the next time she saw you, you said you had lost it.'

'Yes. She tried to tell me that my baby didn't die and that it was stolen from me but I couldn't believe her. I didn't want to believe her. I just simply could not believe that Ernie would do that to me, to lie to me about my baby dying. It was unthinkable. Franco, he was by then my husband. My father had been killed a month before. I had nobody except him. You had disappeared. Katie was dead. I told Ernie what she said and he said she was a lunatic and then we had to leave Malta suddenly. I never saw her again.'

'She was very upset about that,' said Franco, as he poured another glass of wine for himself. Ana still had a full glass in front of her, though he was glad to see that she was picking absent-mindedly at the food. At least she was eating. 'There is something else,' he continued.

Ana looked at him with a worried expression; 'Please don't give me any more shocks tonight,' she warned, 'I don't think I could handle it.'

'I was going to tell you about the baby.'

Ana's face looked so bereft that he immediately put his arms around her. Their embrace was awkward as the chairs were in the way, but Ana to his happiness put her head on his shoulder and he felt brave enough to finish his story.

'As I said, I found the baby in Gozo after the war. She was 14 months by then. She was a pretty little thing. Dark haired and I could pick her out immediately by her eyes. She had your eyes and God help her, my big wide mouth.'

Ana gripped his hand and he took this as a sign to continue so he did.

'I took the baby to live at home with me. You know that I had a lot of younger brothers and sisters so nobody passed much remarks of a fourteenth arriving.'

'Yes,' Ana replied, 'I couldn't believe it, thirteen children. Did they all survive the war?'

'Yes, every one of them, thank God.'

Ana looked up at him and tightened her hold on his hand.

'I am so sorry Franco. What happened to all those children?'

'Oh they were alright. The married ones took the little ones and me, well I took Rigalla. She was brought up as my sister.'

So far Ana had not asked if he had brought the baby home. She was afraid. If he had done, then it was possible that her daughter was now living right here in Valletta. She may even meet her. Then she realised something.

'But, does she know that you are not her brother, but actually her father?'

'Yes. She has known for a long time now.'
'Where is she? Is she in Valletta?'
'Yes. She is in Valletta.'
'Do you think she would like to see me?'
'I am sure she would want to see you. I did not even know that you were here until today. I realise now I will have to tell her of course.'
'How is she? Is she happy? Has she had a good life?'
'Yes. She is very happy in her life. She has had a good life.'
'I am so glad. Is she married? Does she have children?'
'No. She is not married and no, she has no children.'
'She is alone then?'
'No, she is not alone.'
'Does she live with you still?'
'No. But she lives quite close.'
'Please,' Ana asked, 'Go to her. Ask if she will see me.'
'I will.'

Franco then excused himself saying he had to make a call. When he returned he suggested that he bring Ana back to the convent. As he put his blue blazer across her shoulders they both made eye contact, smiling as they realised the significance of this simple act. On arriving at the convent Ana went first to her room to check on her grand-daughter. However she was not yet back. She enquired of the other guests if they had seen Jessy and they replied that they had not seen her since they left Floriana, but that she had stayed until the end of the Pope's Mass and the waiter from the restaurant had stayed with her.

Just then Franco came into the reception room where they all sat having coffee and beckoned to Ana to join him in the kitchens. Puzzled, Ana got off her chair and followed him in to where Sr. Lucija was seated at the wooden table, looking intently at Ana. And she knew in an instant that this was her daughter.

14

The next morning Ana slept until almost 11am. She had sat up until the early hours of the morning. First with her daughter, Rigalla, or Sr. Lucija and then when Jessy arrived in, at quite a late hour, she joined them and was astounded at the news that her grandmother imparted.

'I just can't believe it. It doesn't seem real,' she exclaimed two or three times.

She kept staring at Sr. Lucija who was laughing and smiling back at her.

'You are my aunt. It is unbelievable. I don't know what to say or what to think. I feel like somebody stole my Gran and now I have this new person to get to know all over again. I can't take it in. I just can't.'

Jessy was shocked beyond words. When Ana told her the whole long sad tale of her time in Malta and the war, then meeting Franco and marrying Ernie, she just listened, but it seemed like a story that a stranger was telling her. She couldn't acquaint it with the elderly woman sitting next to her, holding her hand. This woman had brought her up and she thought she knew her inside out.

Today Franco was taking both Ana and Jessy on a day trip. Ana wished to see Mtarfa hospital and the graveyard there, where her father and other friends were buried. She had very mixed feelings about her father, after the revelation that it was he who had had Franco arrested. She knew her father did not think he was suitable for his daughter, but having him deported to Egypt and then as far away as the Orkney Islands was a horrible thing to do to him and his family. Never mind how it had affected Ana also.

She hadn't had a very close relationship with her father as he was away during most of her growing up and she hardly ever saw him when she was in Malta. However, she knew he was there if she needed him until that terrible row they had on that New Year's day. Nevertheless when he was killed in the air raid at Ta-Kali six months later she had been devastated. First Franco had left and now her father was gone. Then not long after, her baby also died. She had no family left. In England there was nobody except Kitty. She had never been close with her parent's friends. The only people who cared about her were Ernie and Jeany. Or so she thought.

~

As they got dressed and prepared for breakfast Jessy directed a barrage of questions at her grandmother. She wanted to know everything and although Ana was quite happy to divulge the answers, she was still trying to take in some of the things that Franco had told her. She was angry to know that she had been lied to for years about her baby. She didn't even know if it had been a boy or a girl. Ernie had told her not to ask any questions as it would be too difficult for her. He simply said that the baby had died and he and Ted had buried it.

Discovering that the lovely nun Sr. Lucija was her daughter was unbelievable and they had sat up for hours chatting the night before. She wanted to know everything about Rigalla and knowing that she was very happy filled Ana's heart with joy. However, try as she might, she could not entirely take in the fact that this was her own daughter.

Sr. Lucija had told her that she had suspicions about Ana's real identity. It was too much of a coincidence that an Englishwoman of the same age her mother would be, who had previously lived in Malta and with eyes just like her own would turn up in Valletta. She had wanted to question Franco but was wary of upsetting him. She had been shown photos of her mother which were hung on the restaurant wall, but it would be impossible to identify the girl in those photos with the slender elderly lady who sat with her now. When Jessy told her how her grandmother's name was spelled, the amazing truth became clear and Sr. Lucija realised that Mrs. McGuill was the mother she had never known.

Sr. Lucija agreed to accompany Ana and Franco, her parents, to Mtarfa. Salvatore was not able to come as he was needed in the restaurant. When Jessy heard this over breakfast, she asked if she could stay in Valletta to help him out, to which Ana gave consent.

'Just don't distract him,' she said, smiling at her granddaughter.

When Franco arrived and the women got into the car, Jessy walked down the hill towards the restaurant. She wore jeans and a plain navy t-shirt with a pair of flip flops and she laughed when she saw that Salvatore was wearing the exact same outfit. Although as she pointed out, the only difference was that he had black flip flops whereas hers were blue with little diamante stars on them. Before they opened the doors to the public they shared a cup of strong espresso coffee and a pastry.

'Do you think we will have a busy day?' she asked him.

'*Iva*,' replied Salvatore. 'For sure we will. Also we will serve a lot of fish as many people still stick to the tradition of not eating meat on a Friday. My father was out fishing this morning very early so we now have a large amount of fresh fish to be served.'

On asking what her duties would be for the day he replied that he would need her to deliver the food to the different tables. She need not take orders as her little knowledge of Maltese was not strong enough to converse with the customers, at least not yet. Also she could help prepare the food. Jessy was quite excited. She was looking forward to spending the whole day with

Salvu. She told him all about what had transpired last night when she got home and he also told her that his father had given him the same story.

'It is extraordinary,' he said, 'what do you make of it all? I had no idea whatsoever that Lucija was not my aunt, but in actual fact my half-sister. It doesn't make a whole lot of difference really, but it is a bizarre story nevertheless.'

'I just find it hard to take in,' Jessy replied. 'I have so many questions in my head.'

'You will have to keep them there for now,' Salvatore replied pointing at the doors, 'because here are our first customers.'

~

The day went by very quickly and Jessy had never worked so hard in her life. The little café which was attached to her small village library would never have more than four or five customers at the one time. Here in '*L'Artiste* Restaurant' there was a constant stream of hungry people to be served. Obviously the busiest time of all was lunchtime, when Jessy was run off her feet. She didn't know how the other staff did this all day, every day. Helping in the kitchen was what Jessy liked best. Franco's brother Pawlu was just like one of those fiery chefs you see on the cookery programmes at home. When Jessy came back to the kitchen with a dish, because she couldn't remember who it was supposed to be for, he had let a roar which caused Salvatore to run back into the kitchen and remind his uncle that Jessy was just helping them out. Pawlu had apologised and Jessy assured him it was fine, but he had nearly made her jump out of her skin with fright.

At six o'clock that evening, Salvatore told her that the day staff now went home and that the night staff would arrive in their place. Each shift consisted of a chef's assistant, normally

Pawlu or another man named Matteo and one waitress. The waitress during the day was named Elena and the other one at night was Krista. None of Franco's other children, of which there were a son and two daughters, worked in the restaurant. Ana thought that it was extremely understaffed.

'If we are short staffed, they will help out of course,' Salvatore informed her. 'But they all have their own jobs and their own lives and have no interest in the restaurant. That's why my father is anxious for me to take over, but I don't want to work here full-time. I don't think it is fair that I should have to, when the other three don't. My father has promised to leave the restaurant to me, including the living quarters, but I just don't want to be tied here for the rest of my life.'

'I suppose it's because like you said, you always helped in the restaurant when your mother was alive while the others left home. Have you told your father about how you feel?'

'Yes I have, many times. To be honest I think he would be quite happy to get rid of the restaurant completely. He keeps it going out of respect to my mother and her family, but I know he would prefer to retire and spend time on his boat. If I don't take over the business I'll be preventing him from doing what he wants. That makes me feel guilty.'

'Have you ever sold any of the paintings that you keep on the wall?'

'Yes I have, many. As soon as one is sold I replace it with another.'

They finished eating their meal of a mouth-watering fish pie and drained their cups of coffee before the next onslaught of customers arrived for the evening meals. The menu changed now also and Matteo arrived to take over from Pawlu. Jessy had hoped that she and Salvatore could then leave but it looked as if they were going to be here all evening as well. She really enjoyed working with him. They didn't have much time to talk but she was aware that he was watching her, just as she watched him. As they skirted around the kitchen together or on the restaurant floor, they each caught each other's eye a few times and they exchanged a smile. Occasionally Salvatore would come up beside her and give her a quick kiss or grab her hand. She loved it and wished they could do this every day. Despite his saying that he didn't like working in the restaurant, he was very good at his job. He could do anything and everything, from cooking delicious meals to serving customers or even just cleaning. He knew all the regular people by name and just as she did in her library café, he often sat and had a few minutes chat with them. He appeared to be well liked and she also couldn't help but notice the female customers vying for his attention when they came in for a coffee and cake.

It was hard to believe really that she had only been here a week. It seemed as if she had known Salvatore much longer than that. They were very comfortable with each other and never ran out of something to talk about. She also thought he was absolutely gorgeous. He was so handsome and kind and funny and she found it odd that he didn't already have a girlfriend. Salvatore told her that he had had some girlfriends over the years but that there was always something missing. He said that he didn't feel that with her. She was perfect. Apart from the fact of course, he reminded her sardonically, that she lived in a different country!

15

Ana was having another strange and emotionally turbulent day. Just being in the car with Franco in the driver's seat next to her, with her daughter Sr. Lucija sitting behind her, was incredible. A week ago she hadn't known whether Franco was alive or dead or where he was. Not only that, but she had always believed that the child she had given birth to in an air-raid shelter during the war had died. Now she was united with a daughter she never known about and her first and only love was right here also. If this was a dream Ana never wanted to wake up.

As they passed through the familiar towns and villages inland on the way to Mtarfa, Ana thought about all the journeys she had made so long ago just like this one, journeys she had taken mostly by bus or sometimes in Franco's cart. The landscape was the same. Nearly all the buildings were new of course. Those she remembered had been either completely or partly destroyed in the incessant air raids. The roads on which they now travelled far surpassed the bumpy dust tracks filled with potholes and bomb craters that Ana remembered. For this reason it was a much quicker trip to Rabat and shortly afterwards they arrived at Mtarfa.

They all got out and Ana stood for some time just looking up at the place that used to be her home. She linked her arm through Franco's and they walked around the huge building which looked so different since she had last seen it. The entrances to the air-raid shelters under the hospital were still visible and she shuddered, remembering some of the terrifying times she had spent in them.

Ana pointed out some places she recognised to Franco and Sr. Lucija and then they walked the short distance to the large cemetery. Franco said that he vaguely remembered where her father's grave was.

Sitting down on a low stone wall, he gestured to the two women to join him. He explained when he returned to Malta after the war, he came here to reassure himself that Ana hadn't died and been buried beside her father.

'You must remember that for the Maltese people the war had been over for a while. People were re-building their homes and their lives. I didn't know what I was going to find out when I came home.'

Franco recounted how he had learned on the ferry about Laurence Mellor's death in an air raid at Ta-Kali airfield. It was after this that he made the journey to Mtarfa in search of Matron Saliba. She didn't reveal much information, except to say that the last time Ana was here she had been a patient, but she would not tell him any more than that. When Franco asked for Miss Castelletti, in the hope that she would know what had happened to Ana, Matron told him that she had gone to work at the children's hospital in Valletta. That was where he went next. Fortunately Jeany still worked there. This was how he discovered that Ana and she had argued and Jeany never heard from Ana again.

The two women he loved most watched as Franco's face darkened and he began to re-live those heart-breaking days when he returned from exile.

'I thought she would have kept in touch with you,' he said wearily to Jeany. 'It seems to be impossible to find out what happened to Anabel. I have been to the Barracks and there was hardly anybody about. All the women and children went to the underground tunnel at St. Andrew's when St. George's got badly bombed. The caretaker at the Barracks remembered Ernie McGuill and Ana though and showed me to their quarters. I found some things belonging to Ana. I can't believe she married him.'

Franco's voice shook as he recalled how he had showed Jeany the tattered suitcase, not revealing what was inside.

'The caretaker told me that Ana went to St. Andrew's during the bombing of the Barracks and that a baby was born but as far he knew the child died. He said he never saw her after that but he told me that Ernie had been wounded and he heard that they went to Egypt.'

Jeany nodded her head as he spoke. 'Yes, they did go to St. Andrew's tunnel. I heard from one of the nurses in Mtarfa that Ana had been brought in after giving birth and that she almost died.'

Franco looked aghast at her. 'Why? What happened?'

'She gave birth in the tunnel and she lost a lot of blood. She hemorrhaged. It was something to do with an inherited heart condition. Some women delivered the baby but they had no idea how to stop the blood. By the time Ana was brought to the hospital she was almost dead. When I went to see her a few days later she was still unconscious. Matron told me she was extremely weak and that they had to sedate her because at one stage she came to and starting wailing for her baby.'

Franco by this stage had tears running freely down his face and didn't make any attempt to even brush them away. 'But where is she Jeany?'

Jeany didn't know. Then she told Franco about their argument.

'The same night that she had given birth, a baby was brought here to this hospital. She was obviously just born as she was still covered in blood. The man that brought her was Ted Langley. He said her mother had been killed after giving birth and they didn't know what to do with the baby. I didn't ask a lot of questions. Babies were often left with us under such circumstances. It was I who looked after her and named her Rigalla. She was wrapped in a blue jacket. When I heard about Ana giving birth the same night I went to visit her. I was sure that the baby was hers. When I got back that day I went searching for the jacket. I was afraid it had been thrown out or given away. It wasn't though. It was still in the laundry room with all the other belongings left behind by patients. I looked in all the pockets to see if I could find anything that might give me an idea of who the baby belonged to.

'I went back to the hospital and thankfully Ana was up and walking about, though Matron wouldn't let her leave yet. She would have only had to go back to the tunnel and she wasn't strong enough for that. We sat outside and I told Ana of my suspicions, but she went crazy. She started yelling that I was a liar and then one of the nurses came running out and Ana started screaming at her to make me leave. So I did. I never saw her again. I heard that Ernie took her out of the hospital and I think they went to Egypt.'

'Why did they go to Egypt?' Franco asked.

'I don't really know. I was told that Ernie had been injured and wasn't able to fly, but Matron said he looked fine when he came to take Ana out of hospital. She said that she tried to convince him to let her stay but he wouldn't listen.'

'My poor, poor girl,' Franco whispered, shaking his head. Then he cried out; 'The baby, where is the baby now?'

'I took her to the convent where I lived, St. Ursula's Convent on Republic Street in Valletta. Do you know of it?'

Franco indicated with his head that he did.

Jeany continued. 'The garden at the convent was bombed however and the nuns and children were all sent to the Santa Guisseppe Convent and orphanage in Gozo for safety. She is still there now. I have been to see her. I try to keep an eye on her. If I was married they would let me adopt her, but I am not. I asked my family to adopt her, but they refused. I suppose in a lot of ways they are still worried about their status in the town and they wouldn't want anybody to think that perhaps I or one of my *sisters had the baby. That happens a lot doesn't it? That an unmarried girl has a baby and it is brought up by her parents, so people will think it is their child to save the honour of their daughter.'*

Apart from the birds chirping merrily in the trees above their heads, there was silence in the graveyard as Ana and her daughter listened to Franco tell his tale. Each woman wanted to put their arms around him and give comfort, but something in his face told them that he was no longer with them in this moment. He was re-living something he had kept buried, kept to himself for so many years. It was almost a reverent moment, as though they were cast in a spell, that neither wanted to break by speaking or moving a limb. Instead they waited as he looked to the sky, as though seeing something there that they could not.

'Franco,' Ana whispered gently. 'Go on. I need to hear this.'

The touch of Ana's small hand against his face brought him back to the present. Taking up his story, Franco told them that he didn't want to wait for the ferry leaving for Gozo the next day.

'I didn't even take time to see my parents. Instead I sailed to Gozo on my own fishing boat which was still moored at Sliema and used by my brothers. When I arrived at Mgarr it was quite late. As I didn't want to knock on the convent door at that time, I slept on the boat.

The next morning I climbed the hill to San Guisseppe's Orphanage where I was welcomed by an elderly nun. After hearing my story the nun brought me to the office of the Mother Superior, who explained that I could not remove the baby from the care of the orphanage without any papers or documents. I argued and pleaded, but to no avail.

The nuns steadfastly refused to give me any information and even threatened to get the *Pulizija* if I did not leave. I was exhausted. I didn't know where to turn. Then I thought of my uncle Father Cauchi who was a priest on Gozo. I made my way to

Ta'Pinu to see if I could find him.

He was standing outside the huge Basilica chatting with some of his congregation when he saw me approaching.

'Is that you Gianfranco? What are you doing in Gozo? When did you get home? Are your parents alright?'

I simply told him I needed his help. So we walked down the long hill towards the town of Victoria where my uncle lived with two other curates. On the way, I told him everything and he just listened and didn't say anything. When eventually we arrived at the house he took me into a large kitchen. I'm just remembering now how bare it was. There was just a small wooden table and three chairs. When he saw me looking around my uncle told me that most of the furniture had either been sold to help out their parishioners during the war, or else had to be used for firewood.

I remember the sadness in his face when he told me how the war had affected that island.

'People think that Gozo largely escaped the war Gianfranco, but that is not the case, not at all. It is true that not many people here were killed in air raids, but they starved, literally many of them starved to death. The convoys that made it to Valletta did not make it here. We also had all the people who arrived over from Malta to feed. We gave them the food out of our own mouths. Also, we had a terrible polio epidemic that wiped out many of our people. My own brother Alfredo, your uncle was the doctor who looked after them. He believes it spread rapidly in the air raid shelters where people were so crammed in beside each other.'

I didn't know about any of this. I felt bad that I didn't spend time listening to him talk but all I wanted was for him to help me get my baby out of the orphanage. But he said he couldn't just go into an orphanage and take a baby out to give to a relative. He told me to go home and that he would see what he could do and write as soon as he had news. I nearly went crazy waiting. It was nearly three weeks before I heard anything. My uncle wrote to suggest that my parents adopt the child because the nuns would only allow her to go a Catholic home where both parents were alive.

Thank God my mother was happy to adopt my little girl, though she was shocked to hear about Ana's pregnancy. She said she was reminded of me as a child. I still hadn't even seen her yet. The nuns wouldn't let me into the children's dormitories. I had to wait in reception room for my parents to bring her in. Oh Ana, as soon as I saw her, I knew she was ours. Your big blue eyes shone out at me when I took her in my arms.'

16

When they came across the grave of Laurence Mellor, Ana felt bad that she hadn't thought of bringing flowers. However, Sr. Lucija had brought something, a packet of seeds, which she dug securely in under the earth.

'He is my grandfather,' she said quietly.

She had asked Ana the night before if she had any photographs of her grandfather. Ana replied that she had, but they were back in Ireland. She had found them at her home in Yorkshire after the war and took them to Ireland with her when they moved there. She promised to post some to her daughter. She also told Sr. Lucija about her other daughter, Maria. She did have a photograph of her. She carried it always in her purse.

'She was beautiful,' her daughter murmured. 'It was such a sad thing that happened to her.'

Ana nodded, 'Yes. I feel the guilt all my life since.'

'Why do you feel guilty?'

'I feel guilty for how Ernie treated her and for not going to look for her, or not being there when she had her baby and died. But more than that Rigalla, I have lived with guilt all of my life. I did not investigate the things that Jeany told me all those years ago. Every single day since, I have felt remorse and sorrow because of that. I kept going over in my mind, what if what Jeany said was true? What if Ernie had lied to me and my baby was somewhere in Malta?' Gulping back tears she was grateful when her daughter threw her arms around her and kissing her face said:

'None of those things are reasons to be guilty. Because you conceived Maria, you now have Jessy. Without Jessy, you probably would never have returned to Malta and met me, or seen Franco again. God works in mysterious ways.'

Ana smiled at her daughter and took her hands in her own. 'Your words give me comfort,' she said quietly. 'It is part of life that decisions and things that we do on the spur of the moment sometimes have far reaching consequences in our lives that at the time we never think possible. The fact is, during those moments, often we don't think at all. We act out of impulsiveness or a need or a want that we have at the time.'

Sr. Lucija laughed. 'I for one am very happy that you had one of those impulsive moments. I have been happy in my life. Franco told me when I was in my late teens and already thinking of a vocation, that he was my father. Obviously, I always thought he was my brother. The papers from the orphanage simply said that I was the adopted daughter of Nikola and Margarita Vella. I was brought to a very large but happy family. Sadly Margarita died of the polio and Nikola died not long after. It was very hard for Franco. My brothers and sisters were divided out among the older siblings and Franco took me to live with him.'

Ana now knew the story about Franco's wife. She was called Serenella and was a Sicilian woman, from the same town of Ragusa as his mother. Her family Inglima, were business people and had owned various businesses and restaurants in both Sicily and Malta before the war. After the war Serenella was in disgrace for having had a baby out of wedlock to a German soldier. Her parents were friends of Margarita and sent her to live with the Vella family. Up until then she was kept hidden by her family as she was under threat by the Partisans in Sicily, who were at the time hunting out women who they portrayed as traitors to their country and many of the women were killed for this. Franco agreed to marry her and in doing so he acquired the restaurant in Valletta. As a married man he was finally able to fully take care of Rigalla and bring her up as his own daughter.

Even now, many years later, it pained Ana to think of Franco with another woman. She knew that he felt the same way about her marrying Ernie. However he did not yet know anything about their marriage. She knew it was ridiculous for a woman of her age to be jealous of another woman who had been dead for years, but she found that she was jealous. She didn't desire to see a photograph of her, in case she was beautiful. She didn't want to even hear Franco mention her name. She simply did not want to know anything about his life with Serenella whatsoever.

Over the many years, she had thought of Franco almost daily. If he was alive, she knew he would probably have married and had children. When she thought of him, she imagined him living in Sliema and working as a fisherman. But it was easy to put thoughts of a wife out of her head as she was a nameless person. Now she knew all about her and she wished she didn't. When Franco spoke of his wife, she wanted to tell him 'Enough', but felt it would be unkind and unreasonable. But she couldn't help it. In her heart, Franco always belonged to her.

Now at her father's grave she felt once again guilty, that she felt nothing. Well, that was untrue. She felt anger. She was so angry that she could not challenge him and ask him to explain to her why he did what he did and send Franco away from Malta, his home, his family and most of all from her. Ana was well aware of his feelings about his only daughter being romantically involved with a humble Maltese fisherman. She never imagined in her wildest dreams that he would take such strong action to tear them apart. It was horrible to know that he could do something so cruel, to her. When Franco told her about the day he was arrested she was filled with such a rage that she found it difficult to let go of it since then.

'I was in my boat at St. Julian's all day. Remember, we were to meet there that evening?' he reminded Ana.

'Yes, and you never turned up,' she replied sadly.

'I was just coming into the harbour when I saw the soldiers on the shore. There were quite a lot of them. I thought perhaps I was in trouble for going fishing, but at that stage nobody passed any heed of us going out from there. It was different in Sliema of course. It was impossible to take your boat out there. When I tied up my boat and walked along the shore carrying my catch, the soldiers began to approach me. I innocently waved at some of them that I recognised, men that I had had a beer with at times and often shared my catch of the day with. But this time they did not smile or even acknowledge that they knew me. They had guns and I knew there was more to their interest in me than just fishing. I began to feel really worried and I could feel my heartbeat in my eardrums, it was beating so fast. Some of the other fellows, friends of mine around me started shouting and asking them what they wanted with me. I was taken to Grand Harbour and put on a ship. I was lying in the hold there for hours and I had a terrible headache. I had no water or food and nowhere to relieve myself except where I lay. There were some other Italian men there also. One of the men was just about sixteen or seventeen and he was crying because he was so afraid. Eventually the door to the hold was opened and that was when I saw your father. He was just standing there and then he looked in and I caught his eye, hoping that somehow he had come to free me. I had hoped that perhaps you had got word of where I was and asked him to help. But before I even tried to speak to him I could tell immediately that to do so was pointless. He just looked at me with a satisfied expression and nodded his head to another soldier. I understood very quickly that he was there only to ensure they had the right man.'

Now when Ana remembered all that Franco had told her about his arrest and his deportation to Egypt and then to the Orkney Islands, she wanted to knock the headstone to the ground. She wanted to take a hammer and bang at the stone where the words about him being a brave British serviceman dying in the service of his country were written. He was a bully and a liar and she shook with the rage that built up inside her.

'I want to leave, now,' she cried.

Franco understood, but first he spoke and said 'There is another grave here that you may want to visit before we go.'

Ana knew straight away which grave he spoke off. It was Katie's. She nodded her head and allowed him to once again take her arm and guide her to where her cherished friend now lay. Sr. Lucija stayed at the grave of her grandfather, wishing to pray there privately for a while.

Katie's grave was actually quite close to her father's. It was a simple white stone, with the words:

Katherine Bowden Cortis, London. Beloved wife of Billy Cortis, St. Julian's.

Born 1919 – Died 1942.

And her son Mikel Cortis. Born 1941 – Died 1942.

At this grave Ana wept openly. For this grave was different. Here at this spot lay the body of a much loved friend and her baby son, who was not even a year old. Franco cried with her, sharing her grief and she was grateful for his strong thick arms around her.

'I am so grateful for being able to be here,' Ana whispered. 'Thank you so much Franco.'

And together they stood as the sun began to set behind the cemetery in Mtarfa. A place which held many of those brave people who had made it possible so that when the sun rose again the next day, it now brought with it the promise of a peaceful day on this tiny island.

17

By the time that the last customer had left the building, Jessy could barely stand with pure exhaustion. As she flopped wearily onto one of the white wooden chairs, Salvatore laughed at her and dragged her once more to her feet.

'Oh we can't sit down yet my darling,' he cajoled her; 'we still have the cleaning up to do.'

Jessy thought he was joking, but unfortunately she soon realised that he wasn't. Pawlu didn't do any of the cleaning, so he left after he put away all the foodstuffs in the huge fridge and cupboards. She and Salvatore tackled the dishes that were still stacked up to be washed, with Jessy washing and Salvatore drying and storing them in the dressers that lined the kitchen walls. Then the counter tops and tables all had to be wiped down and the floor brushed and mopped. When this had all finished Salvatore told Jessy that he then had to begin counting the day's takings, making sure that all the orders taken corresponded with the till receipts. By now it was just after one in the morning and Jessy curled up on the soft armchair in the tiny office while Salvatore did the accounts. He didn't speak as he counted the notes and coins and she enjoyed watching the absorbed expression on his face as he entered the amounts into a large red hardback notebook.

'Why don't you use a computer for the accounts?'

'I wish,' Salvatore replied drily. 'Pop won't hear of it. See how we also use the old fashioned type of cash register still. That one has been there since I was a child. He is so traditional and doesn't like to change things. Me, I would like to change everything.'

Jessy had to agree with him. A computer would make it so much easier. She used one for accounts at her library and café and only for Excel she wouldn't be able to keep everything correct. Maths had never been her strong subject at school and she dreaded to think what state her accounts would be in without the use of technology.

'Excel adds everything up for you,' she explained, 'You should really try to get your father to move into the twenty-first century.'

'You can try,' Salvatore answered, 'he has a soft spot for you.'

Jessy smiled back at him and snuggled down against the soft velvety cushion which Salvu had placed under her head. She continued to watch him as he worked, until eventually the exertions of the day overcame her and her eye-lids began to drop until she was fast asleep.

~

Salvatore raised his head as he heard the sighs coming from the armchair opposite him and smiled to himself as he saw that Jessy was fast asleep. He thought it endearing how she lay with both her hands under her face and her legs curled up under her. She looked so young and so pretty. Yawning, he stretched his arms up over his head and then locked the cash box and put it together with the accounts book into the little cupboard in his father's desk. He thought it a bit ironic that his father locked the cash box but not the cupboard and also hung the key inside the cupboard door on a little hook.

'If somebody wants to steal from me, they won't let a little lock stop them. I prefer they help themselves instead of bashing through this antique desk that belonged to my mother,' was his father's simple explanation.

So, just like the issue with the computer and the cash register, everything stayed exactly as it was and as it always had been, according to his father's wishes. He woke Jessy gently by placing his large warm hand on her face and she opened her eyes instantly.

'It is time to go *hanini,*' he said quietly, as she began to unfurl her legs from underneath her.

'What does that mean?' she asked.

'My love,' replied Salvatore, taking her hand and helping her out of the armchair.

Jessy then blushed. He had never said anything to her like that before. She felt embarrassed, but also wildly happy and she felt something like a bubbly feeling inside her tummy or chest. Kind of like when she was really excited waiting on Santa to come as a child.

'I really enjoyed having you here with me, working with me, all day. It made the day so much better than it usually is. I think if you were here every day, I wouldn't mind working so much. I don't think I would try to find excuses to go off for an hour or so, unless it was with you, of course.'

He smiled down at her and she threw his arms around his neck and leaned up to kiss him. Once again, she marvelled at how she had only known him a week. As he put his arms around her, his smell was already so familiar to her. It seemed as though he and everything about him was part of her. Not just in the last few days, but as though she had known him before. Salvatore felt the same way. Until now, when he had girlfriends he found their company tiresome after an hour or so. He always felt as though he was entertaining a customer who never seemed to leave. He felt as though he had to be on his most polite behaviour when all he wanted was them to stop talking. With Jessy he found he enjoyed her constant chatter and also the times when she went silent all of a sudden and stared into space, as though away in some other world. Then she would catch his eye and smile and he would have her back again. He wondered where she went in her mind during those moments. Was she thinking of home, or somebody at home? He knew she didn't have a boyfriend because she told him so, but somebody as beautiful as her must have somebody back in Ireland she is thinking off. He knew that she sometimes felt lonely as she had confided this in him also. She told him about her home-life and what living in a parochial house was like, also about having been brought up by her grandmother with no brothers or sisters, or indeed any other family.

It was so different from Salvatore's own home-life. He had two brothers and a sister as well as a profusion of cousins, aunts and uncles and also nieces and nephews that he loved to spoil. Knowing this about Jessy made him feel sad for her. He felt he wanted to look after her and take her into the bosom of his family, letting her experience the security of having so many relatives who all loved you. He had no doubt that anybody who knew Jessy would love her and although she said that the priests were very kind to her, they weren't family. To him, it was unthinkable that somebody could be all alone in the world apart from one living relation. Sometimes though, his own family drove him crazy and he longed for peace and quiet but he loved them really and now that there was just himself and Pop at home, he had plenty of privacy.

When Jessy finally got back to her room her grandmother was fast asleep. Now that Ana knew who Salvatore was, she did not have the same reservations or worries about Jessy spending time with him as she would have had if he was a stranger. As far as Ana was concerned, Salvatore was suitable for her granddaughter simply because he was Franco's son. He looked just like his father when Franco was a younger man and she could fully understand Jessy's attraction to him. However, she worried about the fact that in a few days they would be returning to Ireland and it was a prospect that she dreaded. She couldn't bear to leave Franco now that she had found him again. He had already asked her to stay in Malta with him but it was a preposterous idea. She couldn't just walk out on the priests like that after all the kindness they had shown to her and Jessy over the years. She was quite sure however that Jessy could be very tempted to stay. She knew that young woman's feet were itching to get out of the small village they lived in and although her grand-daughter appeared to love the job she was in, Ana knew she would have no hesitation in giving it up for love and the chance of life in a different country. Sighing and lifting herself up on the pillows she switched on the lamp on the bedside locker and lifted her handbag off the floor, where it lay beside the bed. She fished inside for her sleeping pills. Today had been a long day and she believed sleep would come easily without them. Instead she found she had lain awake for what seemed like an age waiting on Jessy's return and her heart was doing its usual somersaults. While trying to sleep, Ana kept going over the events of the day, and all the things that Franco had revealed and this kept her awake. She also worried about Jessy and what might happen now that she had evidently fallen head over heels for Salvatore.

18

The next morning both women were in high spirits. Ana eventually managed to sleep nine hours straight and Jessy didn't waken until nine o'clock, so she was full of beans and looking forward to the day that Franco had planned for them all.

'Pop wants to take us all on some secret journey,' Salvatore informed her the night before. 'He said it's a surprise for Ana and he doesn't trust me not to tell you, or trust you not to tell your grandmother.'

Ana was excited about the trip and did indeed question Jessy relentlessly about what she might know, so it was a good job she was innocent of any knowledge about what the day would entail. Her Gran always managed to wheedle information out of her, whether she wanted to tell it or not. Jessy had thousands of questions for Ana and while they sat out in the orchard waiting on Franco to pick them up, she interrogated her grandmother so much that the older woman had to tell her to calm down and let her give the story in her own time and in her own way.

'I never even knew you were a nurse,' Jessy said, 'or that you lived in Malta or that my great-grandfather was buried here or ever was here. I feel like I don't know you at all. It is fascinating, but I'm wondering why you didn't tell me anything about your life?'

'Oh, I was too busy trying to forget all that myself love,' her grandmother replied. 'And I was too busy also, working and rearing you. Sure you know what it's like at the house. I barely get a moment to bless myself.'

'I know all that Gran, but I know you said something to Joyce about it. I heard you mention once or twice something about Malta, and that's what gave me the idea to send you here to see the Pope when Fr. Sean started talking about going. But I thought you had just been here on a holiday or something.'

'I will tell you anything you want to know pet, but not now.'

'Where is Fr. Sean anyway?' Jessy enquired. 'I thought we'd be seeing him every day over here and we haven't seen him once.'

'Rigalla, I mean Sr. Lucija told me that he got food poisoning almost as soon as he arrived and has been in bed over at that other convent ever since. I'd say he overdosed on chocolate from duty free. I don't envy whoever is looking after him. He can be a terrible patient, bless him. But she says he is over the worst of it now so we'll probably see him soon. Oh look, there's Franco's car coming up the hill. I can't wait to see where he is bringing us. Come on, lift those bags like a good girl and don't forget your cardigan.'

~

Franco had a couple of surprises up his sleeve. The first one was to take them out on his boat at Sliema wharf. Jessy was touched when she saw that it was called 'Anabel'.

'Wow,' she gasped, 'Gran, look at that.'

'Yes, I know,' her Gran replied smiling. 'He showed it to me.'

Salvatore told them that he had heard his father mention Ana over the years but all he knew was that she was a girl that he had met during the war. It gladdened Ana's heart to hear him say this. She also wished that she had known this during the times that she had hardships and felt very alone over the years. It would have eased her heartache to know that there was somebody who was thinking of her and still loving her. The wasted years gnawed at her heart and she could only accept that it was God's will. However, looking at Jessy she knew that she would go through it all again to have this beautiful young woman in her life. Holding on to Jessy's hand with Franco holding her elbow she climbed aboard the little fishing boat that was her namesake and sat down on the bench which ran along inside it.

When Franco went into the little cabin at the front, she gingerly got up and walked over to join him. He asked if she would like to take the wheel and she eagerly nodded her head. As he placed his hands over hers on the wheel, she gently felt a warmth go through her. This reminded her so much of how she would hold the horse's reins while his hands covered hers, many years ago. Ana knew he was remembering too, because he looked down at her and smiled tenderly with those same eyes that she had fallen in love with so long ago.

Franco navigated his boat into the harbour at St. Julian's and he and Salvatore helped the women to get onshore.

'Oh it is so beautiful here,' Jessy exclaimed, as she took in the views of fishermen sitting on the shore tending to their nets and arguing cheerfully with some women who had come down to inspect and buy their catch.

When they all were assembled at the busy harbour Ana looked around eagerly. Although many of the buildings were new, she recognised some which had stood the test of time. Suddenly Franco began to wave and following his gaze she noticed a tall woman waving back at them. She looked very distinguished, dressed smartly in a white suit and wearing a broad black hat brimmed in white. The woman began to walk towards them and Ana shaded her eyes to see who this might be.

Suddenly, she put her hand up to her chest and grabbed Franco's arm.

'Is that…?'

'Yes love. It is,' he answered. As the stylish woman came closer Ana felt that her heart was going to burst out of her chest. It was dear Jeany that she hadn't seen since the war years. She would know her anywhere by that stately walk and huge smile.

'I had never heard of her,' Jessy said to Salvatore later. 'I had no idea who she was.'

Her grandmother and the woman who met them at the pier ran to each other and were still wrapped with their arms around the other when they approached the waiting car. It was a huge black one, Jessy had no idea what make it was but it was bigger than any car she had seen in her life. They all piled into it and her Gran and the other woman were chatting ninety to the dozen in the seat behind while Jessy and Salvatore sat in the seat in front. There was yet another seat in front where Franco and the driver sat. In just a few minutes they entered a long driveway which had huge stone gates at the entrance with some kind of coat of arms on each pillar. Then Jessy gasped aloud as they drove up to an enormous palatial home. There were balconies at all the windows from which flowers tumbled, and every window and door at the front was ornately decorated in the traditional baroque design.

'Where are we?' she asked Salvatore who shook his head.

'I have no idea,' he replied.

When they all stood outside the huge car the strange woman came over to Jessy and introduced herself.

'You must be Jessica. I am Jeanette Castelletti-Borg. I am an old friend of your grandmothers. A very old friend,' she laughed and hugged Jessy close to her and Jessy got a whiff of very expensive perfume.

Ushering everybody inside Jeanette called out and a young woman came out of nowhere and showed them into a huge room where many other people were gathered. Jeanette still had her grandmother by the arm and gestured to the waiting guests.

'Here she is. Here is my dear friend of whom you have all heard me speak about many times. Here is Anabel.'

Ana was lost for words as Jeany introduced her children and grand-children, her husband Alexander whom Ana recalled meeting at a dance many years ago, as well as Jeany's extended family of brothers and sisters and their families. Ana remembered some of Jeany's siblings and marvelled at the fact that she could still recognise some of them. All she wanted to do however was sit with Jeany and talk. They had a chance to do so about two hours later after a sumptuous dinner. The two ladies excused themselves and went out into a sunlit courtyard, shaded by many trees. They sat on a carved stone seat and they began to chat, just as they had so often done in days gone by.

'Franco told me all about the baby, my Rigalla, and the part you played. I am so sorry Jeany for doubting you,' Ana cried to her old friend, as she grasped her hands in her own.

'Oh Ana, it doesn't matter now. All that matters is that you are here. We are both here and we can discuss everything now at length about those times.'

And discuss they did. Until the sun began to go down and the air got chilly and Franco and Alexander came out to look for them. It was too dark now to return by Franco's boat, so Jeany offered the use of her car and driver to take them back to Valletta. The two old friends hugged and kissed each other and promised to meet again in two days before Ana returned to Ireland. This time Jeany would meet Ana in Valletta and they planned to spend the whole day together, which Ana was really looking forward to already. On the journey back Ana was very quiet, causing Franco to ask if she felt alright.

'Oh, I never felt better,' she replied. 'I am just thinking that so much has happened in the last few days. So many questions I had in my head over the years have been answered and...' turning to her grand-daughter, who sat in the seat behind, she said, 'it's all thanks to you love. Everything is down to you and you taking me back here.'

Jessy laughed and replied, 'Well, I thought we were coming on a pilgrimage to see the Pope. I didn't realise it was going to be a personal pilgrimage for you at the same time. But I am glad how it's all turned out.' Then turning to Salvatore who sat beside her she whispered, 'Especially as I got to meet you.' And in return he kissed her chastely on the cheek seeing as they had company. 'Me too,' he answered, as he pulled her close.

19

When the driver left them at the convent, Franco told Salvatore and Jessy that he was taking Ana out for another small surprise. The younger couple where quite happy to be left alone for the evening. Salvatore had to work that evening and Jessy enjoyed working with him and was happy to join him. Ana watched them fondly, holding hands as they began to walk back down the hill.

'Don't they remind you of how we were?' she asked Franco, to which he agreed that they did.

'What is this other surprise you have for me?' Ana asked, 'I can't believe there is more to come.'

'There is, but first I must ask you to go inside for just a little while. I will meet you back here in maybe fifteen minutes. Oh, and bring a warm jacket.'

Ana happily walked through the convent doors and made her way up the stairs to her room. She had to stop half way up as she began to feel quite breathless and her heart was racing. 'It must be the excitement,' she thought to herself, 'these last few days have been one surprise after the other.'

Fifteen minutes later as promised, Franco put his head around the door where Ana sat inside the tiled hallway patiently waiting for him.

'Your carriage awaits my love,' he grinned, holding the door open for her.

When Ana got outside she stood mesmerized at the sight in front of her. It was a horse and cart. Granted this one was a bit more elaborate than the one Franco had driven all those years ago. In fact it was a *Karozzin,* the traditional mode of transport used in Malta in the days before motorcars.

'I don't believe it,' Ana exclaimed excitedly.

Franco laughed at how Ana clapped her hands like a child and gallantly held out his hand to help her into the carriage.

'It is magnificent,' Ana cried. 'But where are we going?'

'To quote what you used to say to me Ana dear, patience is a virtue,' replied Franco with a chuckle.

It was natural that Ana would hold the reins along with him and he clasped his strong warm hands over hers as they trundled along the city roads. Soon they were leaving Valletta and travelling the road to Pieta. Ana was very quiet on the journey, as was Franco. Like it always had been years ago, they were just happy to be in each other's company, taking in the scenery around them, enjoying the close proximity of the other. Occasionally Franco would stroke her hand with his thumb, just to let her know he was aware of her. When they reached Birkirkara Ana was reminded of that fateful day when she had changed buses here, a simple action that had saved her life. Remembering this, she turned to Franco and asked him if he ever thought of the war now.

'Every day,' was his simple reply. 'I believe everybody who lived through those times thinks of it daily. Every time I eat I am reminded of the hunger there was then. When I fish I am reminded of the times it was forbidden to take my boat out, or fish and swim in the sea. We don't all talk about it though. I know myself that I rarely spoke about it to my own children. I suppose I wanted to shield them from the knowledge of what we suffered. There are times when I got frustrated with them over the years, especially Salvatore I have to say, when I feel he has such an easy life and yet he seems to want to waste it. But I have to remind myself that these are different times, and they have different worries.'

'Yes. I know what you mean,' Ana agreed, nodding her head, 'Jessy seems quite upset that I never spoke to her about my having been in Malta or about my nursing, or of course about you. For the same reasons as you, I wanted to protect her. She has only ever known me as her Gran and the person who looks after her and nags her sometimes. She has also only ever known me as being a housekeeper. I know she was shocked to hear I was once a nurse because she knows how I hate the sight of blood, but she said she is proud of me, and that means the world to me.' As she spoke Ana suddenly realised where she was being taken.

'Mosta. You are taking me to Mosta church aren't you?' she exclaimed joyfully.

'Yes,' Franco replied, squeezing her hand. 'We are almost there.'

They passed through the town of Iklin and then they were in front of the magnificent Church of the Assumption, or the Mosta Dome as it was known locally. The church was beautifully lit up by floodlights discreetly placed outside the church and Ana didn't need help in climbing down of the *Karozzin,* so eager was she to see inside again.

'Is that the same bomb?' she asked Franco in amazement as she pointed towards the sacristy where a bomb was mounted against a brass plaque.

'No. It's just a replica,' he answered. 'The real one was dumped at sea. You can still see the hole in the roof, look,' and he pointed up towards the high round ceiling above their heads.

Ana shivered remembering that terrifying day on 9th April, a Thursday if she was correct in 1942, when a huge bomb dropped through the ceiling down into the church where she and Franco and about two hundred and fifty unsuspecting other people were waiting for the priest to arrive. She recalled that Franco had thrown her to the ground and covered her with his body. Some people ran outside screaming, others sat still in shock and some had bravely continued to pray. She and Franco ran outside where he insisted they take cover in a shelter, but thankfully no more bombs fell.

She remembered too what had happened between them afterwards, the feel of his strong protective arms around her body as she trembled with fear. There was nobody else in the shelter except them. Franco lit a match to see exactly how big the shelter was and if it offered any kind of comfort, a blanket or make-shift bed. It did. Taking Ana into the darkest recess of the shelter and laying her down on the pile of blankets on the dusty floor, he reassured her that they were safe. Ana had been terrified. Seeing that bomb fall through the roof, she was sure this was the end and in hindsight she recalled that although she felt afraid, she also felt safe as Franco threw himself over her. She was quite confident that he would always be there to protect her. Feeling this, she pulled him down on the blankets beside her.

She had asked him to hold her, and he did. They held each other all night, despite the fear of more bombs being dropped and in the dark and cold of the thick bastion walls, Franco and Ana celebrated their love together for the first time.

'Now Ana dear,' Franco said, as he steered her towards the back of the church and in through a tiny door just of the sacristy, 'I want you to watch your step, and also button up that jacket you have on you.'

Ana did as he asked and a few seconds later they arrived at the top of the twisty flight of steps and out onto the roof of the Dome itself. She gasped with delight as she looked down at the millions of lights that illuminated the town of Mosta and stretched far into the distance.

'I am sorry love that I couldn't organise a brass band or fireworks,' Franco said as he mysteriously rushed over to a low table at the back wall of the huge church, 'but I have something that I hope will make do.'

Suddenly the sound of music filled the air and Ana smiled

broadly as she realised the song was 'You Are My Sunshine,' the very same song that she and Franco had danced to on the night of August 15th, 1940.

'I can't believe you remembered it,' she whispered, taking his hand as he led her into a gentle foxtrot.

'How could I forget?' he asked her, 'Sometimes I play it over and over and other times I can't bear to listen to it at all.'

Ana nodded her head. 'I was once watching a child's movie with Jessy, I think it was around Christmas one year and the song played and I thought I was going to choke. I had to run out and pretend to Jessy that I'd swallowed my tea the wrong way. My eyes were streaming.'

'I know. The memories of our time together could really catch me unawares too,' Franco agreed as he and Ana tentatively followed each other's steps.

'Maybe it was harder for you, because you were here. I could never have stayed in Malta without you.'

'Why did you marry Ernest McGuill? I know your father approved of him and was always forcing him on you. Did he force you to marry him?'

He could feel Ana nod her head against his chest and he stopped dancing to look down at her.

'Come here,' he said, and directed her over to where he had set up two deckchairs with rugs. He had organised all this on his own as he didn't want anyone to tell Ana what he had planned. The only other person in on the secret was the young sacristan who had set up the CD recorder and chairs for him. He was very curious as to exactly what the old man was preparing and for whom. When Franco had Ana settled down, he took a seat himself and put his hand out for Ana's which she accepted and placed them both under the warm blanket.

'So, your father did force you to marry McGuill?' he asked again.

'Yes,' Ana replied quietly. 'When I told him I was having a baby I expected him to go crazy. Instead he told me very calmly that he would sort it all out. The next thing I knew Miss Honeyman called to the hospital and spoke with Matron and I was taken by car to St. Paul's Church in Valletta. I was to get married, to Ernie McGuill. I couldn't believe it. I started crying and screaming that I wouldn't, but Miss Honeyman calmed me down. I didn't know until then that she and my father were courting. She said if I wanted to keep my baby it was the only way. Matron had already told me you see, that I couldn't continue at the hospital as an unmarried mother. She said that Ernie was a good man and that he showed this by agreeing to marry me under my circumstances. Then Ernie came into the sacristy with my father. He didn't look too keen about the marriage either. I kept thinking I was having a bad dream and then Fr. Raphael came in and they all left and he heard my confession. I was crying but he kept telling me that it was the best thing, for the baby. I tried to explain that Ernie wasn't the father, that it was you and I was waiting for you to come back, but he said that you had obviously run away and this was the best thing to do.

'Run away?' Franco hissed angrily. 'As if I would do that to you, I had no choice in what happened to me. Didn't somebody tell you I was arrested from the harbour? Several of the other fishermen saw it.'

'When I went to your home, your mother said that she had heard soldiers took you. But I when I asked Ernie and Billy to investigate they said that they couldn't find out anything about you being arrested and that more than likely you had got your friends to cover up for you. But your mother insisted that you wouldn't run away. She just blamed herself. She knew there was a chance that you could be arrested because you were born in Italy, but she said that because you only lived there a short time, she didn't think anybody would find out. As you know, your mother was already ill at that time and I didn't want to worry her more by telling her about the baby.'

'I think people kept it all quiet as they were worried that my mother would also be arrested if too many questions were asked.'

'I can't believe you were in England, well Scotland anyway. I was back there in October 1943, in Yorkshire. Imagine, you were so close to me and we didn't know.'

'Yes. That's what makes me so sad, all those years that we could have been together, and we weren't. You didn't get to see Rigalla growing up.'

'Oh, but to know now that she lived and that you looked after her, makes it all so much more bearable,' Ana cried, 'I am sad too though, for the wasted years. But, I would never have had my Maria or Jessy.'

'I am so sorry about your daughter,' Franco said, tightening his grip on her small hand. 'What happened to her?'

'She had a most terrible fight with Ernie. He said some awful things to her and she took off. She was always leaving the village where we lived at Ernie's home-place, for sometimes months at a time, or other times just a few weeks. She hated living in a small village. She was very musical and travelled around a lot with a band she had got involved with. I was sure she would just turn up again when she had calmed down a bit. But, then I got word from the parish priest that she had died. It broke my heart. When I went to Dublin to take her body home, I found out that she had died in a mother and baby home there from a condition called pre-eclampsia. She had the same heart condition that my mother had. She had given birth to a baby girl, Jessica. I was never able to find out who the father was. I presume it was one of the young men she travelled around with, but none of them turned up at her funeral and I'd never had an address or telephone number for any of them.'

'What was the fight about?'

Ana didn't answer for a minute or two. Then she looked up at Franco with sad eyes and replied; 'Ernie told her that he wasn't her father.'

'But why did he say that?'

'Because it was the truth,' she answered. When Franco didn't respond, she continued quietly. 'She was Billy Cortis's daughter.'

At this Franco jumped up in his chair, the rug falling to the ground.

'What?' he shouted. 'How could that be?'

'Sit down and I will tell you,' Ana commanded, picking the rug up from the ground and placing it around his knees. Settling herself down again, she continued.

20

'As you know Billy and Ernie were good friends. I also was very fond of him, being Katie's husband. He was very suspicious about our getting married. He asked me several times whenever he could get me on my own, if everything was alright, but I pretended that it was. To be honest, nobody believed that my pregnancy had anything to do with Ernie. Everybody knew that Franco and I were promised to each other and that he had mysteriously disappeared. Also the fact that my father did not approve of him was not a big secret. But that was in Malta. When I returned to England of course there was no baby and nobody over there knew anything apart from the fact that I had got married to Ernie in Malta. Not even Kitty bless her, guessed anything was wrong.'

'But how did you end up having a baby to Billy?'

'He and Ernie kept in touch, for a while. Billy got a transfer to Britain after the war you see. Ernie had got an honorable discharge. I'm not really sure why or what happened. He hadn't been injured, but he did leave the RAF and we got a pension. Ernie and I lived on our estate in Yorkshire until 1946. Kitty said it had been used as a military hospital, but that my father had incurred huge debts due to his gambling whilst in Malta. Ernie tried to negotiate with the creditors but he was no businessman and in the end the estate had to be sold to honour my father's debts.

Then a solicitor in Ireland contacted Ernie through the RAF. His father and brother had been killed in a farming accident and we moved to Ireland to take over the farm after selling the estate. My life there was miserable.'

Ana stopped talking for a few seconds, her breath coming in little gasps but when Franco asked if she wanted to stop talking she shook her head. Her heart had begun to race again, but she felt relieved of a great burden in just being able to tell Franco all these hidden memories. She felt as though a great load had been lifted from her in finally being able to share her story.

'No, it is good for me talk about it. When Ted Langley was killed while flying after some row he and Ernie had just after we got married, he took to the drink pretty badly. When we moved to Ireland he was looked on as a traitor by our neighbours for serving in the British army and also his marrying a British woman only confirmed that he was not to be trusted. We were basically outcasts. Ernie loved being a pilot and finding himself back in his home village which he hated was awful for him. I never found out why he was discharged or why he never tried to fly again. He became more and more of a recluse and turned to the drink and he stopped replying to Billy's letters. So, Billy began to write to me. I told him after some prodding, how it was with Ernie, about his drinking all the time and his depression. We continued to write to each other for years and his letters were a great source of comfort to me. He was the only person in the whole world I felt I could relate to. There were one or two women I got friendly with through church activities that I had got heavily involved in, mainly as there was nowhere else I was welcomed. I was extremely lonely. Ernie was also violent at times in his drunken rages.'

At this information Franco again went to jump out of his chair but Ana pressed his arm, urging him to stay seated.

'It was more psychological stuff Franco. Actually, the thing that I found most humiliating of all was when he would throw dinners at me that I had prepared for him. The slightest thing wrong with the meal would be enough to set him off. I can't tell you the amount of times I swept up broken dishes and washed gravy out of my hair.'

By now Franco was furious. Inside his chest was a huge

volcano of anger ready to erupt but the only person that he could vent it on was dead. So instead, all he could do was sit there with the hand which wasn't holding Ana's, closed in a tight fist.

'Billy knew all about this of course. He also sent me money from time to time as he knew that Ernie kept me short. Anyway, in 1956, in November, I got a letter saying that Kitty had died. I was heartbroken. She hadn't been in good health for some time but knowing she was still there, in Yorkshire, made me believe in a way, that I still had a home there somehow. It was too late for me to go to her funeral, by the time I had got the letter she was already buried. But I really wanted to visit her grave and visit her children and grandchildren. Billy sent me the money for the ferry. When I disembarked at Holyhead, he was standing there waiting for me. I couldn't believe it.'

'And you had an affair with him?' Franco asked.

'Well, it was hardly an affair. I was only there for a few weeks. But it resulted in Maria.'

'Did Ernie know, or did he just assume she was his?'

'Oh, he knew there was no chance she was his. We had never consummated our marriage.'

Franco looked at her aghast. 'What?'

'Let's just say that Ernie had no interest in me or any other women for that matter. His tastes lay elsewhere.'

'Do you mean he was a...'

'Yes,' Ana confirmed, 'he was.' They didn't need to elaborate.

Franco shook his head in disbelief. 'My God, what a life you led,' he said sadly. 'When I was in the Orkneys, I thought about you day and night. I sent letters to Mtarfa and my mother, didn't you get any?'

'No. Of course not, otherwise I would have stayed in Malta somehow until you came back.'

'I drew pictures of you in the Orkneys you know, from memory. A lot of the time we didn't even have writing materials.

We built this little church and I did a lot of the drawings on the ceilings and walls. Just in pencil of course, I was never much good at the painting. You must remember, I didn't know that you thought our baby had died, or had in fact been given away. When I thought of you over the years while I was a prisoner, I thought of you with a baby, our baby.'

'Oh, I would love to see that little church someday Franco. You suffered so much too. But we are so lucky that God has given us this chance to meet and to talk and for me to find my Rigalla. Imagine, if it wasn't for Jessy, we would never have had this opportunity.'

'But what did Ernie say about you having a baby?'

'All he said was, 'For a woman who proclaims to be a good Catholic not even you can explain that particular miracle.' That was all. I said nothing either. After a few months of my coming back from Yorkshire I began to show signs of a pregnancy and then people started to congratulate us both. They were saying rude things like 'Oh, you finally got around to it then,' or to Ernie they'd say 'You found out what it was for did you?' Somehow my being pregnant made me more acceptable to the other women. But Ernie never said another word about it. He just drank excessively. He ignored Maria for the most part. The locals began to acknowledge me and shunned Ernie completely. Maria could never bring friends to our house but she was always in and out of the neighbour's houses. Then she started hanging around with different bands from Dublin and one day after she'd spent the night out Ernie went mad at her. He'd been up the whole night drinking and when Maria crept in he hit her. I heard her screaming and Ernie was saying that she was a whore like her mother and that he wasn't her father. I tried to intervene but she ran out the front door and I never saw her again. Ana grew silent and when Franco looked at her, he could see tears on her cheek. He leaned over and brushed them away;

'I think enough for tonight my Ana.'

'I am okay Franco really. It is good for me to talk about these things. Ernie never forgave himself for Maria running away because of what he said. He went downhill very quickly after that. He drank himself to death basically, but when he was nearing the end Fr. Sean spent a lot of time with him. I know that he emptied his heart of the guilt and sorrow he had held inside for so many years. A few days before he died he asked me to forgive him, which of course I did. He was only sixty-nine when he died and then I lost Maria not long afterwards. Jessy has been a huge comfort to me.'

While Ana was speaking, Franco sat with his arm clumsily around her shoulders and rubbed her back as if to help her get the words out. He knew these were things that she had pondered in her heart for many years and the telling of them was therapeutic. However, listening to her talk of what she went through tore at his heart and he wanted to protect her, just as he had wanted to do many years ago. If he had anything to do with it, he would make sure that she never suffered another day of pain in her life.

He decided that it was time they both went back down now. It was growing late. As they stood up he offered his hand to Ana and then wrapped his strong arms around her frail body. They both looked upwards at the same time and took in the majesty of the millions of little stars twinkling above their heads, as if they were smiling down at Ana and Franco, together again.

21

Jessy and Salvatore had had another busy evening at the restaurant.

'What do you think those two have been up to tonight?' Jessy wondered out loud.

'Oh, there is heat in those old bones yet you know,' Salvatore laughed, tickling Jessy as she put her cardigan on after removing the apron she'd been wearing all night.

'Ew, don't say that!' she giggled. 'They are old.'

'Yes. But you can see they are still in love.'

'I know,' Jessy agreed. 'And it is so lovely to see. I am happy for Gran. I still can't take in all that I've found out about her though. I know when I go home I will have her tormented with questions.'

Locking the door behind him, Salvatore said quietly, 'Don't talk about going home.'

'I know. I can't bear the thoughts of it Salvu, but what can we do? I can't let Gran go back there alone and live over there on her own, and she'd never leave the priests. I know she wouldn't.'

'Would you stay, otherwise?' he asked.

'Yes, in a heartbeat.'

'Maybe something will happen so you can,' he replied wistfully, taking Jessy's hand as they walked uphill towards the convent.

When they arrived Sr. Lucija was still awake.

'Fr. Sean was here earlier looking for you,' she informed Jessy. 'He said he will be back in the morning and said he is sorry he hadn't seen you since you arrived as he has been ill as I told you.'

'Oh grand,' Jessy replied to her aunt. 'Though I think Gran has enjoyed some time away from him.'

She kissed Salvatore good-night before he reluctantly left and

Jessy climbed the stairs to her room. She was amazed that her grandmother was still out at this hour. Giggling to herself she thought of what Salvu had said and left a note on Ana's bed to let her know Fr. Sean had called. She added a quick note to say that she was getting up early in the morning to go fishing with Salvatore before he started work, and would be back in time for breakfast.

Ana was indeed home late and she was happier than she had ever been in her whole life. As she lay in bed that night listening to the sounds of her grand-daughter gently snoring, she pondered on all that had occurred over the last few days. She couldn't help but smile when she thought of Franco gingerly getting down on one knee as he asked her to marry him and chuckled to herself on remembering how she had to help him get back up when she replied that he was an old fool but that yes, she would. How to break the news to Fr. Sean was a problem she would worry about tomorrow. Somehow she didn't think Jessy would be too concerned about a change of residence. This time, Ana was going to do exactly as she wished and she drifted off to sleep with that thought and the knowledge of Franco's love in her heart.

~

'Did you wonder who the Anabel was that is painted on the boat?' Jessy asked Salvatore, as they took Franco's boat out of the harbour in Sliema, so that Salvu could catch some fresh fish for the menu that day.

'It was I who painted it on, but I had heard about Ana before. It was never a secret that there was a girl during the war that he had loved and lost. He would never have named it that while my mother was alive though.'

'What was she like?'

'She was gentle and quiet. She was quite posh really. She came from a wealthy family in Ragusa. She just worked and kept the house and looked after us. She and Pop had a very polite kind of relationship. But I never saw any real spark or anything between them. They didn't talk an awful lot. It was like they both were acting the part of husband and wife but not really together, if you know what I mean?'

'Sure what would I know about a husband and wife? I never knew my father or mother and I never met my grandfather.'

'Maybe you will know one day,' Salvatore whispered into her ear, making her blush deep red.

It was chilly in Malta that morning. The sun hadn't quite woken up yet and Jessy was grateful for the rug that was under the benches of the fishing boat. She groaned inwardly as she had forgotten her camera for the wonderful sights of the different fishing ports they passed. It was a beautiful time on the island, when the day hadn't yet properly started and for the first time she really took in the splendour of the tiny island and all its wonder.

'It is so beautiful here,' she said, as they entered back into Sliema, 'I could live here forever.'

'Then do,' was Salvatore's simple reply, as he steered the boat in between the others moored at the water's edge.

When they got back to the convent breakfast was over, but Sr. Lucija told them to sit down in the empty dining hall and she would come back with some food.

'I suppose Gran is out with Franco again?' Jessy asked as she removed her jacket, for it was now getting warm.

'I haven't seen her this morning yet,' Sr. Lucija replied as she left the room.

As they sat tucking into platefuls of cheese, fruit and bread Franco came into the room.

'Good morning you two,' he said happily, giving them each a kiss on both cheeks. 'Where is Ana?'

'Oh, Sr. Lucija said she is still asleep,' Jessy answered, her mouth full of the prickly pear she had taken a liking too, despite its seedy bits which stubbornly stuck in her teeth.

'I don't want to go into her room. At least not yet,' he winked. 'Will you go and see if she is awake?' Franco asked, as he poured himself a coffee.

Jessy wrinkled her brow quizzically at his remark and made to get up when Sr. Lucija said:

'I will do it,' as she placed more pastries on the table for the two hungry young people. 'I won't be a minute.'

'So, what have you planned today then?' Jessy asked Franco. 'I hope you will have my grandmother back at a reasonable hour tonight,' she joked. Turning to Salvatore she said, 'Do you know, when I got home last night after 1am, Gran still wasn't in her bed.'

She wagged her finger comically at Franco and he laughed, 'Oh, we had much to talk about,' he replied innocently.

When they had all finished eating Jessy stood up to go to her room to see what was keeping Sr. Lucija so long, but was stopped at the door by her aunt and Fr. Sean who was with her.

'So is the sleeping beauty awake yet then?' she asked.

The nun looked first at Franco and then down at Jessy who stood in front of her.

'Hi l-irqad ma 'l-anġli,' she answered and took Jessy's hands in hers.

'I can understand that,' Jessy laughed. 'She is sleeping like an angel. I'd say she is, after the time she came in last night.'

When Salvatore and Franco rushed over to her and gently maneuvered her down into the chair she had just got up from, she looked at them bewilderingly.

'What's up?' she asked.

Salvatore knelt down on the floor in front of her, while his father began stroking her head and murmuring something in Maltese.

'Jessy love, what Sr. Lucija has said is your Gran, Ana, is sleeping with the angels.'

~

It rained the morning that they carried Anabel Mellor McGuill's coffin out of the little church in St. Ursula's Convent in Valletta. When they reached Mtarfa cemetery the sun had come out and shone down on the many people gathered to say goodbye to their friend, grandmother, mother and lover. Fr. Sean had given in to her funeral taking place in Malta and not returning her body to Ireland where he believed she would have wanted to be laid at rest.

'She was Maltese in her heart,' Jessy told him. 'I know that now. She would want to be here, with Katie and Mikel. She wouldn't want to be next to Ernie. This is where she thought of as home. This is where she would have lived, if she had had the choice.'

Jessy anguished over the decision however, wondering if perhaps she should take Ana home to be buried next to her daughter. As she helped Sr. Lucija pack up her grandmothers things in their room, she found the rosary beads which were on the locker next to Ana's bed. When she took them downstairs to give to Fr. Sean, so they could be placed beside her where they always were, Franco gasped as she passed them over.

'Our ring, that's our ring,' he cried, reaching out for the beads. Jessy had seen the tiny ring hanging from the rosary for years and had often asked to try it on but had never been allowed to.

'Do you recognise the ring?' she asked Franco. 'She never wore it. Not that I remember.'

'Oh but she did,' he replied. 'It was the ring I gave her when I asked her to wait for me, to marry me,' he whispered, as tears ran down his cheeks.

That was what made Jessy decide that her grandmother should be buried in Malta. Ana should have married here and lived out her life with Franco like she wanted to do, but that was a choice taken away from her by people who thought they knew better. It was enough. This time Gran would get her wish. She would stay on this island where she found love and was loved. She would be buried near her good friend Katie, in a country where people cared for her, who would visit her grave and remember her life and her suffering and to whom she had given so much love back in return. Ana would want to be here, lying under the warm Maltese sky.

The End

~ History of Malta ~

How does one describe the island of Malta to somebody who has never witnessed its beauty? Arriving into Valletta harbour by ship is a wondrous spectacle never to be forgotten. The majestic walls of high limestone rock which solidly protect its shores only add to the awe one experiences on entering a country of history, culture and bravery. This tiny country, only becoming a Republic in its own right as recently as 1974, has fought more battles and won more wars than any other nation under the stars.

The State of Malta consists of three small islands with Malta being the largest. Gozo is the second largest and then there is its baby, Comino. It lies in the Mediterranean between Tripoli, 195 miles away and Sicily just 60 miles away. Because of its strategic position Malta has always been in the middle of the trading and combative path of this land-locked sea. The small state comprises an area of just 316 sq.km with a population of approximately 400,000. This alone gives us an idea of the density of its country, also of how resilient its people have remained, despite its ever-changing governance and the constant conflict from other nations. The Maltese people largely choose to remain in Malta. They are proud of their stalwart little island and in the face of so much discord throughout its centuries they have held on to their traditions, making this a most special of places.

The name Malta comes from the Latin word *melit* for honey, which is just one of the things that the island is famous for. Its national symbol is the eight point cross which had been brought to Malta by the Knights of St. John when they arrived in 1126.

In its lifespan, Malta had been part of many empires, finally becoming independent from Britain in 1964, who had governed it since 1800. In 60 AD The Apostle Paul was shipwrecked off the coast of Malta on his way to Rome making this the island's earliest written reference. He brought Christianity to the Maltese people and Catholicism has remained the official religion of Malta. Many churches and cathedrals, streets and indeed its people have been named after St. Paul, one of the country's patron saints along with St. Publius and St. Agatha. Valletta is its capital city, named after the Grand Master La Vallette from the Order of St. John who laid the first stone in 1566 after the Great Siege. This exceptionally beautiful city is a world heritage site recognized by UNESCO.

If you fly into Malta you are greeted on its south-west by the sight of soaring steep cliffs reaching into the sky and as you descend a little lower you see a patchwork of thousands of tiny fields, bordered by roughly built limestone walls. On its northeast, yachts, fishing boats and cruise liners hug its coasts and the sparkling aquamarine sea twinkles in welcome.

The sunlight in Malta I believe is different than anywhere else. It can blind you with its intensity the minute you land on her shores, taking your eyes some moments to adjust to its brilliance. It is relentless in its search for you, seeking you out even when you believe you are in the shade. But like a temptress it draws you in and leaves you yearning for its heat when it has gone to bed for the night.

Malta during the Second World War

On 10th June 1940 the Italian dictator Benito Mussolini declared war on France and Britain from the balcony of Palazzo Venezia in Rome and the Siege of Malta began. Up to this time, the people of Malta had felt relatively safe from the war. The Italians wasted no time in their attack as the very next morning at quarter to seven the majority of people who were still in their beds were rudely awakened by the scream of the air raid siren. The Italian air force had begun their frightening assault on the small and practically defenseless island. The target was the island of their friends and neighbours, who were now suddenly enemies due to the horror of war. The sky came terrifyingly alive with the sound of planes firing guns and dropping bombs, looking like silver birds of steel taking over the skies. The bombers were chased by the island's three British planes, later affectionately to be named Faith, Hope and Charity who flew out in defence of their country and chased them into the sun, back from where they had come. However they returned *en masse* continuing to mercilessly bomb the island eight more times that same day, killing six soldiers who were manning the guns at Fort St. Elmo. Malta was ill-equipped for war, even though the island had been preparing defences for some time. It had just 5,000 troops who were not properly equipped, almost no fighter aircraft and only fourteen or so guns to defend its coast and only enough food to keep the island going for about a month. Malta's strategic position in the Mediterranean Sea was strategic to the island's importance. Royal Navy ships and RAF aircraft used the island as a base to attack Axis convoys that were trying to supply their forces in North Africa.

In early 1941 German forces had by now also begun to strike. They bombed the island relentlessly for 154 consecutive days in 3,000 bombing raids, concentrating on supply ships in an attempt to bomb and starve its people into submission. They did not succeed.

Without any doubt the Maltese people had showed exceptional courage during nearly two years of persistent shelling. Almost all their beautiful island lay in ruins. The Three Cities of Senglea, Cospicua and Vittoriosa and its capital Valletta, had been devastated. Grand Harbour was practically inoperative. Towns were simply mounds of rubble and most historical buildings were wiped out. In fact some are still undergoing rebuilding to this day. The people now lived underground or in slit trenches, their homes no longer existent. Families who once proudly owned their own homes now lived in dirty cramped conditions and those who survived had to begin making a new life again.

There were severe shortages of food and necessities like fuel and medical aid. The Victory Kitchens were set up simply to stop people from starving. These people were left destitute and yet they survived to make Malta what it is today. When the Axis finally withdrew from Africa in May 1943, the siege of Malta, the most systematically bombed island in the war finally ended, with 1,493 of its people having been killed and a further 3,764 wounded.

'With Malta in enemy hands, the Mediterranean route would be completely closed to us...this tiny island was a vital feature in the defence of our Middle East position.'
General Hastings Ismay - 1942

Because the people of Malta showed such extreme bravery in the face of severe threat and hardship King George VI made a unique and well deserved gesture. On 15 April 1942 he awarded the George Cross to the Maltese nation.

'To honour her brave people,' the citation read, *'I award the George Cross to the Island Fortress of Malta to bear witness to a heroism and devotion that will long be famous in history.'*

This is an honour which is still borne by the Maltese on their flag.

~

Acknowledgements

I would like to thank my faithful proofreader and editor, Tony O'Connell (author of *Atlantipedia*) who spent many hours labouring over my work. Others who gave me much support in my research are David Petters *RAF Transport and Command Memorial UK, Inniskillen Barracks NI, Mtarfa Military Hospital Historical Group Malta*, Don Pace and especially Andre Brincat from *Malta WWII Living History Group* for his advice and sharing his wide knowledge of Malta's history, Paul from *Malta Historic Military*, and my two tour guides and faithful taxi drivers in *Sicily*, Carlo Vasquez and in Malta, Michael Sultana. A very special mention to author Daphne Kapsali for her support and advice (daphnekapsali.com). Finally, I owe a debt of gratitude to my parents Nicholas and Mary Kearns, brother and sisters. Their belief in me kept me going when I sometimes became discouraged. My novel is dedicated to my two sons, Darragh and Adam. They are my inspiration and proudest achievements in life.

Thank you for reading this book!
If you enjoyed it, please take a moment
to post a review on Amazon.

~

Read on for an excerpt from Nicola's new novel
The Azure Window.

Excerpt from *The Azure Window*

Malta, January 2003

Jessy typed 'William *(Billy)* Cortis' into Google. Within minutes a colour photograph popped up on the computer screen and she felt her heart leap in delight. With excitement, she scanned quickly through the English newspaper article and was relieved that it wasn't one to announce his death. Instead the newspaper report was about a recent event to honour past R.A.F. servicemen and women. Under the group photo was a long list of names. William Cortis was one of them. He was the man seated at the end of the front row. Jessy enlarged the photo and gasped to see her own brown eyes gaze back at her. Finally, after months of searching, she had found him.

'I don't know why I didn't think of this before,' she exclaimed to Salvatore who was seated at the other end of the antique oak desk, reviewing the restaurant's accounts. 'All those letters I'd written to that address in England hoping for a reply for months, when all I had to do was type his name into the search engine.'

Her boyfriend thought it a good idea that Jessy track down the grandfather she had never met. However, the fact that he was now in his eighties meant that it had to be done both carefully and soon.

'Perhaps you could contact the R.A.F. office closest to where he lives in England, now that we know he is a member of the Past Serviceman's Club there,' he suggested. 'Or maybe you should write to one of the newspapers. You have nothing to lose.'

Jessy did just that.

~

Would you like to read more? *The Azure Window* is available to buy on Amazon, in paperback and on Kindle.

About the author

Nicola Kearns has contributed many stories and articles to women's magazines over the past years. She has two sons and works in a heritage centre, which gives her the opportunity to develop her interest in people and in history. She has published two novels, *Under a Maltese Sky* (2015) and *The Azure Window* (2017). Both are available to buy on Amazon.

Contact Nicola Kearns:

Website: **nicolakearnswriter.com**
Email: **nicolakearns3@hotmail.com**
Twitter: **@nicola3mary**